# Lesser Prophets

BLUE FEATHER BOOKS, LTD.

*I wish to dedicate this book to my cousin, Wes "Smoky" Phillips, who showed me the stars and shared my love of SF.*

ALSO WRITTEN BY KELLY SINCLAIR:

❖ ACCIDENTAL REBELS

AVAILABLE NOW FROM
BLUE FEATHER BOOKS, LTD.

www.bluefeatherbooks.com

# Lesser Prophets

A BLUE FEATHER BOOK

by
## Kelly Sinclair

This is a work of fiction. All characters, locales and events are either products of the author's imagination or are used fictitiously.

LESSER PROPHETS

Copyright © 2010 by Kelly Sinclair

Cover design by Ann Phillips

A Blue Feather Book
Published by Blue Feather Books, Ltd.

www.bluefeatherbooks.com

ISBN: 978-0-9822858-8-6

First edition: January, 2010

Printed in the United States of America and in the United Kingdom.

# Acknowledgements

I want to thank Karen Smith for her unfailing expertise and literary advice over the years, and most of all, for her friendship.

# Chapter 1

*Debra Shanrahan, 35, veterinarian*
*Moree Region, New South Wales, Australia*

Duroc 29b appeared to be recovering from his bout of bronchitis. He gulped down his morning tucker, whuffled in Jack Ducket's direction as if to say, "Seconds, please," and settled in a wallow by the isolation shed.

Ducket rated as a quality manager. Some piggeries knock you down from that methane smell, but Dausco Agro had a clean, well-kempt operation, one that didn't altogether wreak havoc on your nasals.

What I remember about that October was that it had been raining pretty steady, but a warm day in the 20s. Perfect weather for mud racing. I owned a buggy and had been competing in trials for years, so looking at Duroc 29b made me envious. He got to roll in the bog with no one looking at him crosswise.

I'd been working in the Moree Region for about five years, coming here from outside of Sydney, where I was raised. People in the Moree, they'll take the crust off of you. It took me awhile to get used to it.

Ducket seemed in a livelier mood than usual. He told me that a Dutch couple had been by a few days before, looking over the operation. They worked for Korteweg Investments, which owned Dausco Agro. Ducket bragged on how they said he had a better-run operation than the ones they'd just come from visiting in China.

When I called later in the week, Ducket told me he had returned Duroc 29b to the sheds. That was a drongo thing to do, as the boar shouldn't have been released yet. When I told him that, he laughed. He wouldn't take me seriously. His voice sounded raspy, he even had a coughing fit on the phone, but he claimed he felt fine. I reported his actions to the Chief Veterinary Officer and to the Stock Inspector. I thought a call from them might get his attention.

Then, when I read his obituary in the *Daily Liberal*, which gave pneumonia as the cause of death, I thought, hang on. I'd seen him less than a week ago, and here he was dead. I figured he must have had a preexisting condition. The man smoked like a demon the whole time I was out there.

The next morning, I was enjoying a Sunday fry-up with a friend. That's when we heard on the radio about the deaths of a ranching couple that had lived next to Ducket. Right on cue, Neil Jepson, a vet over in Dubbo, rang me up. With so many rural families sick at home or in hospital, stock was suffering. Volunteered or drafted, the same result: no mud bogging for me.

When we came into the first farmhouse, the wife offered us cups of boiling tea and stale biscuits on an unwashed plate. She appeared agitated, and her face was flushed as though she had been out in the sun all day. Needless to say, Jepson and I passed on the refreshments and went out to the paddock. Both the owner and his foreman were in Dubbo Base Hospital. The wife seemed likely to join them, although she refused our offer of a lift into town.

The other visits were much the same, ending with a brief visit to Ducket's piggery—brief, because there was not a soul left on the premises. The sheds had been left unlocked, and hogs were everywhere. This made travel a bump-the-snout proposition. I happened to spy Duroc 29b scuffling with his mates. After we topped off their water and put out some feed, Jepson called the Department of Primary Industries office in Orange to report a stock crisis.

He said, "That'll get Animal Welfare out here."

I noticed then that Jepson himself seemed off form. He had been out to several operations in the past few days, a fact that made me regret not packing a mask in my kit.

Jepson died eight days later. He drove himself to Dubbo Base Hospital just in time to crater from cardiac arrest. My friend texted the news to me, since I was too busy with stock to keep track of anything except supplies and petrol. Then the authorities put the whole Moree Region under quarantine. They took too long, in my opinion. Sixteen deaths reported by that point and loads of sick people, but I didn't know how sick until I went back to the first farm I had visited.

There were no checkpoints yet. The authorities thus far had been content with mandating masks for anyone traveling on the roads. I may not have been an ambo driver, but I did have on my gloves and mask. That's when I saw what the news reports had been leaving out.

I didn't venture past the bedroom door. The wife had bled out days ago, from the look of it. Dark patches all over her body. That and soaked linens and crusted floors told me it was disseminated intravascular coagulation, possibly caused by a hemorrhagic fever. DIC's a symptom you find on rare occasions with the worst cases of flu, but you almost always see it with such viruses as Ebola and Marburg.

African Swine Fever had never gone zoonotic—meaning it had never crossed over from pigs to humans—so I saw no reason to consider it as a causative factor, especially since I hadn't seen any symptoms amongst the hogs at Ducket's place. I did ring up the Veterinary Officer to suggest we take blood samples from stock in the area. Just to be on the safe side.

The next day, I read an article on my iPhone saying that the British government was investigating the deaths of a Dutch couple. They had fallen ill on an Air France flight to Amsterdam that had stopped over at Heathrow Airport.

They had been admitted to Hillingdon Hospital in London in critical condition and died only days after admittance. There were allegations of a cover-up, whether by the airline, the Dutch couple's employers, the British government, or Chinese investment partners. Frankly, I didn't care who took the fall.

The Dutch couple had visited Australia less than three weeks earlier. I made some calls to health officials, but the most important one was to my mum, who lived in a suburb outside of Sydney. I told her to wear a mask and gloves, drink filtered water, and stay away from people. My sister laughed when I called her. She said she would stay on holiday at Bondi Beach, no matter what. She deserved a good bake in the sun, says her. I said she rated a tanning of another sort.

By then, hundreds of cases had been reported, officially, in Australia and along the Pacific Rim. The Chinese were still trying to zip their coverage, but word was starting to leak out.

Symptoms began with a low-grade fever that lasted for days. Then came gastric upset, a persistent cough, even hiccups, and, strangely, a mild mania that worsened as the fever escalated until dark spots appeared on the torso and spread to the arms and legs. Mania ebbed into malaise, then came bleeding through all orifices. Death, some small mercy, arrived soon after.

# Chapter 2

*Wylie Ann Halverson, 61, high school teacher*
*Stevens Point, Wisconsin*

Someone snapped an image of a woman who had been carried off a plane at O'Hare. Although there weren't any spots visible, her hands were a blur in the picture, and she was trying to get up from the cart. Most of the people around her were wearing cloth masks, but I don't recall whether they were wearing gloves.

In my view, it's not fair to blame the crisis completely on the airlines. A great number of people who had been exposed to the illness flew into the States from Asia and Australia before the Feds halted international flights.

You'd see reports on TV of people dying of swine flu. That's what they kept calling it, even after the World Health Organization started calling it Variant Swine Fever. Let's just say that's a clue, right there, about how well organized the Feds were to deal with this. They couldn't even get the name right at first.

I thought the best thing to do with my class was to allow them to pass the student's cell phone around so everyone could see the pictures. Who could concentrate on history class anyway, what with Fox News telling us to expel every Australian from the country?

I didn't think Portage County was in much danger, to be honest, given that we weren't near any big cities and weren't a major hog producer. I wasn't worried about foreigners of any kind. The President came on television to tell us to remain calm and keep to our normal routines, to go shopping but use precautions. Even though you saw people on TV wearing masks and goggles, the locals didn't seem all that concerned. I did hear that gas stations and convenience stores were refusing to serve customers from out of town. That caused a big stink because a couple of students from the University of Wisconsin—Stevens Point had a branch—were turned away at a Kwik Trip.

We had a good discussion in class about civil liberties, but kids were more worried over whether the school would cancel the basketball game against Merrill that night. It had already been rescheduled from Thursday due to a totally unrelated reason. I believe there'd been a power grid problem affecting the gym.

I attended the game. Chelsea Thoresen was a starting forward for our girls' team. We won on a last-second shot by Chelsea, so three cheers for the red and black. After the game, one of the referees keeled over with an asthma attack. He had to be taken by ambulance to St. Michael's. I heard talk later on that he had been the source, but he wasn't the only out-of-towner at the game. Besides, several locals had already been exposed while traveling. You can't put it all on the ref, no matter how tempting that is.

*Dreya Underhill, 26, gardener*
*Chula Vista, California*

We were surprised they didn't cancel the Starlight Parade. Rita said all it'd take was one person with a coughing fit to set off a stampede. She worked in IT at Southwestern College. We'd been living together for about three years. We had an apartment in Terra Nova Villas that was on the small side but decent on the rent. Considering what houses were going for, we thought we had it pretty good.

Rita was a lot older than me and had an ex-husband she still talked to, even though she knew it pissed me off. Be that as it may, most of the time we got along great.

We went over to Otay Ranch Mall after work, picked up my sister on the way, did some shopping, and then ate at PF Chang's. Just your ordinary TGIF. I didn't notice anybody wearing face masks.

The next day I took a call from a prospective client. On the way over to her house, I heard on the radio that the Naval Station and Miramar were closed to civilian traffic. That's when we started thinking this might be serious, even though we still went to a birthday party at a friend's house in North Park that night.

Traffic didn't seem any heavier than usual. Somebody at the party said there was a gated community in Del Mar where residents had loaded up on supplies and weren't letting in the hired help. I think some of the rich ones, the insiders, got a special heads-up so they would be prepared for trouble.

Rita and I left early from the party, stopped at a store, and stocked up on canned foods. I had the bright idea to buy several five-gallon jugs, which I filled up at the gas pump the next morning. That's when I noticed people in masks, although not everybody had a handle on the right kind to wear. One couple, I swear, was decked out in Halloween masks, and one boy had punched holes in a plastic bag he was wearing. Maybe they meant that as a joke, but I don't think so. I had some masks and goggles I wore for gardening that Rita and I put on when we were around the public. We called friends and family, making sure everyone had masks.

I remember by that afternoon when my sister, Leesa, came over to pick up her mask, it took her ninety minutes to get from her place to our apartment, although part of that was because she was checking on her ex-girlfriend. Traffic was picking up. Grocery stores were jammed, and there were long gas lines. We had her spend the night. No sense fighting the crowds. We made plans for her to drive up the next day to check on our parents.

It probably sounds stupid looking back, but I had a schedule, I had clients, and until notified otherwise, I planned to stick to it. I guess the people running things had the same attitude, but they should have known better. They knew more than me, or they should have known.

On the one hand, you had our mayor saying he would take it day by day on whether to shut down mass transit. On the other hand, Leesa worked at the La Quinta in Chula Vista, where they were already at capacity with people from Mexico, the ones who had some money, coming across the border. Rita's aunts and cousins were due in any day. Her dad was going around buying beds-in-bags because he didn't think there'd be a spare room in town by the end of the week. He was right.

*Analyn Orante, 46, Under Secretary for Democracy and Global Affairs, State Department, Washington, D.C.*

That Friday was frustrating by any standard. I doubt that anyone has ever heard of the North American Plan for Avian and Pandemic Influenza. It can probably still be found on a website somewhere. My predecessors had worked on it for years. I had worked on it. All that labor for nothing.

We stood ready to implement it, but the White House wanted their people to deal with the state agencies. Never mind we already had an interagency task force in place to coordinate such groups. It didn't matter that the crisis turned out to be Variant Swine Fever and not avian flu; people were dying. Cases were being reported in cities across the country. It was absolutely imperative we cancel all domestic air service, not just international.

It wasn't until Monday noon that domestic flights and Amtrak were ordered to stand down. By then, you had people stuck at their offices trying to figure out how to get to the suburbs and exurbs if their train was affected. Buses kept running. So did trolleys and most subways. It was left up to the cities and states to decide. A nationwide shutdown wasn't ordered until the next Friday.

I remember my contact at the White House saying that as long as everyone wore their masks and gloves and used their disinfectant sprays, we would experience a rough couple of weeks, then the cases would taper off.

Inside the Beltway, there was a misperception based on media reports that Australia had dropped the ball on protective measures. The news blackout in China certainly didn't help the situation.

I said to the guy at the White House, what about the United Kingdom, what about the EU?

He said to me, "They're alarmists about everything. Look how they flipped out about genetically modified foods. This'll blow over."

The first big wave of deaths was about to hit in Europe. I still suspect he knew something about that. Denial, such denial going on. No one wanted to take the initiative to stop everyday life in its tracks before the virus did it for us.

We had supplies in several locations across the country prepositioned to handle a pandemic. Meals Ready to Eat or MREs as the military calls them, isolation gear, medical supplies. Nowhere near enough of anything, as it turned out, but we had a system in place. To their credit, FEMA staff did fly out to prepare the distribution system. It took until Wednesday for them to receive authorization to release supplies to the state agencies. But that was all ahead of me, ahead of us.

Friday night was when I decided to destroy my career, which surprisingly enough, concerned me at the time.

I arrived home pretty late that night. I lived in a condo in Rockville, up north of D.C. Normal traffic. Typical commuters. At the stops I'd look over at their faces. They were talking into their phones, listening to their iPods. Were they worried? I didn't think so. I called Bill Levine, my assistant, and told him to grab as many boxes of masks and gloves as he could find. We needed to go door-to-door at the State Department, stand out on the street if we had to.

We had staff doing that Monday until we ran out of masks and gloves.

I had been putting off returning calls from the media, but after I finished with Bill, I called my contact at the *Post*. I told her on the record that our citizens needed to get off the streets and not report to work unless they were critical personnel. We had burned past the alert period and were well into pandemic level four. I couldn't wait on Homeland and the White House to act, not when the UK and most of Europe were battening down the hatches. Canada and Mexico already closed their borders, thank God, but our ports remained open to international shipping, by my recollection, for three more days.

I've been asked did I know what was going to happen. No, I didn't, but I was trained to expect the worst-case scenario. Preparedness, prevention, and containment. Those are words to live by, then and now. The Ambassador, our Special Representative on Avian and Pandemic Influenza, had flown to Geneva for a UN meeting on avian flu, ironically. He couldn't get a civilian flight out, so he drove to Germany and came back to Washington via military transport, but we were in close contact, coordinating with our counterparts overseas.

Along about five a.m., I got dressed, packed some things, and drove into D.C. The streets were quiet. I called my parents in Atlanta and my older brother in Wilmette. My little brother, Michael, who was a junior at the University of Texas in Austin, was partying with his buddies in Jamaica. He took his own good time answering the phone. I laid out for them what was happening.

During the drive, a cousin in Manila called me. She heard a rumor the government there was about to declare martial law. There hadn't been many cases reported in the Philippines. She was thinking about staying with some friends who lived in a fishing village up the coast. I told her to go.

To this day, I believe that Friday represented the tipping point. Maybe it couldn't have been stopped; maybe nothing could have been done. We all see twenty-twenty in the rearview mirror.

*Dora Navarro, 24, piano teacher*
*Belton, Texas*
I remember that Friday. It had been a warm autumn, not at all like winter was right around the corner. Shorts weather. I was at the hospital visiting my ex-boyfriend. He was there recovering from knee surgery. We were on good terms, considering.

I overheard one of the resident doctors, an Indian man, tell the nurses that everyone should double-glove and wear masks and gowns from the moment they came to work to the moment they left. I asked one of the nurses if I should wear a mask myself. She acted like that was a stupid question, but later she did bring me a mask. I decided to carry it with me from that moment on.

That night I went to a club in Killeen to hear one of my piano students play in a band. I'd read online about cases in Texas, but no one around me, including the soldiers from Fort Hood, was wearing any kind of protection. The soldiers were easy to pick out because of their haircuts. Even though I felt kind of silly, I wore my mask the whole time.

When I got back home, I found a message on the answering machine from my older brother, Mark, who lived in Abilene. For Christmas we planned to give our mother and stepdad plane tickets for a trip to Las Vegas, but he was worried that flights would be cancelled. That's what happened the next day. We had talked before about giving them a Wii game console, so we decided to go back to that idea.

I remember writing myself a reminder to tell Mama to buy a mask and gloves. She had asthma. I thought she would be at risk if it spread to Odessa. I should have told them to hide out at their vacation cabin. That doctor at the hospital, he didn't mess around. He told us what to do. If only the people in charge had been as on top of things as he was.

# Chapter 3

*Debra Shanrahan*

Oh, and that's good fun, isn't it. They stuck me in an isolation room whilst doctors argued over why I was so cheeky as to still be alive. National emergency, that's why I quote-unquote volunteered my services.

They shipped me weeks ago to Fitzroy, which is a suburb of Melbourne. The entire trip I'm in the back of an ambulance under armed guard, full hazmat all around. I'm thinking to myself, you call this gratitude? I confirm the link between Ducket and the Dutch couple, I send in the first stock samples, I'm sounding the alarm as best I can, and where do they stick me? In a bloody clinic with no telly and no radio, not even allowed my laptop and cell phone. It made me wish I'd gone to bush.

Meantime, a steady stream of lab jackets from St. Vincent's Institute, the National Serology lab mob, was doing me up in tidy little slices. I was on the high horses of all high horses about it.

I remember telling one girl, "I may look like a footballer gone to seed, but I am a physician. A boonie hog doc as far as you're concerned, but I have something to contribute."

They did let me have one monitored call to my mum, who was terribly concerned. She lived right outside of Sydney.

Finally, after days and days of needle sticks, one of the lab girls told me the truth. Canberra believed terrorists could be behind it all, or that some country leaked a bioweapon on purpose or accidentally. Several of the hog samples tested positive for swine fever. The Chinese weren't talking, so at this point, all we knew was that the Dutch couple contracted the virus somewhere in their travels and spread it in Australia.

Most of the hogs showed few symptoms, meaning that they were mildly sick from a variant of a virus that, full on, usually killed them. It meant they could spread the virus that much easier. Every pig in New South Wales was destined to end up dead and on a burn pile, and that was just for starters.

The next thing she said took me aback. I tested positive.

"No telling how many people you exposed to the virus," she told me.

I had experienced no symptoms whatsoever. Ducket gave the fever to me, and I passed it on all those weeks, thinking I was pitching in. I stayed a proper little monkey after that.

I can't say it mattered much to me that loads of individuals took the virus worldwide. I did my part and didn't even know it.

*Wylie Halverson*

The referee died at St. Michael's, which goes to show he probably wasn't the first one who spread it to Portage County. Several were dead already in Stevens Point and more in the surrounding communities. At first, the patients were those who worked at dairy farms, convenience stores, and restaurants.

My theory? Our Patient Zero had been a milk-truck driver on a collection run. He felt under the weather but kept on working, kept on coughing, and spread the plague all the way back to the processing plant. Those who had it, they didn't fall over and die on the spot. It took awhile.

One of the other teachers, I saw him at the faculty meetings when we were deciding on how to handle the crisis. He had the plague even then, but no one knew it at the time. He had been a quiet, laid-back kind of guy, but not that day. He blabbed on and on, mostly about what to do with kids in the after-school program. He had some idea about busing them over to the Lutheran church where their parents could pick them up when they got off work. Boy, did he have the gift of gab.

I saw him in the teacher's lounge later in the week after the school board voted to suspend classes. He was still talking, and coughing up a storm, and that's when I noticed dark spots on his hands. While I talked him into putting his mask back on, the principal called his wife and the paramedics. It turned out his wife had been in bed for days. Their kids had been left to fend for themselves.

We weren't at the panic stage, but getting close. From what my principal told me, the schools might not reopen until February, at the earliest. I guess a lot of us thought that the doctors—the miracle workers—would get the situation under control. Every day you heard rumors of a breakthrough.

People were dying. How terrible the symptoms were was obvious from the news and from rumors about patients in St. Michael's, but not everyone was catching it. I saw reports about Australians who had been exposed for weeks and weeks without any symptoms, people like me.

One of my neighbors, I knew at her age she couldn't deal with shopping, so I went by the store to stock up for the both of us. Parking lot was jammed, so I parked across the street at the athletic supply store then walked over. I was making my way across the parking lot when Coach Kobold and his oldest boy called over to me. They were loading up their SUV. The parking lot was a death trap, really, with people driving like maniacs.

Coach gave me one of their empty carts and had his son come with me to help deal with the crowd. There, at the entrance, a couple of security guards gave everyone the eye, making sure we behaved. But we're 'Cawnsiners. We may run you over when we're behind the wheel, but we're friendly on foot.

The store looked like it had been hit by a well-organized riot. No perishables at all, except for a few apples the produce manager brought from the back. Those went quickly.

I went over to the canned goods shelves, and they were pretty well cleaned out, too, but then I saw that the ethnic foods section had barely been touched. I loaded up on coconut milk, rice noodles, lentils, gefilte fish, and boxes of paella mix. Some things I'd never heard of before, like halva and dried cuttlefish.

Pickings were slim everywhere else. You couldn't buy a bean of any kind, canned or dry. I did find some canned dog food, which I knew my neighbor would appreciate. For her peekapoo, not her. I saw shoppers with carts full of bottled water, but this is Portage County. As long as you have an axe to break up the river ice, you'll not go thirsty, believe you me.

Coach Kobold and his son helped me load the pickup, which is hard to do when we're all trying not to touch one another. I was about to drive off when I saw it in front of me. Athletic store. Supplements.

I went in there on a hunch and found the sales clerk sitting by the door watching the excitement across the street. The kid was wearing a ski mask—as if that would block a virus— but the store appeared open for business. He accepted my credit card, thank heavens. I made three trips to the pickup with canisters of protein powders, vitamin bottles, cases of protein bars, beef jerky, whatever looked edible, and some that didn't. It was a good thing my pickup had a camper shell, since a light snow was beginning to fall.

On an earlier trip to the store, I'd bought plenty of food for my cat. He's not a picky eater. He does like the occasional potato chip. I had a feeling he would be missing out on that for a while.

*Dreya Underhill*

You don't put the President of the freaking United States in the hospital just to be on the safe side, not when you've stashed the veep over at Camp David and half your senators are calling in sick. Our mayor's dead, the governor's in intensive care, and you don't want the American people to see the big boss on TV? No, we knew what was up on that. They were lying to us like they'd been lying all along.

Rita and me had our hands full anyway. We couldn't be bothered worrying about anyone else's troubles when both our families were in bad, bad shape.

See, I blame it on football, basketball, all those games people kept going to even after we knew cases were being reported here in the States. When that finally got stopped, you know some fans bitched about it, crazy fools, even Rita's dad, who knew better. He was into the Chargers big time. It didn't surprise me he got sick. He and his brother had attended a game right when the walking fever hit.

And think about the malls back then, and Wal-Mart. All the stores were big, bigger, biggest. Everywhere you went, you'd see people trying to get what they needed and trying not to bump into each other.

Rita was taking care of her parents and her grandma, her *abuela*, in National City. She was good at being a caretaker. Me, I ended up with her relatives from Mexico. You couldn't take a step in our apartment without tripping over someone. They were nice people, just scared all the time, afraid Immigration was about to bust down the door. Then they started getting sick.

It was weird how the thing would hit. They would be acting okay but kind of flushed, kind of excited. Not wild acting, not like that, but revved up. What was up with that, I don't know, but if you ever touched them, how warm their skin felt, you'd know they were sick.

I was talking on the phone to my sister, Leesa, who drove up the week before to Riverside to stay with our parents, and something about the way she talked had me worried.

She said my mom was cooking a bunch of casseroles, and Pops's emphysema was giving him more trouble than usual, which could have meant nothing. I knew my mom. She was a career civil servant type who took a transfer to Riverside for the pay raise since Pops had to put in for early retirement. She didn't cook. Woman had a giant fridge just for frozen meals.

I jumped into my van right then and drove as far as Escondido before I had to turn back. You had to deal with roadblocks if you wanted to come off the Interstate. Trooper told me Riverside wasn't letting anybody in, so no point continuing.

I did pick up an old lady and her grandkids off the side of the road coming back. Their car broke down, and they were waiting on the National Guard to rescue them. Good luck on that. I took them all the way back to their place in El Cajon, where I found a gas station still open. When I gassed up, I filled all my jugs, even bought some more jugs and filled them up. It hit me I better not get back to smoking, not unless I really wanted to blow myself up.

I had a bunch of messages from clients canceling out on me, as if anyone had to tell me keeping up their begonias was no longer a priority. The weirdest call came from this lawyer over in Lemon Grove who lived in a gated community. He had been a client of mine since my high school days, back when I was still working for the property management group. He told me he and two other families hired extra security guards for protection, and did I want to move in during the situation. That's what he called it, the situation.

You want me to take care of your greenery, like that is important now? I didn't bother asking him if I could bring Rita. I knew what his answer would be.

Rita called me just as I was getting into town. She said that Scripps Mercy had taken over Parkway and South Bay Community Centers for patient overflow, and that her boss at the college wanted her to go in to work. Before I could say anything, she explained that it had nothing to do with computers. County needed a location for something or other. A lot of her coworkers were sick or not coming to work, which meant Rita needed to step in.

She told them no. She couldn't do for the county, not when most of her family had the walking fever.

*Analyn Orante*

Bill Levine and I couldn't figure it out. It turned out we both had been exposed almost from the start. We read in the *Post* about a group of lobbyists who visited Australia then flew back to

Washington in November. The paper listed a steak place in Georgetown where Bill, his partner, and I ate the same night they did.

The newspapers made such a fuss over this, as if the lobbyists were the only individuals who had flown that route, as if they were the ones who killed our President. It was common knowledge that the President was on life support and not expected to make it. Our Vice President? Supposedly no problem, but other than an appearance on the official website, he might as well have been down the rabbit hole.

My boss, the Secretary of State, conducted business via intranet and videoconferencing. Not that I blame anyone for ducking for cover. There was an option for high-ranking officials to go to the underground complex. A few people went there: for instance, the Supreme Court, their clerks, and their families. Interestingly enough, the decision on that was made before the official declaration of an emergency. Make of that what you will.

My mom kept calling me, asking me what to do. I gave everyone the same advice. Stay home. Don't answer the door. Pray.

My brother Michael's flight never left Jamaica because the United States wouldn't allow it into our airspace. He sounded fine on the phone. He was more worried about his girlfriend in Austin than anything else. I didn't have enough strings to pull to get him home.

From what the people at the National Institutes of Health and the Center for Disease Control were telling us, there were two categories of infection: apparently asymptomatic and acute. And by acute, I mean fatal.

And what about Bill and me? In the weeks since we ate at the same place as the lobbyists, we had been in news conferences, dashed in and out of stores, even flown to New York for a meeting with UN officials. We were both perfectly fine, and perfectly infectious.

Bill worried about the presidential line of succession. President about to be dead, Vice President, who knows, Speaker of the House looking sicker by the day, President pro tempore back in his home state not taking interviews, not a good sign. And we had our suspicions about the Secretary of State. When we went through the chart, it looked to us like the healthiest person still in town running her department was Secretary of the Treasury Rebecca Budin, who was next in line.

Bill said Budin's husband and son were sick, but she refused to hide in the underground shelter or go to Camp David with her family. It took all of my nerve to not hop on a military flight to Atlanta because I was so scared for my parents; yet Budin took her responsibility seriously. A lot of us did, including the ones who made it and the ones who didn't.

*Dora Navarro*

I decided to start for Odessa early in the morning so that in case of problems on the road, I wouldn't break evening curfew. I drove the entire way like I was a contestant on *The Amazing Race*. We all were driving recklessly, everyone on the road. Highway Patrol wasn't about to stop anyone unless they noticed you not wearing a mask. The news said they would give you a warning, throw you a mask, and record your license plate. Second offense, they were authorized to shoot to kill.

I knew of a kid in my neighborhood who got shot in the leg by a neighbor when she wandered onto his yard, and there was a mail carrier murdered a few blocks from my apartment. No one went anywhere on foot unless they absolutely had to.

On the radio, they were telling people to wear their masks and gloves. They ran bilingual announcements on all stations. Talk shows were going berserk over this, blaming illegal aliens, blaming Australians, blaming pigs, NAFTA, everything. I couldn't bring myself to listen after a while. People would have been rioting in the streets if they hadn't been afraid of getting infected.

I made it into Odessa with plenty of time before sunset. I drove over to my mother and stepdad's house, and there was my brother, barbecuing on the driveway. His kids were inside playing Nintendo. They had come over from Abilene.

Mark and his wife quit wearing masks the week before. One day at work his boss coughed up a lot of blood, which got all over my brother. He said they were making the kids wear masks and gloves, but "it's really up to God at this point." Their church kept an online prayer chat room going round the clock.

I walked down the hallway into the bedroom where Mama and my stepdad were sitting up in bed. It was obvious they were sick. They couldn't keep any food down, they had bad coughs, and Mama's asthma was giving her problems, but they both were so... upbeat. That's the word for it. Did I have a good drive? Had I had something to eat? Was I able to reschedule my piano students, and were the Methodists still going to pay me even though services had been cancelled? This wasn't what I expected.

While I was helping my sister-in-law load the washing machine, she told me the next-door neighbors were in the hospital.

She said, "Doctors are telling everyone with symptoms not to go anywhere, not even to the hospital, until their fever gets to 103 and stays there."

"Why 103?"

From what she had heard on the news, once the fever kept at that level, aspirin wouldn't bring it down. Or, as she put it, "Their bodies go all to pieces. Families can't manage it at home anymore."

After supper, I flipped open my laptop, eager for a breakthrough, a ray of light, only to see what ordinarily would have been the biggest news story of the year. The President of the United States had just died at Walter Reed Army Medical Center. The Vice President, still at Camp David, had just been sworn in as President.

My oldest nephew asked me, "Does the Vice President get paid for doing both jobs?"

# Chapter 4

*Debra Shanrahan*

I have always found it bloody hard to sleep in a plane. When you're stuck in a C-17 Globemaster III with nothing to wee in but a rigged-up loo, about as far from the others as you can be and not be perched on the wing, airmen shooting death at you with their eyes, and you can only cross your legs for so long—try doing that in full hazmat—you're damned well not going to sleep, are you?

Dr. Sinlop, the project head, ordered the soldiers to let me visit the loo. Dr. Sinlop had a way about him for a skinny fellow. You didn't want to brook him.

It'd all gone crooked, a great wanking debacle. He told me some of the details once we were in the air. Despite keeping me cozy in isolation, most of the staff tested positive for VSF. They had been exposed, which meant, by all odds, they were done for. He had to keep the project going. There were contacts in Canada, which hadn't yet been hit too hard.

Canberra didn't want him to leave at first, but I suppose they realized they had no choice if they wanted to crack it. He didn't say this, but he had me, alive and kicking, a walking blood bank. Longest-lived survivor. We made a mad gallop to Amberley, Queensland, then we went on board the C-17, which wasn't the first choice they told me, but other craft were busy rescuing our nationals from places like Indonesia and Thailand.

Canberra had arranged a refueling in Hawaii with permission to fly over the continental U.S., but when we left out from there, our pilot received orders to change his flight plan. I thought for sure the Americans were going to shoot us down.

I may look like the sturdy type, but you wouldn't have thought that at the time. I felt shaky on my pins. We got redirected to Lackland Air Force Base, which is in San Antonio, Texas. All the way in, and I know I wasn't the only one thinking this, it went through my head, they blame us for what happened. They'll blow us out of the air, or worse yet, wait till we land and then line up a firing squad.

Then there we were on the ground, in Texas of all places. The plane smelled a trifle ripe by this time.

One of the airmen kept complaining, "They ought to give us a fair go. We're not in with that lot."

"That lot" meaning Dr. Sinlop, his two assistants, and myself. The airman looked feverish to me. Maybe they all looked that way to me by that time, whether or not they really were.

Dr. Sinlop told me the Americans must have found out what was on board and decided to boost us from the Canucks. Along about four in the a.m. their time, the Americans deplaned us and stuck us in their ambos with all the grace of delivering a load of kibble, not that I expected a warm welcome from anyone. Then they took us to a building there on base.

I don't know what I was expecting, a room in isolation or jail or a coffin, but they put me in a regular patient room with one of the assistants. I didn't know what to do then, take off the suit or what. She said go on since she had tested positive. Matter of time. It turned out the Americans made the entire floor isolation protocol. They came in wearing the gear, took the samples, Dr. Sinlop's records, even his laptop, and told us to sit tight.

It wasn't until the girl mentioned it that I realized I missed out on Christmas. She let me borrow her cellie, and I tried to call my mum. No answer so I rang up my sister, and who answered but her boyfriend? Bad news all around. Bad as you can get. I couldn't even cry by that point. I had been awake going on three days straight. Who knew when I had eaten more than a stale crisp? The boyfriend didn't sound angry. He sounded tired, more than anything.

I might have apologized, I don't recall. The girl said later I fell asleep with the phone still in my hand. Next thing I knew, it was still daylight, or maybe the next day, and some bloke wearing hazmat was sticking a needle in my arm. I would have volunteered my spleen, my liver, anything they wanted.

*Wylie Halverson*

I had been too busy volunteering at the hospital and checking in on neighbors to pay attention to the holidays, but one day I went by the church and lit a candle. I sat there watching it melt down, and I guess I drifted off.

Next thing I knew, Selma Steicher was tapping me gently on the arm, asking the last time I had eaten anything. I couldn't remember, so she drove me back to my house and heated us up some leftover pad thai. Then she broke out the snow blower. I hadn't had time to work down the drifts in my driveway, and the neighbor boys I usually paid to do it... they were dead by this point, or about to be, or holed up with their families.

I knew Selma, not well, but we collaborated on some of the same church events over the years since I moved back home. Selma and her brother ran a dairy farm. I knew her brother and his family had been taken because Father Jerzy mentioned it on the radio. There was a long list of obituaries by then, plus he was asking for canned food to give to the shut-ins.

People who weren't sick yet, they were staying away from the rest of the world. Trying to keep from getting infected. Some of them had stockpiled enough groceries; others were already running low. Back in the day, people who hid out in the wilderness were called survivalists. That's what these families were trying to do.

Since one of my neighbors needed food, I had spent that morning gathering up some items. I disinfected the outsides of the cans and boxes as best I could, then I left it on their front porch. I saw the husband looking through the shades, his mouth moving, saying "thank you."

The snow felt hard under my feet, like crunching down on chalk. Snow on snow, but still easy to get around on if you were used to it. We hadn't had what one of my sisters used to call a foot-long, a blizzard. That was a blessing, I suppose, maybe the only one I can think of during that time. There were so many darkened houses by then on my block, but several of us were still hanging in there, keeping our outside lights on day and night. Look at us, we're alive.

It was a strange kind of disaster. Everyone had light, heat, and water. The TV shows were still playing in between announcements; you had the Internet. There had been lines at the gas stations at first, but since most people weren't allowed on the street except for short periods of time, you didn't hear much about gas shortages, not in our area.

Food was beginning to be a problem. Donald Metzger, who used to work with the Red Cross, organized teams to visit homes where people had died, to gather up food and other necessary items. He said on the radio and TV that it was important to respect personal property.

I had picked up another cat, one that used to belong to a family down the street, and my neighbor's peekapoo, who got along fine with my cat. The way things were headed, it looked like I might end up with a lot of pets.

I knew I had to be contagious. I didn't need a blood test to prove that. I tried not to think about whether I would eventually come down with the plague. You would see reporters on CNN and Fox talking about how people who felt healthy still needed to take precautions. Those reporters had to know they were describing themselves, as well.

I was one of the lucky ones, although I didn't feel that way. I couldn't raise up either of my sisters on the phone in Milwaukee, or my nephews and nieces, or their families.

I knew what that meant. I was sixty-one years old and in pretty good shape from yoga class, but I never expected to outlive my sisters' children. I never expected to see so many of my students go to their graves. So many lives taken.

At night before going to bed, I would pray the Stations of the Cross. My mind kept going blank on the words. I kept thinking, why was this happening? God, why?

By the time Selma came back in from snow-blowing, I had cups of hot cocoa ready. She sat across from me at the table. She looked like a strong woman. Thin like me, but strong. I knew that from helping her carry out the vats on fish-fry nights down at the parish hall. Then it occurred to me: all those cows. She had to be doing all the milking, but where was the milk going? There weren't any trucks running those days.

We worked it out on the spot. I would come out and help with the milking, the usual five a.m. and five p.m. It's all done with machines, of course, but still so time consuming. You have to clear the lines, maintain the pumps, and keep the entire procedure as antiseptic as possible. Milk gets stored in a stainless steel tank, big jobber, so I was talking with Selma about how to get the milk out to the shut-ins. She said that their father had put their old milk cans in storage. He never bothered to get rid of them, which meant we had a means of carrying it to the families. We were talking about the logistics of it when my doorbell rang.

It was Chelsea Thoresen, standing there in her letter jacket with a boy it took me a moment to recognize. Coach Kobold's youngest son, Dixon. He was thirteen years old, but a tow-headed fellow who looked younger. Father Jerzy sent them to me. They were both shell-shocked, so the main task at hand, as I saw it, was to feed them something warm and familiar, something other than the packaged pad thai I had been living off. Selma cooked some bratwurst I'd been saving in the freezer, while I made up the spare bedroom and the davenport. We took care of their immediate needs, then Selma drove me back over to the church so I could take my pickup back home.

"Got yourself a ready-made family," she said.

I told her it was probably a temporary situation.

"We don't know how long this thing is going to last. You might as well plan on having them for the duration, don't you know?"

Four a.m. sharp, I bounced out of bed and got ready. To be more accurate, I crawled out of bed, dragged some clothes onto my body, and tried to prepare my mind for the day to come.

Chelsea heard me rustling in the kitchen while making a thermos of coffee. She said she wasn't about to be left behind. We both had heard gunshots during the night. In some cases, sheriff's deputies were going around shooting abandoned dogs; other cases, well, the plague had a way of making people choose a faster way to die.

I wound up taking both of them out to the farm with me. It kept them busy. Took their minds off their troubles for a while. Chelsea, being an athlete, was in pretty good shape to help out, while Dixon, he mainly played with the cats. Selma, she was easy to work with. She has those deep brown eyes, a grave expression as though she had already witnessed a world of trouble, yet she would let loose with some silly cow sounds, trying to make the kids smile.

*Dreya Underhill*

I didn't want to see Rita's symptoms, so I didn't, at first. We had barely been around each other since it began. We'd been so busy dealing with family issues. I didn't know these people, but they were Rita's family. I couldn't leave them, and I couldn't get through the roadblocks to my parents. Stuck all around. And the way I saw it, I was going to come down with it myself at any time. I might as well stay. I did my best to keep them clean and fed them aspirin, which was all I had.

I couldn't think of anything else to do, so I started pouring whiskey down this one lady's throat (Rita's great-aunt, I think), and that's what helped more than anything.

I rounded up bottles of booze from the neighbors. To tell it right, I stole the bottles, since most everybody in my neighborhood was either dead or hiding out in the hills, and I didn't see any point in keeping Rita's relatives sober. According to the Internet, everyone died once they started showing symptoms, so why should they suffer? I already tried to get the first couple into a hospital, but every one of those places was batshit crazy. Idiots pulled guns to try to get ahead in line, doctors worked until they dropped dead themselves. The patients...

I remember those zombie movies I used to watch. Some of the old-school zombies might stumble around while the new-school would jump in your face, but these people weren't zombies. They were human. They were real. Until they couldn't move anymore, they went around trying to get help for themselves and their families, which made it worse, I think, in the way it spread. Booze at least slowed them down. I didn't have any drugs to give them other than aspirin, which amounted to nothing. I kept them clean, and when they died, I hauled their bodies down to Southwestern College, which was one of the collection centers. That's what the officials had wanted Rita for, to record the bodies.

One morning, Rita called me and said she was coming home. I took that to mean her dad had died. He was the last holdout in her immediate family. She didn't sound like herself. When she got home, she tried to help me move her cousin's body to the bathtub so we could wash off the blood. She almost fell down, so I told her I would take care of it.

She said we ought to go for a drive through Balboa Park, to get the stink out of our noses. It was hard enough to get around town those days, and she's asking for a Sunday drive? When I touched her arm, I could feel the fever. She didn't want a hug. I knew what that meant. Victims would get those tender spots on their chest and stomach, and it would spread over the rest of their body.

I managed to load her cousin into the back of the van, found a bottle of Rita's favorite rum I'd been holding back, and then she and I went for a drive. National Guardsmen stopped us, but I yelled that I was taking a body for collection. They were fine with any story that kept them from touching somebody.

We went in by way of Sixth, which took us by the eucalyptus and pine trees. It made me remember my parents taking us on a road trip up north when I was a kid so we could see the redwoods. It's why I wanted to become a gardener. I wanted to grow something like that, to be the one to get a giant like that started.

Balboa Park creeped me out. Place was totally empty. I mean, no one.

About the zoo... I'd heard on TV that the zookeepers had moved some of the animals out to private homes, but it was still up in the air what to do about the larger animals. As long as they had staff to take care of them, they'd hold off on killing them.

Rita made me stop the van over by the friendship garden. I had no clue how many people were left in town, who had died, and who had made a run for Somewhere Else. As for my friends, it was hard, just hard. Some of them were sick, some of them weren't answering their phones anymore, for whatever reason, and the ones who did were in the same boat as me, taking care of their loved ones.

When I talked to Pops the last time on the phone, he could string words together, but they didn't make any sense except on this one point: God placed this fever on us as a final judgment. God was doing this to us. Not the terrorists and not some Australian messing with a pig. This was the Lord's business. God had no use for us anymore.

Rita and I walked into the Japanese garden. It's supposed to be serene, supposed to put you in a better place, spiritually. She was having trouble walking, so when we came to a bench, we sat down, the two of us and a bottle of rum.

That's when I got up my nerve to take an honest look at her. She had on a long-sleeved shirt, but you could see those dark spots on her hands and neck. She started talking about how I needed to get out of town, and that in our neighborhood anybody left alive was going to be either pissed off, or crazy, or both. You heard plenty of gunshots by then. Sirens going all day and all night. Not a lot of bodies on the street. Crews were still doing a good job picking them up.

Rita was a real strong woman. If she had an opinion on anything, she let you know it. I told her, no freaking way I was going to leave her.

I had to carry her back to the van, and by the time we made it back home from dropping off her cousin's body, she was stone drunk, her skin on fire from the fever.

She died two days later.

Early the next morning (I had been drunk off my ass with Rita that last day, so I was hung over, badly hung over), I called Leesa and told her to get ready, I was coming up to get her. I packed some bags and drove to Riverside, and this time, I didn't stop for nothing, not even roadblocks.

The closer I came to my parents' place, I saw more houses burned out, store windows broken in, and bodies in the alleyways with sheets over them. Leesa cried when she saw me, but I didn't.

Mom and Pops dead, our uncle down the street, dead. The neighbors. All I could see was a bad situation bound to get worse.

On the Internet, it sounded like San Francisco was still holding it together even though victims had overwhelmed their hospitals. Seeing the houses burned out made me think about how bad it would be if another big fire hit. Who'd be left to fight it?

I pushed Leesa hard, real hard, to finish up on her packing while I grabbed supplies and pictures, whatever I thought we needed to hang on to. I found Pops's old service pistol. I piled everything in the van. I told Leesa, "We're leaving and we're leaving now. We're going north."

*Analyn Orante*

Although I had visited the White House any number of times over the years, dating back to my intern days, I had never been down in the Situation Room. But then, I never thought I would receive this type of job promotion, Secretary of State, and that I would be sitting across the table from our new President, Rebecca Budin.

Good thing all those cameras and microphones in the ceiling were recording history in the making. This marked the first time the line of succession came down to the Secretary of the Treasury. The first Jew, the first native Oregonian. Just name the category, she had it sewn up. In her late forties, with short gray hair and a dynamic presence, even at this moment, she gave off a vibe that was more laid-back Silicon executive than dry bureaucrat.

There was one person ahead of me in State still healthy, but the President promoted me anyhow, pointing out that I had been right about Variant Swine Fever, or VSF as everyone was calling it now. She wanted my expertise. Expertise in what, I wondered.

Despite having worked at the State Department for fourteen years, I was hardly God's gift to diplomacy. In every department, you need technocrats, men and women who get things done, but aren't born politicians. That's why I never had illusions of being appointed to an ambassadorship.

But there I was in the Sit Room, thanking the petty officer for a perfect cup of coffee. I sat in a soft leather chair while admiring the cherrywood cabinetry, gazing down at a table on which you'd be proud to serve Thanksgiving dinner.

At the same time, there were Army and Guard units stationed through the capitol. They were deployed a virally safe distance apart from each other, but yes, we had not ruled out the possibility of terrorism, whether as biowarfare or in hostile elements wanting to take advantage. Intelligence told us there was no solid evidence that VSF had been released deliberately, but we simply didn't know what could happen next, here or abroad.

Fatalities in D.C. alone were over fifty thousand, minimum estimate. There were neighborhoods that emergency medical techs and police couldn't easily penetrate, whether due to gang activity or because they were gated communities.

I couldn't get hold of my little brother, Michael. I hoped it was because his cell phone service had been disrupted and he was lying on a beach in Jamaica, sipping a rum drink. I clung to that image with all my might. My older brother had fallen ill, as had his family, and my parents. It doesn't even bear discussing when you think about everyone else's losses.

I felt transfixed by the multiple screens on the wall before us. On one panel, we were in the midst of a report from the commanding officer of the *USS Ronald Reagan*, a Nimitz-class supercarrier, home-ported out of San Diego, but on deployment to the Western Pacific.

It had been a major stroke of luck that a Pentagon admiral ordered the *Reagan* to remain at sea early on in the pandemic alert. You couldn't say the same for the *Stennis*, which had been preparing for a training cycle at Norfolk, Virginia.

*Stennis* represented but one line on a long list of compromised assets. The *Reagan* was our one completely unaffected supercarrier and Carrier Strike Group that we could confirm, but how long could we keep it out at sea?

The commander estimated that, based on current ship's stores, the carrier group could comfortably stay out three more months.

"After that," he said, "we'll need to break out the fishing nets."

The President thanked him for the presentation; then came a short, painful news summary on screen two, delivered by the Acting Joint Chief of Staff, a hastily unretired admiral.

We managed to transfer more of our troops from the Middle East Command onto our ships, but all ports in the region were closed to foreign vessels. The Egyptians had shut down the Suez Canal, and our remaining soldiers on the ground were dying by droves while we flew the uninfected home by way of Europe. Each flight had to be cleared by EU member countries. This took entirely too long. With all this going on, options appeared limited.

I tried to imagine what it would be like on a crowded vessel, limping to Diego Garcia or making the trans-Indian Ocean trip to

Perth. Australia welcomed our Yankee firepower. President Budin sent word to the various heads of state in the region that attacks on our troops would be met with maximum reprisal.

"I don't care if we're down to one officer with his bleeding finger on the trigger, we'll make good on the threat," she told the admiral before dismissing him.

I tried to be subtle about peering at the people gathered around the table. It marked the first time in several weeks I had been around a group of people where no one was wearing protective gear, not even the watch officers in the surge room next door. All of us, right down to the petty officer serving us coffee, had tested positive for VSF.

In person, a nameless woman representing a joint-intelligence task force briefed us on what more had been learned about the virus's origins. In short, next to nothing. The Dutch couple had, indeed, visited a slaughterhouse in the southern Chinese city of Guangzhou. More important, we knew of a government biological research facility located near Guangzhou.

Pigs share certain physical similarities with humans and are easier to acquire and maintain than apes. One could speculate as to how a sick research subject ended up at the slaughterhouse; however, Beijing's current leadership, who were issuing faceless communiqués in lieu of appearances, rejected outside requests for investigations.

My assistant, Bill Levine, had learned from associates within the Pentagon that there was some truth behind the current rumor that a Defense Department research project back in the late 1990s focused on the zoonotic potential of certain viruses. If one such virus had become a weaponable biological agent, I doubted that anyone sitting in the Situation Room, our nameless intelligence official included, knew how it got to China. I suspected anyone still alive who had been associated with that project had covered their tracks, even at the cost of hiding potential treatments.

Ms. Nameless finished her report and left the room. I heard the sound of a throat clearing from the direction of the far wall.

Screen three, the acting head of the CDC, Dr. James Tofill. He possessed a craggy face, and as I soon realized, the body of a little person. It was a sign of the current upheaval that another milestone had been reached without a celebratory moment. Bill Levine told me earlier that Tofill and the President were in the same class at Harvard.

Smoke from a cigarette off-screen wafted through the air above his head. Even compared to present company, he looked exhausted. "Madam President, I truly wish that I could give you good news right now."

"I'll take a kick to the head, James, with both feet."

"We haven't finished analyzing the Australians' records we seized in San Antonio, but I can tell you it's not likely to change my take on it. This is a designed virus and a damned efficient one. We're looking at a protein triggering sequence that normally should kick in..."

"For a pig," said Defense Secretary Clayton FitzGerald, a bullet-shaped projectile with a similar degree of patience.

"Yes, I believe we were discussing pigs, and not manatees. Your average, God-fearing pig contracts the virus, fights the hell out of it, and either dies or does a damn good job at trying to," said Tofill.

"What about humans?"

FitzGerald and Tofill were not going to rate glowing mentions in each other's autobiography. That is, if they lived long enough to write the books and any potential readers survived.

"If all we did was fight like a pig, we'd have a serious kill-rate, perhaps sixty to eighty percent. But what happens is that we fight it so hard that the immune system ends up attacking the body, which initiates a cascade reaction. If the virus doesn't kill you outright, your reaction will. Something like this happened with the Spanish flu, but this variant form of swine fever produces a kill-rate of over ninety percent, if current projections hold true. Then again, one could compare it to the medieval expression of the bubonic plague."

I could tell from Secretary FitzGerald's body language that another aerial assault was planned, so I stepped in.

"Dr. Tofill, to bring the discussion into this century, could you tell us why we're still alive? I haven't had so much as a sniffle yet."

"Do you know when you were initially exposed?"

"Early November."

Tofill took a drag off his cigarette and set it down off-screen. "Madam Secretary, are you gay?"

"Pardon? I don't see what that has to do—"

"Everything. It has everything to do with why you're still alive."

"What are you driving at, James?" President Budin's voice sounded steady.

"The Australians noticed it first. The longest-lived survivor is a lesbian veterinarian. Also, a gay volleyball tournament took place at the same time that the Dutch couple frolicked on Bondi Beach. The Australians tracked much of the viral traffic in Sydney from Bondi, but they discovered that few of the volleyballers, or for that matter, the gay neighborhoods they came from, have been affected. Then they deliberately infected two gay researchers. Their blood looks the same as the hog doctor: the virus is present, but inactive within the blood stream. We don't fight. We coexist."

I heard the "we," as did the President.

Almost gently, she said, "James, there's a flaw in your logic. Noah is dead." For the first time, I heard her voice tremble. "I don't call that coexisting."

Tofill looked somber.

"Becky—Madam President—some of us are as sensitive as the heterosexuals. I don't have enough information yet to speculate as to why. Perhaps there's some truth to the nature versus nurture theory; I don't know. We're hampered by the lack of reliable numbers on gay populations worldwide. Anyhow, about the disease: we're looking at the role of proteins, of triggers existing in what used to be called junk DNA. Somehow, it's connected to our sexuality, but more than that appears to be involved."

"What can we do, James? How soon can we develop a vaccine, or a treatment of some kind?"

"That's the problem, Madam President. We've already identified seven variants or mutations of VSF from the Australian samples alone. Think about how we deal with influenza. There's an elaborate network designed to predict which variants will spread and how long it will take to produce the prototypes. It's a mammoth, worldwide effort that has taken decades to fine-tune, and yet people still die by the thousands, if you include contributing factors.

"Now, let's say we develop a vaccine, not a cure and not a treatment, but a vaccine. Given the number of chicken eggs that have to be used in the manufacturing process, it boggles the mind how we'll ramp up production in the current situation, even if we do find an effective prototype."

"Are you saying, because it's hard, we shouldn't even try?" Secretary FitzGerald slammed down his folder.

Tofill's eyes flashed. He started to say something, stopped, then took a different tack. "We're doing something that would have been impossible a few years ago. In only a matter of weeks, we have identified the viral mechanism and are working on the mother of all kitchen sink strategies. Anything, everything, and I guarantee you every functioning medical and genetics research lab in this country is trying to beat this thing, whether with drug combinations, blood treatments, animal trials, or volunteers. It's like that last part in 'A Day in the Life' where the orchestra plays every note in the book. I'm rambling. Sorry."

He took a drag from his cigarette. "The only people who are able to travel safely are us, and we're infected, either currently or potentially. This isn't HIV, where it's hard to catch and slow to develop. It's not Ebola, where you contract it in a matter of days, then essentially die where you fall. This is the ultimate killer cold, one that takes weeks to destroy its carriers. One or more of the strains might evolve into a less virulent strain the way syphilis did in the Middle Ages, but that could take generations."

"Madam President," Secretary FitzGerald said before Tofill could go on. "I don't believe we should inform the public about homosexual resistance to the virus. It would create a panic."

"More than the panic we already have, Clay?" Her aura of confidence had returned. "This does explain why some places are handling the crisis better than others, and also why rural areas are so hard hit. Look, we have who knows how many caregivers out there killing their patients and families without knowing it, and let's not forget the children out there."

With a start, I remembered she lost a child to the virus less than a week ago. A teenaged boy who had been sent to a friend's farm in rural Maryland. Had he caught the virus from his mother?

She turned to her assistant. "I want you to set up a live remote. I need to lay this out for the public."

This time I jumped in. "Madam President, there's going to be a backlash. Anyone who is gay or perceived to be gay will have a target on their back. We're staggering over a cliff as it is. This can't possibly help."

"I'm not going to hide in here and sing 'Kumbayah.' I'm going to tell them what's happening. Face it, people. Right now there are several million of us in this country who can keep things running, who can try to protect the ones who aren't infected, while James and his crew develop a cure."

Tofill lit another cigarette, a spectral smile crossing his lips. "You know what the press is going to ask you."

The President gazed at us, her spirit unflagging. "I have always believed God made me this way for a reason, and now I know why."

*Dora Navarro*

The knock on the door totally surprised me. I almost fell down, although part of that might have been exhaustion. I had been cleaning the house from top to bottom, trying to scrub away traces of blood. Maybe it's because I'm my mother's daughter. When in doubt, get out the bleach.

That's why I took so long getting Mama ready to take to the Odessa Convention Center, even though she would be just another body to them. Mama had been the first infected, yet she was the last to go. My brother told me to use the gun if necessary. I couldn't do that.

Mark couldn't see the percentage in staying around, not when they were all so sick, him included. That's why he killed himself. First, he took our stepdad's deer rifle and shot Nicole and the boys. He made me help drag Nicole into the folks' camper. The boys were already there. He had shot them first. I had three nephews. Daniel was the baby. When he was born, Nicole swore she would try for a girl the next time.

I couldn't go back into the garage, even though I knew at some point I needed to drive the camper over to the Convention Center. If I had any plans, it amounted to leaving it there with the key in the ignition and walking all the way back to the house. It had been three or four days since the deal with the camper. I thought maybe three or four days. I wasn't sure about the date, or about when I had last eaten.

I hadn't heard from my stepbrother, who was in Afghanistan, since right after the infections started. Maybe he was alive and hiding in a cave somewhere. Two of the local TV stations still had news anchors, even if you couldn't recognize them. Every day they would give the local scores. That's the way it looked to me. Today's sports results: Death, 500; Odessa, 0.

I opened the front door, and there stood Miguel Contreras, wearing stained overalls and a cowboy hat, smiling at me. We were in the same graduating class from Permian High School, even sang in choir together one year. We didn't hang out together much. He was in with the theater crowd, and I was a band nerd. But we liked each other, and when he saw me at the local gay club with this girl I had a crush on, he didn't out me at school.

Odessa, you were either gay or straight. Bisexual freaked everyone out. Throw in multiracial and no, not a great senior prom, but Mama said things had changed since I graduated from high school. There were gay kids in her classes who didn't automatically get beaten up, who were popular, even.

I found one Pepsi left in the fridge, and we split it while we talked in the den. Miguel had seen me drive by his block earlier in the week, probably when I was searching for chicken bouillon broth, something I might get Mama to drink.

"I wanted to call 'bring out your dead,'" I said. "A little Monty Python for you, but maybe this isn't the best moment for that."

"Is that what you've been doing, collecting bodies?"

"Part of the time. My sister and her kids went camping weeks ago. I just came back from looking for them over by Goldsmith. She had friends there who were going to let her pitch a tent in the backyard."

"It's getting pretty cold at night."

"I checked at the friends' house, and the only reason I don't have a bullet hole in me is because they're lousy shots. Her car was there, but I couldn't see a tent, and I didn't feel all that welcome, to be honest."

Athletic-looking, Miguel could have played football, which was the town's leading obsession, but decided on cooking school instead. He told me later on that when he moved to Dallas, he ended up working at the Mansion on Turtle Creek.

I told him about my situation. He instantly volunteered to drive the camper to the Convention Center.

"I've got my mother to move, too," I said. "I don't want her in the camper. It's messy."

I realized how silly that sounded, given all that was going on, but Miguel understood.

"I took my dad over a few days ago, and man, I got so pissed off while I was there. It took me an hour just to find somebody to register him. Maybe it sounds stupid, but I wanted it to be written down before they dropped him in the pit. There's no time, no space for anything like a funeral."

"I saw a preacher there praying with the families. Make that near the families."

Just then it hit me. Neither of us was wearing a mask. My hands went to my face automatically.

Miguel tried to put me at ease. "If you're not dead yet, you're not going to be. I've been reading online, and there's some crazy rumors going around. I'll tell you more in a bit, but right now, we've got to get over to the Convention Center before dark. Patrols may be too overwhelmed to mess with enforcing curfew, but I don't want us getting hit by a stray bullet."

After helping me move Mama into the back of his SUV, Miguel drove the camper as I followed. He wouldn't let me come with him as he rolled the cart through the center doors.

"You don't want to go inside now. It's gotten worse. Fire department brought over a unit to hose down the floors, which helps, but so many of the people coming in are sick themselves. They'll pull a gun on you if you come near them. It's like they think they can retroactively hold off the disease."

Afterward, we went back home where I packed my bags and drove over to his place. He had some food to share. I wasn't afraid of dying of the epidemic anymore. Exhaustion does that to you, but the thought of being alone was unbearable.

He baked a tater tot and blue cheese casserole. "It's not haute cuisine, but the freezer's a bit lacking in options at the moment," he said. I cooked a pork chop for us to split.

We sat in the living room, plates balanced on our laps, and watched President Budin's scheduled address to the nation, to whoever was left.

*Transcript of broadcast:*

Announcer: And now, from the Oval Office, the President of the United States.

President Budin: Good evening, my fellow Americans. Tonight, I look out upon a nation that has suffered unimaginable losses. In my home state of Oregon, where I was elected to statewide office three times, it is estimated that over one-hundred-and-fifty-thousand citizens have died.

In my hometown of Portland, where I ran a company dedicated to innovation, high school and college gymnasiums are now operating as morgues. Losses across the country have well exceeded total casualties in all our wars combined. This is a crushing burden that every single one of us shares.

Like many of you, I, too, have experienced personal losses. My heart is saddened, my soul is weary, but I know upon whom I rely. My help comes from the Creator. My faith strengthens me, as I am sure your faith has been a beacon to you, whatever tradition to which you belong.

All of us, regardless of our religious background, share a common faith in our beloved country, the shining stars we call the United States of America.

We are the best hope for humankind. Tonight, much of the developing world lies in chaos, while our partners in Europe, the United Kingdom, and the Pacific Rim struggle with the terrible impact of Variant Swine Fever.

As Americans, we must work together as we have in the past. We must become once more the strong, vital center around which our planet can rebuild. The battle has only just begun, but with me at this moment are able soldiers for our cause. [Camera scans those seated in chairs next to her desk.]

In recent days, you have been introduced to Secretary of Defense Clayton FitzGerald, a decorated Gulf War veteran who has extensive experience within the Pentagon. You have also met Secretary of State Analyn Orante, who courageously warned us of the pandemic in its early stages.

Also here tonight is Dr. James Tofill, representing the Center for Disease Control. Dr. Tofill has given me news about VSF. It is news that has both positive and negative implications for how we will conquer this virulent foe.

Many of you are wondering: where are your local leaders, your statewide elected officials? Are they in hiding, are they sick, or are they dead? I have informed the leadership of all fifty states that they are to convene, via the Internet, both party and legislative sessions to select replacements for all vacant positions in their home states, as well as in Congress. I signed an executive order to that effect this afternoon.

I have also cancelled all retirements within the past ten years of military service for those currently residing in the United States and have so ordered that they resume active duty within their state's National Guard or Reserve units, whichever is the best fit for their services.

This is not the time for partisan politics or for the placing of blame. I am calling for an end of violence toward all visitors to our shores, a pledge backed up by mobilized National Guard units patrolling the streets of our major cities. As previously announced, we are transferring our overseas military personnel back to their home bases, but this is a process that will take time.

I mentioned earlier that Dr. Tofill, an eminent researcher internationally recognized in his field, has given me news regarding VSF. You may have noticed that some of our citizens who have been exposed to the virus have not as yet displayed symptoms. Dr. Tofill explained to me that their lack of symptoms does not mean that they are immune.

VSF is highly contagious, so there are some among us who are infected but may never develop symptoms, which is why even those who by all appearances are healthy must still take protective measures.

Dr. Tofill tells me that research begun by the Australians, and continued by the CDC, indicates there is a small population existing worldwide that can act without fear. These people, who are members of a group that includes infants, children, adults, and elders, are individuals possessing a wide variety of skills.

It is a group comprising, at best, seven to nine percent of our population. They are of many ethnic and religious backgrounds. They are your neighbors. They are in your hometown right now. They're working to make a positive difference in this unimaginable tragedy.

This group is made up of members of our gay and lesbian community. Not all gays and lesbians, however, have been spared the ravages of VSF. It appears that some are as susceptible to the virus as heterosexuals. This was the case for my husband, Noah, whom I loved very much.

Although I was infected at the same time as my husband and our only child, I've shown no symptoms. I'm sure you understand what this means. I have long believed that a person's orientation has no bearing on whether he or she should participate in our democratic process.

I still strongly believe that, and that is why I encourage all Americans like me, who have tested positive for VSF and have remained free of symptoms for a minimum of three weeks, to become active in your communities and to take roles to which you may feel unaccustomed. Become foster parents, caregivers, Red Cross volunteers, and neighborhood watch officers. Your country is counting on you. We can and must weather this storm.

In these times, I'm reminded of what Abraham Lincoln said during the darkest days of the Civil War, a conflict that took so many lives.

He said, "The dogmas of the quiet past are inadequate to the stormy present. The occasion is piled high with difficulty, and we must rise with the occasion. As our case is new, so we must think anew and act anew. We must disenthrall ourselves, and then we shall save our country."

Friends, this is the stormy present. We must think anew, and act anew. We must free ourselves of the past, and so shall we save our country.

God bless the United States of America, and God bless each and every one of you. Good night.

# Chapter 5

*Debra Shanrahan*

I didn't consider it to be relevant, my orientation, whatnot. How could it be? I was asked back at the beginning about sexual partners, which I disclosed quite readily. Why would anyone care, other than my mum? She always had her heart set on a traditional white wedding.

I barely got used to San Antonio, then off they took me to Atlanta, where I met a wee man with a cocky attitude, and it's nonstop lesbian this, gay that. Then, to discover it actually matters what I am, and matters greatly. My gay friends back home, I hoped this meant they were still alive, but at the rate I was going, I didn't expect to ever get back home, and why would I want to? I had read the newspapers when I was stuck in isolation, with reporters saying I had been spreading the fever around.

Poor, sad little Dutch couple. They got all the sympathy, all the crocodile tears, when they infected half of Asia and Australia, for Chrissake. If anyone deserved tears, it was Dr. Sinlop, the project head, who died in his traces and never made it to Atlanta.

After a very short visit with a very short man, I did get my wish granted to actually do something useful, by working with pigs, at first. It's sort of my specialty, after all.

To me, it seemed rather obvious that you could blame swine all you want, but you have to look at the soft ticks. They're the biological vectors, the real reservoir population, you might say.

It worried the hell out of me that VSF was transmittable human to human. Right there's a clue this wasn't normal swine fever. But once we had the population in lockdown, so to speak, I felt pretty certain we could contain our losses until the virus died out from lack of human carriers. But I couldn't stop thinking: how did Ducket's hogs get infected? It had to be from humans. Or ticks that fed on humans.

38

I'd heard that the virus had been tracked to a slaughterhouse in China, but I also heard that the virus originally came from the Americans. Lots of rumors going around, but I didn't see the traction in worrying over it. No matter how the virus got out, I figured it still had to obey the same rules, which meant vectors.

I thought it likely that soft ticks here in America had already contracted VSF from infected humans, but what really concerned me was where else it could go. Could this zoonotic swine fever now latch on to other animal hosts by way of the ticks?

I was telling Bao-Zhai, the head of my lab section, about the habits of ticks, how some species can transmit a virus to their progeny, through the generations, and that as nesting ticks, they can survive for months, even years, without food.

"Without us, you mean?" She frowned as she downed the last of her Coke. "What would VSF do to other animals, I wonder."

"VSF specifically jumped to us. It would have to mutate yet again to attack other animals."

"We can't rule that out. As fast as this thing spread, I think the Chinese are lying about when they started seeing cases. Besides that, they're not telling us anything, truth or lie, about whether they were using other species besides pigs in their project."

"So you think they're the culprits."

"I'd say they're more like the co-conspirators and the co-victims." Bao-Zhai crumpled her can. "In the meantime, if this thing can be carried by vectors besides ticks, we need to know ASAP yesterday. We need a lot more animal and insect vectors to test, so get on it. And if you happen to come across a case of Cokes, I want it. The delivery man hasn't been by here in weeks."

*Wylie Halverson*

It was a brutal cold snap, staying below zero for days. Don Metzger said on the TV that he needed more volunteers to check on the elderly.

He had already sent teams around for an accurate census. That couldn't have been an easy task, what with homeowners pointing guns through their windows. Somehow he determined where the survivors were and where they weren't. He then had the power turned off on all unused buildings.

Didn't that upset some people? They called into the radio stations. "Our neighbors don't have power." They're dead. You don't need lights on over there, and if you're relying on your neighbor's freezer for food storage, that entire house is a chill chest.

Metzger had turned into the High Sheriff of Portage County. He ran roughshod over more delicate souls. He said we didn't need all the churches lit up all the time, especially since we had to use some of the smaller ones to store bodies. Ground was frozen down eighteen inches, radio said, and the original pits that had been dug were full to the grim, which was how Selma put it. A malaprop, but accurate.

The dying had slowed down considerably. According to the census, there were about seven thousand people left in the Stevens Point area. We'd grown to over fifty thousand before all this happened. You figure some people left to check on family, some went to the rural areas, smart enough not to stay out in the open, I hoped, and then you count in the visitors.

The recorded deaths were estimated at fourteen thousand. Metzger said that meant that a lot of people were still out there but afraid to get counted, afraid and paranoid. Don't let the government know you're alive, or Uncle Sam'll come after you.

I agreed with Metzger on most decisions, but he didn't have to be quite so pushy. One day, he sent a case of formula and two cases of diapers to us, accompanied by a three-month-old boy named Jarrod, which Selma said was Metzger's idea of a bouquet. We had become one big de facto family at her place. I moved out to the farm with Chelsea and Dixon not long after we started the milking project. I didn't feel safe at home.

I had discovered one of my neighbors siphoning gas from my truck. There was still gas at a couple of stations, if you didn't mind the lines, but he was afraid to be near the others. He said he was taking what was left of his family up north because the plague couldn't live up there. I tried telling him that Canada had the same problem we did. Maybe it was taking longer, but people were dying there, too.

He completely lost it. He started screaming that faggots started the plague by having sex with animals. He waved his rifle around for a bit, then he grabbed the gas can and went back to his place. Back before, we attended the same church and his wife helped out on food drives. We weren't close friends, but still. I'd witnessed enough of the plague that I knew he was sick. I think the dying are entitled to their anger. It was all he had by then.

I went back inside and called Selma, who helped us move out to the farm the next day.

Chelsea kept her dad's pickup, we had our vehicles, and as long as the farm's gas storage tank held out, we would be okay. There were no more fuel deliveries for the time being.

I remember one night at a meeting Metzger called. It was at the high school gym. He wanted us to get better organized at checking on the elderly and getting supplies to the needy.

There were two men sitting on the bleacher in front of me. One of them had his arm around the other's waist. They weren't being romantic. It was something you might do with a loved one during a difficult moment. I thought, oh, they need to be more discreet. That's what you did. You tried not to be obvious. They kept on holding each other, and nothing happened. Nothing happened. That's when it hit me: we were the healthy ones, the normal ones, now.

My neighbor with the gun, he wasn't how all the straight people behaved. We kept finding gifts on the front porches of shut-ins we went to on our milk runs. They left us children's clothes, toilet paper, and other useful items that were in short supply.

Father Jerzy told me about a local man, a print-shop owner, who had recently died from the plague. When one of Metzger's foraging squads went into his house, they found rooms stacked to the ceiling with cases of food, yet the man had been one of the biggest complainers about shortages. Human nature, Father Jerzy said, but I thought human greed was a more accurate phrase, whatever the orientation.

Chelsea wanted to go help with restoring power around the county. Selma and I put the kibosh on that. We still had electricity and a backup generator if that failed. We needed her at home, and not only to help with milking. There were diapers to wash. Besides Jarrod, we had a one-year-old girl named Felicity. Metzger also gave us Reha, a seven-year-old girl with hearing problems. There were meals to prepare and children to keep occupied.

And cows to feed. That was getting to be a problem. We called a major commercial operation north of town, but they refused to come to terms. Selma knew of a dairy farm a few miles away. She had been dreading going over there, afraid of what she would find, so that morning I had Chelsea babysit the kids—and I can tell you, she did not like being left behind—while Selma and I drove over to investigate. We took Dixon along because he was climbing the walls from cabin fever.

We found the farm owner sitting in his pickup in front of his house. He had been dead for some time, frozen in place. There was no one left inside the house, but he had kept the electricity running. I checked out the food and other supplies while Selma and Dixon went over to the barn. You know, I didn't even think about whether it was appropriate for a child to see a dead man. Dixon had seen so much worse by then.

By the time they returned, I had loaded up everything in the back of the pickup. It looked to me as though there was enough on hand that we could make a return visit. I felt sorry about the way we left the man, but there was no way to bury him, and at least he was safe from animals where he was at.

He had shot all the cows. He didn't want them to suffer. I wish other folks had been as thoughtful about their animals. Well, I say that, but people when they're sick like that, they can't think clearly.

The forklift still had some gas in it, so we used it to load up the trailer with bags of feed and other items Selma had found, then she drove the trailer back to our place while Dixon and I followed behind.

We were listening to the radio. The announcer said that enough teams were now in place to work on the power situation, but that volunteers were needed to give blood for a patient down at the hospital.

"Did the queers start the fever?" Dixon asked.

"No, heavens, no. Where did you hear this?"

"I read it on the Internet."

"I thought you were playing games."

"My favorite website won't work anymore," he said. "I found another one, but while I was looking, I read that the queers were spreading the pig fever, that it was their fault."

Dixon would figure out at some point that he was gay. No need to push that along right now, but I did need to clarify his thinking without coming off like a history teacher.

"Dixon, there are quite a few gay and lesbian people who have survived the plague so far. Selma and I are lesbians, and so is Chelsea. We caught it just like you and your family. For some reason, we're not sick. We may never come down with this. The longer it goes on, I think the less likely it is we'll get sick."

"Why?" He burst into tears. "Mom went to church all the time, and she was nice to people, except maybe to that man next door, and he kept his music too loud, Mom said. Daddy said bad words sometimes, but he was good, too, and so was my brother. Father Jerzy says they're all in heaven now, but I'm not. I'm not there. The

Internet said it's the final days. Good people are up in heaven now, and the queers are going to hell."

Dear Lord. He took the handkerchief I gave him and put it to good use. Driving was too chancy for me to stop on the side of the road. I kept on going and glanced over at him when I could.

"What you read on the Internet was written by somebody who's very upset. He wants to find some people to blame. No one's at fault. A virus that pigs used to come down with got out somehow, and it started making humans sick. People who are gay, we didn't know we were infectious at first, but then the government told us we were. You've seen Selma and me around people we think might catch it. We wear our masks and gloves.

"I'm not the judge on who's going to heaven these days, but I'm pretty sure your family and mine are up there now. They'd want us to work hard at taking care of ourselves and looking after those in need of help. You're a good young man, and when it's all said and done, God will know where you belong. It won't be in the other place. It'll be with your brother and your parents. But right now, we have important jobs to do, just like the president said. Okay?"

He nodded his head. After a while, he turned the radio back up. Truck drivers were needed for the Upper Midwest. The jobs offered good money and excellent benefits. Those interested should call or come by the post office in Stevens Point. A recruiter would be there Thursday morning. If we were lucky, Chelsea didn't have the radio on.

*Dreya Underhill*

After two weeks of hauling bodies to the Presidio pits and living in the van, Leesa and I were ready for a more settled situation. She kept agitating for us to go back to San Diego. The news I read on the laptop made it sound like San Diego's leadership was starting to get it together, but we were in San Francisco, supposedly the gay mecca.

If the news was true about us being immune to the walking fever, I wanted to be where I wouldn't get shot by angry and/or crazy straight people. I have to admit I was tired of eating Meals Ready to Eat, or MREs as the military calls them.

The first night in San Francisco, we got ordered by bullhorn to move three different times on a street near Golden Gate Park. After that, I parked us in an alley behind what looked to be a closed business on Geary Boulevard near the Central Richmond area. This plan lasted longer than I had any right to expect. One night, I woke up to find a flashlight shining into the van. I heard the stressed-out voice of a man telling me that the neighborhood watch association wanted me to move.

"I'll move us in the morning, sir. Please don't make me look for a safe place this time of night."

He worked the beam of his flashlight over the interior of the van. "Most folks these days are stealing game consoles and flat screens. You must prefer lawn equipment."

That ticked off Leesa. "She's a gardener. They're her tools. She's not a thief."

This time the man turned the flashlight onto his face. He was a middle-aged black man, with the kind of face that probably didn't need a disaster to look hangdog.

"Is that true?"

"Yes, sir. We came up from San Diego. We thought it'd be safer here," I said.

"Can't say I agree with you. There're a lot of street kids, some of them old enough to know better, running wild right now. Me and my partner just booted a bunch of them out of a place in my neighborhood. People think they can take over a place anywhere they want if it's empty."

The flashlight beam returned to my face. "What're you doing during the day?"

"Carrying bodies to the Presidio. My sister's helping at the soup kitchen."

"Turn on your overhead and write this down." He gave me the name and address of a business farther down Geary Boulevard. "A woman there and her partner have a restaurant. I believe they own a greenhouse around here somewhere. I'll call her in the morning to tell her you'll be coming by."

By next afternoon, Leesa and I were busy at a large nursery, belonging not to the restaurateurs but to their friend, in the Market Street area and well on the other side of town from Richmond. But the hangdog man at least was accurate about the job.

The nursery owner, a frazzled and fortyish woman named Susan Rhee, said she would allow us to park behind the nursery. If we were still around by the end of the week, and working to her expectations, she'd see about finding us a place to stay. In the meantime, free meals and no hauling dead bodies. A deal with growth potential, literally, although Leesa, born without green thumbs, didn't want anything to do with foliage.

She wanted her job in Chula Vista. She wanted her old life back, and she spent a lot of time, that should have been spent working, talking on her cell to friends back home. One of her ex-girlfriends was now working as a security guard for the City of San Diego, protecting downtown businesses. If Leesa could get down there, she had a job waiting. I didn't want Leesa to go. Rita was gone, our parents were gone; I didn't want to lose my sister, too.

When her cell phone minutes finally ran out and she couldn't find a provider to load more time, it made her that more determined to go back home where she could move in with someone who still had a landline. I'm thinking, they've gone through how many presidents in India, riots in European countries I'd never even heard of, Russians shooting their minorities—and that's from me glancing at the news when I have time—the world's in total meltdown and my sister's worried about texting. I had to remind myself she was barely nineteen. But, still.

The market for ornamental palm trees was collapsing before her eyes, which was why Susan Rhee decided to go into tomatoes and other food plants in a big way. Hundreds of starter containers and racks of hydro shoots lined the aisles of the nursery. Even though it wasn't my idea of real, dig-your-hands-in-the-dirt gardening, it'd have to do until the general situation calmed down, if it calmed down. I didn't like having to take sponge baths in the employee bathroom, but it was better than nothing.

By the middle of the week, she had us sleeping in the back of the building. I guess she decided she had to trust somebody. We had yet to see her partner. The woman supposedly was up in Marin County taking care of business. What kind of business anybody would have there besides growing weed, I don't know, but that's the story I heard. Anyhow, my job was turning into a steady situation.

Then came late Thursday night. I woke up hearing noises coming from the alley. That instantly pissed me off. Those days my van served as my storage room, my everything. I was out the back door before I really even had my eyes open.

Bad move, Dreya, bad move.

Five or six people were trying to break through the back door of a jewelry store across the way. Due to a light over the door, I could see them, and they could see me. All of them were teenagers except for a scraggly white woman I spotted as the brains of the organization. She knew I had a gun in my hand but did not lend it any credence whatsoever.

They had a couple of tire irons and a baseball bat, but mainly they had the woman. The moment I looked at her, I knew she could cause trouble.

"You get back inside," she said. "This ain't your deal."

I had the same idea but hadn't talked my feet into moving yet. Before I could back my ass out of the situation, one of the girls lunged at me with the bat. I didn't think; I reacted. I grabbed the bat best I could and dragged it away from her, knocking us both down in the process. The gun went somewhere; then the beat-down commenced, let me tell you, and I was the honoree.

I didn't know how it all ended until the next morning. That's when I woke up at a senior care center where noncritical patients were being kept. I had a concussion and more bruises than a three-month-old banana, but I was alive, thanks to Leesa. She found Pops's pistol and fired it off a few times over their heads. Mostly over their heads. Judging by the trail of blood, she aimed a little lower than she claimed.

After that, Susan Rhee hooked us up with a place the real estate association decided to let go for indigent housing. Terms were that we didn't get into personal items stored in the garage, paid utilities, and kept an eye out for prowlers. The place had a landline. Leesa was happy about that. It turned out she didn't want to leave after all. She said she needed to take care of me, although I think it had more to do with a nurse she met at the center while they were waiting on me to wake up.

Susan said Leesa and I were extremely lucky. Almost all of her friends in town had lost their families to the walking fever. I hadn't thought about whether I was lucky. I was alive, whether or not God had any use for me. I wondered what Pops would have thought about that. I hoped he was happy wherever he was and that he could see I was trying to take care of his baby girl.

*Analyn Orante*

We had lost containment on the majority of our fleet. Personnel were stuck on floating time bombs, every section in quarantine, everyone on edge. Who was IA, who wasn't IA? It stood for Infected/Asymptomatic. IA personnel took care of the infected and tried not to infect the viral negatives. They kept the ships running and ferried supplies back and forth.

IAs took a lot of heat from their fellow crewmembers because it was widely believed that gays caused the crisis. Utterly false. We weren't the ones coughing and throwing up blood everywhere; we weren't the ones in the majority.

It helped that we had people like Secretary Clayton FitzGerald in the administration, because he has such a forceful personality.

He looks like a pit bull in a business suit, which made his statements to the media interesting. Gay people interviewing gay people, each side believing that a lot of the heterosexuals watching on TV and the Internet were petrified over the suspicion that, since we were now in charge, we intended to wipe them out.

It meant we had to make the process as democratic as possible. This meant rough questioning, open records, and aggressive follow-ups that would have led to waterboarding under a previous administration.

FitzGerald's attitude helped, believe it or not. Polls we did showed that heterosexuals by a wide margin expressed confidence in Secretary FitzGerald. And why shouldn't we do polls? They did them in World War II, and this was way worse than that little skirmish.

President Budin grew on the general population. They were aware that she lost her family, but by then, everybody had lost family members. They didn't like that she had been closeted and married to a man. That didn't go down well with her party. The Jewish factor? Not a big deal except for the lunatic fringe. Even VSF couldn't kill enough of them off, it seemed.

Budin is such a confident person. It could come off as cocky on some people, but not on her. And she was on TV a lot. She participated in online town hall meetings and call-in shows on CNN.

Domestically, we were nowhere close to being out of the woods. So many people were still dying, although the first huge waves seemed to be over. Dr. Tofill said it was because of the winter weather.

The CDC was already issuing directives about mosquito netting and insect sprays. Initial tests showed that, in addition to ticks and some types of mosquitoes, certain flying insects had the potential of being carriers. That meant rodents, deer, and other wildlife as well as domestic animals could pose a hazard, not so much from the animals themselves, but from the vectors on them.

As for my action items, some were going better than others.

The U.S. was the only permanent member of the United Nations Security Council calling for an emergency session. I did secure pledges from thirty-two member nations that they would send delegates to a general session, tentatively planned for April.

The plan came up against serious obstacles, not the least one being threats to boycott if Australia sent a delegate. I finessed that one by stipulating the World Health Organization would certify a viral-negative Australian representative. I have to admit I wasn't certain one could be found, but we'd fight that battle when it came.

About the India-Pakistan war: the best you could say was that the missile exchange hadn't gone nuclear. I'm not sure why it didn't. They certainly had the wherewithal to turn Kashmir alone into ashes, but conventional missiles did a more than adequate job of killing anyone who hadn't fallen victim to the virus or civil unrest.

Russia's diplomat in New Delhi flew back and forth between both capitols and eventually helped to bring about a non-shooting stalemate. Call it diplomacy on the fly.

Iran's political climate could best be described as complicated. We had a junior trade representative in Tehran who was jailed twice, freed by opposing factions, and got shot at from a moving vehicle, yet she somehow managed to broker a power-sharing agreement.

I wouldn't have predicted an Iranian-American, and a woman at that, being able to pull it off in that environment, but she did. I take no credit for it.

I told her to make no promises except this: any faction killing gays loses out on the cure we Americans were working on. That proved to be a popular formula for success.

Did we have a cure yet? No. Were they aware of that fact? No. Americans knew vaccines, Americans knew miracle cures. We just had to deliver one. Somehow.

President Budin said we could write off getting a reliable supply of oil from the Middle East for the foreseeable future. There were too many technical and chain of supply issues, besides the political turmoil. No, the best we could hope for in the current situation was to deliver a good old-fashioned American deus ex machina, a last-minute solution.

*Dora Navarro*

In their emails, my friends Barbara Shuster and Beverly Lehrman invited me to come back down south. They owned a property near the town of Salado on the road into Austin, with a water well, two deep freezers, and stands of fruit and pecan trees. It was a tempting offer, one repeated by my other surviving friends back home. The ones I could still contact, that is. Some cell phone companies fell apart over the whole thing, and if you were with them, good luck on adding more hours. My company, I tried to go online and pay my bill, but their website had crashed. My phone kept working, though.

I had a way to communicate on the road and a good car. I just had to figure out how to get back in one piece.

According to online, I-20 was fairly safe, so long as you didn't travel at night. Caravans were strongly recommended, but once off the major highways, you ran the risk of getting hit by snipers.

Miguel said he was needed in Dallas, and from there he thought I could find safe passage. I couldn't stand being in Odessa. It didn't feel like home to me anymore.

But even with all the suffering, the scared faces peering through curtains, there would still be a wave of the hand from an elderly man at the food truck and a half-smile from a woman who looked like an account executive and a 9-11 survivor.

I didn't think Odessa would fall apart the way some places had, but there was a real possibility it might run out of people.

I rode with Miguel out to Goldsmith, where we found his sister's and her kids' bodies lined up in the backyard. They had been dead awhile, it looked like. The birds had gotten at them.

Their hosts, a middle-aged couple, were in their garage, dead from what looked like carbon monoxide poisoning. Miguel had known the husband. He worked for him back in high school doing detail work at a car dealership.

"And yet he tried to shoot you."

"We're the monsters now, Dora, the way they look at it."

No emotion registered in his face.

I helped him dig a grave there for his sister and the kids, but we left the couple in the garage. Maybe they had relatives who would come along someday and bury them, or maybe the locals would. Neither of us cared any more. Too many bodies, not enough time.

The next morning we created our own caravan of Miguel's SUV and my Subaru. We headed east on I-20. I was listening to a mix on my nano of Brandi Carlile, John Legend, and Art Tatum, thinking that I needed to get a keyboard under my fingers, and soon.

There wasn't any traffic to speak of. A few trucks and about eight cars zipped by in a pack. Wrecked cars on the side of the highway. Trash. Stuff people left behind or threw out. Bloody sheets, that sort of thing.

I drove, trying not to pay attention to anything except the back of Miguel's SUV, then I noticed him pulling over. His check engine light had come on. Miguel checked the oil and fluids, and we both looked under the hood. Neither of us had a clue what was wrong with it.

It was a cold, overcast day in late January. I felt the wind biting through my corduroy jacket and wondered again why I hadn't carried Mama's gloves with me.

"Maybe a spark plug?" I ventured.

"It doesn't have spark plugs."

"We've ruled that out, then."

"Thank you, Dora, for your mechanical expertise."

He decided to chance it as far as the next town, Merkel, which had a truck stop on the outskirts. It might or might not be open, but we could at least let the engine run for a while there and see if the problem stopped on its own. If need be, we could cram his stuff into my Subaru and go from there.

The truck stop had a sprinkling of vehicles, each parked some distance from one another, and there were lights on inside the store. No sign of people.

I pulled up to the curb, stepped out of my car, and joined Miguel in trying to divine the mysteries of the check engine light.

"The engine doesn't feel all that hot and there's plenty of oil," he said.

"We could just drive slowly and see what happens."

We both heard the sound. A creaking of wheels from around the corner. I looked up and saw a white man in coveralls. He held in his gloved hands a thick hose with a sprayer attachment. There was a large canister on a rolling chassis behind him.

"Nice SUV you got there." His voice was muffled by the mask.

"Thank you," Miguel said cautiously.

"Ya'll riding together?"

The man spoke quietly, taking a step or two closer as a woman, dressed similarly, came out of the store. Instead of a hose, she held a shotgun in her arms. Just then, I saw a man walk down the steps of his RV that was parked under the pump canopy.

"Yes, we're together. We're about to head back out. Come on, Dora."

"Where you come from?" the RV man said loudly. He was dressed in a bright orange hazmat suit but with the hood partly open.

"Odessa," I said.

I flashed a "let's get the hell out of here" look at Miguel. He closed the hood of the SUV.

"I wouldn't move if I were you." The woman lifted up the barrel of her gun.

Miguel acted so calm, like this was an everyday occurrence. "Yes, ma'am. Would you like my wallet? I don't have much money left, but you're more than welcome to it."

RV man laughed. "You hear the way he's talking, John?"

"Yes, I do. He's one of them," the sprayer man said.

Miguel spoke in my direction, the control in his voice starting to fray.

"Dora, why don't you head on out. I'll catch up when I can."

"We're engaged," I heard myself say.

"Isn't that nice," the woman said.

A miniature sonic boom went off at the same time as most of Miguel's head. A reddish pink section of it landed on the sidewalk in front of me. The smell of fireworks. A ringing in my ears.

I felt a fluid blast knocking me to the ground, chemicals drenching my body. Panicked, I crawled in the opposite direction, scraping my face and hands on the pavement until finally the hose turned off. The smell of bug spray was overwhelming. Stunned that I was still alive, I squinted at my surroundings, only to see the woman with the gun standing a few feet away.

"Get up. You're not dead."

I struggled to my feet, leaning my hand on the SUV.

"The keys are over by the faggot. Go get them," said RV Man.

I wobbled over to what was left of Miguel, found the keys in a puddle of blood, and looked at the men.

"Open up the back and spread everything out."

I threw up.

"You through?" the woman asked after a while.

Gagging, I managed to nod my head. I didn't see how this was survivable. I didn't think they would rape me, given the virus, given the chemical bath, but death looked to be a real option.

"Get to work," John said with the air of a schoolteacher running a computer lab.

I emptied out both vehicles. I spread the contents of our luggage and the few cans of food we'd been able to scavenge out on the pavement. John gave them a thorough spraying.

I sat on the ground next to the Subaru and waited for them to kill me.

"We're done?" RV Man asked the woman, who nodded. "Okay, you need to head on out. Abilene's that way. Don't go into Merkel. They don't want your kind there."

I dry-heaved, but nothing came up. From out of nowhere came a flicker of rebellion. "I don't care what else you keep, but you're not getting Mama's quilt." It was in a large, sealed plastic bag.

John laughed. "You'd die for that?"

My eyes burning pure misery, I tried to look at him without wavering. Miguel would have had a snappy comeback. I had nothing to offer except a small shard of attitude. That, and my jewelry, proved to be enough.

Much later, as I limped along the highway with the quilt bag in my arms, the joints in my body all came unhinged and I fell face forward into the side of a concrete divider. I couldn't open my left eye, which had taken the brunt of the fall.

For however long it took, I sat there in a daze, feeling the wind dry the stinking mess that was my hair. My hands were crusted with blood from the scrapes on my skin, and, maybe, from touching Miguel.

I thought, if I keep going, I might make it to Abilene by nightfall. Or die trying.

I heard the cars before I saw them. Were they from the truck stop? I couldn't remember what the cars there looked like, so I wobbled to the side of the road. Two pickups and a trio of cars hurtled by without stopping. Then another truck, solo. The next truck stopped. A white woman with blazing red hair opened up the passenger door. She looked down at me.

"Sweet Jesus, what happened to you?"

I staggered up the steps into the cab, dragging the quilt bag behind me.

Exclaiming over the smell, she offered me a bottle of water. I drank it down without pause.

She made for the bag. I held on to it more tightly.

"Darlin', I'm just putting it behind the seat, okay?"

I allowed her to take the bag. After failing to get me to eat a sausage biscuit, she got us back on the road.

I wasn't in the mood for talking, but a few educated questions from her, the chemical stench, my pointing finger, and a telling grunt gave her an outline.

"The truck stop?"

I nodded.

She let out a heartfelt curse, then said, "I've heard about something similar to that happening at a station over by Stephenville. Bastards spray the life out of you. The Highway Patrol has a civilian auxiliary operating out of the Skittles restaurant on the other side of Abilene. I'll stop there and see if we can't get something done."

After refusing first aid because I couldn't bear the pain of being touched, I rode with three well-armed men in a Hummer back to the truck stop. John and his partners were long gone, but my car and rifled luggage, stinking of spray, had been left behind.

"Sorry about your friend." The oldest of my rescuers pressed some bills into my hand. His buddies began unzipping a body bag. "Why don't you follow us back to Skittles? I know there's a caravan going to Fort Worth first thing in the morning, and there's always caravans going elsewhere."

I squinted at Miguel's body on the ground, haloed by the headlights. They would have killed him whether or not he was gay. At some level I understood that. But at the moment I hated them, not only for their blind cruelty, but also for still being alive when the good ones, like my family, had died. I wanted all of them gone, the sooner the better.

# Chapter 6

*Debra Shanrahan*

We had very little time, if any, to get a handle on the problem. It's not cold enough in the southern part of the U.S. to completely eradicate potential vectors, which meant we were recording more and more infected samples. You had to expect it to crop up everywhere else the closer we moved to a full-tilt American spring.

Back home, you couldn't totally freeze out the pests except in some of the upper elevations, not that this lot at the CDC wanted to discuss any troubles not happening on their turf. I asked a coworker as we were out scraping up lab critters if she had heard whether the massive chemical spraying going on in the Ukraine had done any good yet.

Some countries were trying the approach of spraying anything that moved, whilst others were relocating their uninfected populations into places that had been certified viral-free. She couldn't tell me a bleeding word about anything going on anywhere outside the U.S.A.

When we returned to the lab, my boss, Bao-Zhai, thanked us for bringing her another case of Coca-Colas. The local cannery was back in operation, although I'm not sure where the ingredients were coming from. The news from her end, not so wonderful, my dear.

We knew about ticks, but when she told us about our old friends, the family *Culicidae*, I thought, that's it for our side. Three more species thus far confirmed to carry VSF. It's one thing to screen your porch to keep out mosquitoes. How do you screen a city, a people, an entire planet? There's not enough spray to do the trick, regardless of what the Ukrainians thought. One bite from the wrong insect, and you've started a whole new round of troubles. Like with malaria. Some countries had been able to contain it, for instance, but you still had cases.

I thought you Yanks had had it easy to this point. You lost scads of people, not at the percentage of population that Australia did, and certainly not like China and India, but no one would deny that you suffered. Even so, your government was still standing, and you were getting some services operational again.

You had even tricked out some potential vaccines. Dr. Tofill authorized simultaneous trials. Why mess around with it? Just try them all and see what works. There were no shortages of volunteers and controls, and no shortage of optimism, even from me.

*Wylie Halverson*

The governor said they were close to certifying Sawyer and Washburn counties, but the main sticking point was the holdouts. People hiding in the rural areas who weren't willing to get tested. They said they hadn't gotten sick yet, so why bother with the sticks, but you couldn't say a county was plague-free until you had every resident on record as being so.

The governor responded by sending out units from the National Guard. They got the blood samples. She then certified Sawyer and Washburn as safe-travel counties. There were still roadblocks leading into those areas. You had to have a recently dated viral card, and it had to be in the computer system so stating.

People in those counties definitely did not view themselves as a safe harbor. They did not want new people moving in. The governor's goal was to certify counties neighboring the first two, and then she was going to move as many shut-ins there as possible, no matter who it upset.

No one can stay stuck inside a house forever, not doing anything, just sitting there being afraid. She said on the news that the only way Wisconsin was ever going to get back to normal was to get healthy, one county at a time. They had shipped in plastic sheeting, sprayers, and air filters, trying to prepare Sawyer and Washburn for the newcomers.

I had my doubts about the project, but I understood the reason for it. There weren't enough protective materials in the world to seal off every single home in every single neighborhood, plus supply them, and monitor their filters, and everything else. You have to do it in groups. You also have to think in terms of how many survivors are available to take care of the ones inside.

Stores were starting to have a few more items on the shelves, even rye bread. That was something Father Jerzy had been missing. I heard that Wal-Mart, which had been knocked for a loop by all this, had gotten something of a delivery system back up and going, although very limited, and it hadn't been able to reliably travel to the smaller cities yet. Not to Stevens Point, believe you me.

Amazingly, a couple of the pizza places and a Chinese restaurant had begun delivering meals to anyone who had the money. I think the pizza places got what they needed from a Canadian supplier. They couldn't deliver to the country, so one day Chelsea went into town, called in her order, put her cash in an envelope, and taped it to the door. A delivery guy brought out the pizzas and left them in the parking lot.

Chelsea said they microwaved the money to kill any germs, which is why they wouldn't accept coins. Too much trouble to disinfect. The kids were so thrilled. Well, I don't know that Jarrod got much out of it, but the older ones thoroughly enjoyed it.

An animal health inspector came out and tested the cows. They came up clean, of course, but the milkers failed, so no more runs to the shut-ins. I thought it was ridiculous. We kept the entire process completely hygienic. No one had died from the milk, but that didn't seem to matter to the inspector. That major dairy operation north of town was still in operation. No one had shut them down, but they were still a big employer. How did they feed their cows, especially during the January crunch? More supplies on hand, I suppose.

We got a call the next day from the new operators of a dairy that was supplying stores in Madison. Selma was thrilled by the news, especially since the Feds had taken away all agriculture subsidies, including for milk. That was another one of President Budin's ideas, naturally. Congress ratified everything she said, including what she asked for breakfast in the morning. That the government needed its resources for relief efforts and the like, I understood. I didn't have to appreciate certain aspects of it.

Her auto exchange program didn't go too well here. I did agree with that idea. It made good sense for counties to seize flex-fuel and hybrid vehicles left behind by the dead and allow the living to trade in their gas-guzzlers. It went swimmingly well in the bigger cities.

Here in Portage County, there weren't enough vehicles of that type available. County did go around and collect the unclaimed cars with good gas mileage. That's another way of saying that we went with the spirit of the law, if not the letter.

Chelsea said you could find a lot of good deals on eBay, although how people planned to ship a car across a country given the conditions, I have no idea. The Post Office wasn't letting a little issue like a worldwide disaster shut it down, and bless the express mail companies for trying, but some schemes simply weren't doable.

Chelsea, who kept track of the Internet for us, found a website that helped school districts organize in-home instruction for students. Don Metzger—him again—had his people scavenging homes for computers until even our poorer students could participate. It seemed like a good plan to me, teaching without ever leaving the farm. No danger of infecting anyone that way.

*Dreya Underhill*

Susan's partner never came back. It turned out there was an ex-lover in Marin County with a cushy estate where they could wait out the end of the world. Susan's explanation. Personally, I still think her ex was growing weed and decided to live with her drug supply, but that's just me talking.

In a normal situation, I suppose we both would have grieved a decent amount of time, then gradually we'd have gone from being boss and employee, to friends, and then maybe lovers. But what happened was one afternoon, I came back from the market telling Susan how much money we made off the tomatoes alone.

See, I thought yeah, go ahead and sell your starters to the home garden set, but I'll baby along my plants, give it all I got, and we'll be the earliest and the best in the market with locally grown produce. Susan had always grown some specialty herbs, edible flowers, and whatnot for her friends at the restaurant. All we did was step it up to meet the need. We weren't the only ones doing that, but I'd put my tomatoes up against anyone's.

So we're hugging, right? Celebrating the fact that we were a team. Then we're kissing, and what went through my mind is that all the people I touched over the last few months had been either dead or dying, and the last woman I kissed was Rita. I lost it right then and there. People who know me at all know I keep it together, no matter what.

Susan took me into her arms and held me. She just held me.

I moved in with her a week later, although the relationship part, that took a while. I felt so damned tired of history. Leesa and her friends called what was happening the Big Delete, after that button on your keyboard you don't want to touch.

On TV and the net, they called it the New Black Death, the Pig Plague, the Aussie Flu, the Gone-Away. They said we were living through the Final Days, the End of History. The last one I hoped for, because then we could all settle down. We could get back to living our lives and not be worrying about what new stretch of hell was out there.

Like in Florida. The government people couldn't get jack done there. People were still dying all over the place and not just from the walking fever. They were starving, too. Get that. They're living next to the water, they own fishing poles and hunting rifles, yet they're starving. Government's dropping food packages from planes 'cause the roads are too dangerous. Somebody's getting the food. Governor refused to let the troops come in; said they would spread the disease.

Finally, the President went, enough with this shit, I'm taking over. She sent the troops in to straighten it out. Governor was some dumb jerk who had gone out on his yacht and stayed there while the worst was happening. When he came back, he and his friends grabbed up all the mosquito nets, air filters, and safe suits they could find, then they set themselves up a sweet ride.

Me, I would have ripped their masks off and said, "Feel my disease, asshole," but the government was planning on trying them in court.

California was hanging in there, and even getting some new recruits. Mexicans that came up—the ones that lived—didn't go back home. My friends back in San Diego said the Mexicans had moved into empty houses and taken over shops and businesses where the owners had died. Border, what border? I didn't care. As long as they were trying to get the town up and going again, I said good for them.

I heard about places like Bakersfield that were practically ghost towns, but that was about to change. The state was trying to move the straights in there, make an entire city like a safe suit. I didn't see how it was possible, but they were going to try.

In the meantime, me and mine, what was left of me and mine, were growing tomatoes, trying to keep the riff-raff away, trying to ignore history.

*Analyn Orante*

Bill Levine said it amounted to ethnic cleansing, but without the roadside bombs. According to the mayor, there wasn't a single heterosexual left in Manhattan, unless someone had his or her grandmother stuck in a loft somewhere. The straight ones, those who survived, were in upstate New York or Canada, or on farms in Connecticut, Vermont, and Maine. That is, if they made it past the roadblocks, still a common feature during travel.

Large urban areas had higher concentrations of gay people to begin with. It made sense that, once past the panic phase, New York City could reinstitute some degree of civic and economic stability, but Budin refused to allow stock market activity and unmonitored corporate reorganizations. Anything major a company wanted to do had to be cleared first by the Commerce Department.

As a former Secretary of the Treasury, she had always been a strong free market proponent, but in this situation, where you had a new Chairman of the Federal Reserve and so many industries in serious trouble, you didn't pour gasoline on a flame.

So the Secretary of State visits Penn Station, visits Times Square, visits the Port Authority, eats a bagel, a knish, a samosa, and a Papaya's hot dog, all the while being tailed by cameras recording a live feed for the Internet and TV. New York City, open for business, the city that never sleeps.

When the mayor suggested we take in a Broadway benefit performance of *Our Town*, I considered declining the invitation, but Bill gave me such a reproachful look I changed my mind.

The scene in the graveyard where the dead spoke made me think about my family. No word about Michael in Jamaica, but I knew he had to be dead, too. It's hard to hide on a crowded island, or to find a way off if you can't buy a ride. Boat people were kept offshore by all coastal nations.

Our nation had taken such a horrendous blow. It was only because we were such a wealthy country before this happened that we hadn't completely collapsed. To me, we were all talking in the graveyard, trying to convince ourselves that the situation was fixable.

Bill and I were seated in the back of a bulletproof limousine, waiting for it to carry us away from the theater.

I leaned over and said, "All this pretending is fun, but tomorrow it's back to the real world."

"As far as I'm concerned, Ana, this is the real world. Why go back to the nightmare?"

*Dora Navarro*

The trip from Fort Worth sent me past a travelogue of abandoned cars, trash, dead animals, and smoking ruins, which I viewed through lacerating flicks of my one semi-working eye. Then the scenery faded, and all I could see through the tunnel was the tailpipe of the pickup in front of me.

I kept to the caravan's blazing speed until I reached Belton, driving more by feel than vision. However long it took me, I made it to the driveway of my duplex apartment. It took a while to unpeel my clenched fingers from the steering wheel and walk inside.

Finally, I had access to a landline. My cell phone had been a lesser casualty from the truck stop attack. But who to call first? Several of my friends and I had phone-tagged each other while struggling with our respective family disasters. Standing there in my apartment, I flashed on the memory of a party at Barbara Shuster and Beverly Lehrman's house.

It was solid brick and on a heavily wooded road well back from the highway to Austin. Gated. Safe. Didn't they already invite me?

Dialing their number from memory, I listened to Barb say hello. She must have checked her caller ID, for she said my name repeatedly, trying to get an answer.

"I'm on my way. Don't go anywhere. Hang on."

Barb, a woman generous in girth and spirit, wasted no time getting me packed into her car, acrid-smelling luggage and all, with her first stop being at the clinic.

The PA, a friend of hers, was reluctant to break away from a child we could hear howling in the back, but agreed to spare a moment for me. I probably wasn't the worst-looking patient she had seen lately.

When she couldn't get me to take off my jacket, I heard her sigh. "I'll do what I can, okay? I'm really backed up here."

She treated my eyes with a saline solution lavage then sent me off with a roll of gauze, antibiotics, and a tube of ointment.

"Bring her back in a week," she told Barb. "By then, I may be able to squeeze her in to see Dr. Krieger."

"What about... she's not talking. What do we do?"

The PA's voice came closer to me. "Whatever happened to you, it's over now. You're still alive. You have friends."

To Barb, she said, "She might get back to talking, and she might not. I wouldn't push it. Keep her busy. That seems to help."

Back at their house, Barb led me to a bathroom, where I gestured that I wanted to be left alone. I got undressed and managed to draw myself a bath. I tried to wash my hair without disturbing the ointment on my eyes. It was slow going.

Barb came in after a while and sat on the side of the tub.

"Oh, you poor—" She stopped herself from finishing the phrase. "You need to turn yourself around in the tub. I have a nozzle I can use."

She used one hand to guard my eyes, and the other to run a soft, warm stream through my hair. I couldn't see the bruises on my body, but I could certainly feel them. Barb's hands were gentle as she picked out the gravel and God knows what else from my hair. Although the shampoo stung tender places on my head, I was well beyond caring.

She helped me out of the tub and onto a chair. As she used a towel to pat me dry, she said with a slight tremble in her voice, "You're safe now. We won't let anyone hurt you."

I slept for what felt like an eternity, getting up only to go to the bathroom or to drink one of Barb's herbal teas. She gave me pills that took away some of the pain.

Bev came in to check on me during what might have been the next evening. She was a psychologist, so I figured this for a professional visit. Instead, she talked casually about how her day went and the weather. Then she came to the point.

"It's hard on Barb being here by herself these days, what with so much going on. If you could stay and help out, I sure would appreciate it."

How was I supposed to be useful when I couldn't talk and could barely see?

But over the next few days, my aches and scrapes began to heal. Antibiotics, ointment, and time brought improvements to my right eye, but the darkness in my left eye remained. Barb found little tasks that matched my current skill set, upping the ante as my health improved.

Upkeep of their orchard, laundry and dishes, charity food drives. Too many errands took us outside their gate as the weeks went by. My holding their gun helped, even if it was unloaded. Barb always kept the bullets handy. Survivors hiding by the river were still staging attacks on isolated homes for supplies. Gone feral, Barb said. I worried about Bev's daily commute. She was a clinical psychologist who worked on Fort Hood under a civilian contract.

Barb used to be a civil attorney, before she became a painter, before she dabbled in rental properties. She had a trust fund is what it boiled down to. We first met when she decided to take piano lessons. The lessons never quite sank in, but she was certainly an artist in the kitchen. She didn't seem to mind me keeping silent when she showed me how to make kugel and other family recipes.

Bev always spoke to me as though I was holding up my end of the conversation. This was our daily routine: every night after supper, she would sit on the front step and tell me about her day. I would listen and withhold comment. One evening, however, I found a piece of paper and wrote down a request.

Bev looked into what happened to my stepbrother. He died at the Kabul airport, one of the victims of a massive suicide bombing. His unit was supposed to be on the next flight out on a journey that would have eventually taken them to Fort Hood. He was that close to making it, that close to me.

Fort Hood was supposed to be one of the safest places around, once the blood test became available. Positives were transferred to a quarantine facility on base, where they waited on results of further blood tests. In twenty-four hours, their blood was tested again for signs of reaction to the virus. By now, everyone knew what that meant. A person might not show major symptoms for days after that, but the blood test didn't lie.

Bev said in her experience of counseling soldiers, no one ever received a false positive.

She told me that most people understood now that working soldiers couldn't be viral negative. They had to be able to go wherever, whenever. Please ask, please tell.

The viral negatives ate, exercised, and slept in quarantine barracks. The air filtration system required for each unit was huge, Bev said.

"I don't see how they can sleep in there with that thing making such a racket." She watched me rock back and forth on their front porch swing.

She switched to another topic. "Barb says the doctor discontinued the eye ointment. Your right eye looks almost healed. She also said that you were very helpful around the house today. She doesn't know what she'd do without you."

I nodded my head. That was a conversational breakthrough I had recently achieved.

Bev got up from her perch on the steps, went inside for a moment, then came back out with a set of binoculars.

"Amazing what kind of presents I get these days. They have night vision."

I now had something new to keep me occupied in the restless hours before dawn, when every rustle beyond the curtains signified a fresh terror.

"Thank you."

Bev said gently, "That's a good start."

# Chapter 7

*Debra Shanrahan*

Bao-Zhai gave me her standard greeting of a kiss when I got back to the lab after running errands. Somehow, what with doing scut work, along with critter care and Coca-Cola runs, I had ended up with Bao-Zhai. The pairing surprised both of us, if not her assistant, who claimed she called it from the outset.

There was no time for connubial bliss, for all of us were racing against the clock. Variant Swine Fever appeared endlessly mutable and impossible to eradicate from the human body. That facet reminded me of HIV, but unlike that deadly foe, VSF's use of insect vectors was a significant and growing risk.

It hardly comforted me that researchers at the National Institutes of Health in Bethesda, Maryland, tasked with finding solutions on the drug side, were having no better success than we were.

A cardiac medication turned out to have properties that slowed, however slightly, viral cell destruction. Its side effects appeared insurmountable. You give a med to slow the course of the illness. The med causes a slow heartbeat, so you give meds for that, but at some point liver failure stops the body from metabolizing all your fine notions. Which means, at best, you're adding two or three days to your patient's wretched life.

"If we had ten years, we might come up with maintenance drugs so it wouldn't matter if the virus was still in the body, but we don't even have ten days," Bao-Zhai said.

I handed her a plate of lamb and tabbouleh from a nearby Lebanese restaurant. Add delivery girl to my list of critical tasks. Not that the blokes at the restaurant looked Middle Eastern, but you didn't look a gift shawarma in the mouth.

It was a major effort to get Bao-Zhai to sit down to eat rather than do her usual gulp and go, but while we were eating in her office, a coworker rushed in and turned on the television.

"You've got to see this, guys," he said.

"Is this about the fire?" Bao-Zhai asked. "I heard about that already."

The grasslands of western Kansas, currently ablaze in a series of set fires, were finally coming under control. Firefighters, initially shot at by some of the locals, returned with federal troops providing backup.

Blame the Internet for providing websites where survivors could share their grievances. Blame cell phones, gun hoarders, and ugly paranoia. Blame fear, most of all, for fostering the belief that fire and chemicals were all that was needed to cleanse the countryside of dangerous creatures. And don't forget bullets to kill any gays feckless enough to venture out of the cities. Gays carried the virus, the thinking went.

You didn't have to go far to see the opposition. Their videos were everywhere online. Dozens of gunplay and handmade bomb incidents had tangled relief efforts across the country, not to mention everywhere else.

In Japan, after the first death waves, their government shipped all known IAs to Hokkaido, the northernmost island. That, and massive chemical spraying, was the battle plan. Some countries, particularly in Africa, South America, and Asia, didn't bother with relocations of known and suspected IAs.

We were dying in droves, gay and straight. I understood the logic of it. If you could eliminate every known carrier, whether animal or insect, then you stood a chance of beating VSF. But you couldn't kill every mosquito, pig, and tick in the world. VSF came from China, so were you going to ban all imports and travel from there? The European Union had already taken that measure, followed by the United States and, pointlessly, Australia, my pariah homeland.

I thought the whole exercise ludicrous. We IAs were fighting like mad to save the world, to keep some vestige of trade and travel afloat. Kill us all, and who are left as humanity's last line of defense?

We were the ones trying to find the cure. We even manufactured the very protective clothing those idiots wore while killing us. We were the ones trying so hard to keep the disease from spreading, and doing a damned good job in the CDC building, I might add. There was an entire upper floor chock full of viral negative researchers.

I wouldn't have wanted to be there, sleeping on cots, living cheek to cheek months on end, but it could be done. There had been incidents outside the CDC building, but none of the nutcases had made it past the receiving area.

On the TV screen, a reporter stood inside what looked to be an office.

"We're expecting the helicopter to touch down on the landing pad within the next fifteen minutes," he said.

The reporter was a thin, deep-voiced young man with unruly hair whose voice reminded me of Mitch Mitchell, a newsreader back home. I almost expected him to give Mitchell's sendoff, "Thanks for your company," but this was no bush fire.

Over a hundred court officers and relief workers had fled to the Florida State Capitol complex in Tallahassee after a series of bombings had gone off in the metropolitan area. Florida again, but worse than the takeover incident. A video had been released warning, "Faggots, this is only the beginning." The wankers had upped their game.

I looked down at my plate of take-out food. So much for our little fantasy world.

*Wylie Halverson*

Selma and I, we didn't see what else the President could do except try to get our people out of Florida. If they could make it to the designated areas, then our sailors could escort them to the ships. I thought it might go all right, but the crazies had gotten good at hitting their targets lately.

Selma said it didn't matter if most of the people down there weren't setting the fires and doing the killing. They weren't stopping it, which was more important in the scheme of things.

We were lucky in our part of Wisconsin. The shut-ins, the ones we could find, that is, had been shipped to the safe towns up north with hardly any incidents. South of us was a different story, but you couldn't do anything about human nature, regardless of what Father Jerzy said at services.

Speaking of human nature, Chelsea and Regina Warfield, a teammate whose family had died in the first wave, had been spending time together. I don't believe they were dating, but they had so much in common.

Regina was an excellent influence. She was smart and levelheaded, always volunteering for anything that needed doing. She ended up moving in with us. It was getting a little crowded in a four-bedroom house with two adults and six children, although Chelsea would certainly disagree with being called a child.

But I have to hand it to Metzger and his minions on the foraging. No one in our county was starving, even if the food was downright boring. I mean, how many ways can you prepare cornbread? Don't get me started about that case of salmon jerky. Gah. Spring planting was going on without a hitch, not just here, but you heard about farms farther south, like in Iowa.

City folk were coming back to places where they had been raised, so they could help out on spring planting. Positively inspiring. I wish I could say all the news was good, here and abroad, but the flavorful results of Dixon and the older girls' food project were already being shared with our neighbors. Kansas might be burning. In Stevens Point, we had fresh cheese curds.

Selma and I... well, I suppose it could have been predicted we'd end up together. But we'd been single for so long, we were both set in our ways. We slept in the same bed because it made sense, given that the number of people and the number of beds didn't quite match up. Made our decisions together, prayed together, worked together, argued at times.

We were so busy there wasn't time for grieving, it seemed like, but then one evening I came into the bedroom and Selma was crying. That day, Dixon played in the yard with Reha. It reminded Selma of her nephews, and then of her brother, and then of everybody she had lost. It piled up on her, the way it did on me sometimes.

I told her, "You can't be strong all the time. Fall apart when you need to. It'll do you good."

She cried on my shoulder, the way she had needed to all along.

After that, it got easier for us. Not the work, or the worries, but being with each other.

Selma liked to say we fell in love while milking the cows, but I think it happened when she had the courage to stop trying to be the superwoman.

She let me in, and I never walked out.

*Dreya Underhill*

The only reason I joined the civil patrol was to keep Susan from doing it. The neighborhood association wanted volunteers, and she's a volunteering fool. My group was fairly typical: some ex-military grayheads, teenagers from group homes, and the rest of us young and mobile. We had some hard-nosed types working to clean the thieves out of our part of town. I hadn't seen that scraggly white woman and her gang yet, but I was hoping, man, I was hoping we would get reacquainted.

Then, one night on the news, it said that volunteers were needed to help in the Salinas reclamation project. Lots of farms and food processing in that area, but most of the negatives had headed farther east. Guess they thought they were too close to the coast, too close to us for comfort. I thought I could do some good in Salinas. My garden project had done so well that Susan had hired a couple of more people. Maybe I was feeling a little guilty about ditching San Diego so quickly.

Anyhow, I rode out with the other volunteers on a touring bus that I think had belonged to some rock star, then it came on the radio that Kern County had kicked out the state people. I believe in calling a straight a straight, you know? State had moved in a bunch of them to Bakersfield, enough so that the straights didn't feel they needed to bow down to us anymore. Not that we were coming on like the Sopranos, but they didn't want our diseased, faggoty little asses near them. Kicked us out. They don't want us? Fine. See if they can make it in their bubble towns without our help.

When we had been in Salinas for about a week, setting up operations, shit started happening. I had a crew under me putting in acres of lettuce and spinach. A late start on planting, but that's the breaks. You never have perfect conditions.

A bug bomb. That's what the news called them. They were big canisters with an explosive charge so that when one went off, it threw shrapnel and chemical spray in the air. Once you saw what they looked like, you knew to look out for dumpsters, abandoned trucks, anything that could hide one. Ours blew up a block away from the warehouse where I was looking at produce trucks. I felt the ground shake underneath my feet. At first, I thought it was an earthquake, but then I saw smoke in the air and smelled this terrible odor. Like the nuclear bomb of roach foggers.

One dead, four injured, and it could have been a lot worse. The bomb went off right before lunch. If it had hit the restaurant twenty minutes later, I don't want to think about our chances. A couple of the locals knew of an area south of town where some straights stayed. There had been problems with them before, shots fired when deputies went by. We had a medical crew helping the victims, but me, I knew I had to protect my crew, so I rode with the posse, went cowboying. You see, the straights couldn't let us get close, even if they thought we were innocent little lambs. Walking fever, remember?

We weren't about to have a handshaking Jimmy Carter moment, so when they lit us up, we gave it right back to them. While working on patrol, a sergeant had trained me on how to use Pops's pistol. I had to wave it a few times but never needed to use it. The deputies had the situation taken care of by the time my crew got in there. My gun was drawn, even if I didn't use it, and I have to admit, I felt absolutely prepared to kill somebody.

Rita used to make fun of me 'cause I felt sorry for the animals at Balboa Zoo being stuck in there. One time, a coyote showed up on the back lawn of this property I was working on, and I ran like it was a man killer. When I told Rita about it, I thought I'd never hear the end of it. Thing is, the straights, they weren't the only ones afraid. We were, too.

*Analyn Orante*

President Budin was reluctant to consider the last option on the table. We had already tried several options short of large-scale mobilization of our forces into Florida. That was not a practical consideration, given our lack of manpower.

You would think states such as Alabama and Mississippi might be major suspects in any separatist movement. They were in the Deep South, had a growing problem with VSF vectors, and a history of being anti gay rights. Even so, we had strong allies there who worked with us in establishing safe towns. They were more like marginally safer towns, in my opinion, but they were better than nothing, and those allies conducted responsible spraying programs, too.

Florida marked such a contrast in attitude. State authorities ordered airborne spraying throughout their urban areas at toxic levels, ignoring long-established guidelines. When contacted, one stalwart reportedly claimed that the next hard rain would wash away the toxicity, everybody was staying inside anyway, except for the homosexuals, and besides, its tree-huggers like you who caused this problem in the first place.

The spraying killed bugs, yes, but the overflow seeped into urban drinking water, and then the bugs came back, because of chemical resistance and their own version of safe houses in the swamps. Water is deep. It hides, it filters, and then it fights back with mosquitoes and ticks even more pesticide-resistant.

Eerily similar to how China was handling the emergency. I couldn't get accurate mortality figures from China, not directly, but my counterparts in South Korea, whose intelligence sources I respected, told me about the number of dead in Hebei Province, which surrounds Beijing. Deaths were believed to be in excess of thirty million, and Beijing had been reduced to, by best estimate, one hundred thousand.

A twenty-first-century Long March, troop-enforced, sent urban residents into the countryside. Missile attacks on the Sino-Russia border had been a constant since soon after the crisis began, clashes replicated on a human level when unfortunates tried to find safe stopping places. As for IAs, those in charge at that time appeared to have the same view as the Floridian outlaws: kill, isolate, or ignore. But preferably, kill.

We had a difficult hand to play in Florida.

President Budin said simply, "We have people down there who are sitting ducks. We have an obligation to rescue them."

Although we broadcast what would happen if anyone interfered with operations, there were incidents, mostly in the Orlando area, where conditions were rapidly worsening. Elements of the $82^{nd}$ Airborne Division and the National Guard took casualties and gave some, too. One would be amazed at how many buses can be commandeered with a firm attitude and a riot gun.

Drive, fly, and ship our people out, but where to take the refugees? It made sense to send them where we needed healthy bodies the most, which was in our ports and manufacturing centers. In retrospect, every step we took had a logical trajectory: separating gays from straights, IAs from viral negatives, who were starting to be called sensitives, but we didn't have the luxury of hindsight.

If I give the impression that my duties as Secretary of State strayed into the domestic side, the impression is partially true. Secretary FitzGerald sometimes called me "Secretary to the States" in Sit Room meetings.

The Department of State had much to deal with during this time: figuring how to make the United Nations relevant in the crisis, sharing vital information with our allies about possible treatments for VSF, and keeping trade and relief shipments going, however minimal.

At the same time, the White House was critically shorthanded. Some of the initial departmental appointments during this time proved not to be good fits, shall we say, for the positions they were asked to fill. I took on a rather broad portfolio. I make no apologies for that fact.

Somewhere in all this, the new government in Jamaica was able to confirm for me that my brother was dead, no further details given. It struck me during the Florida crisis that somewhere in that swamp, there were people like my brother, struggling to survive, people who, through no fault of their own, had been placed in an impossible situation.

*Dora Navarro*

It started with having to endure Barb's clanking on my piano, which they had arranged to move to their house. Over sixty of Barb and Bev's fellow believers were in need of a cantor on Fort Hood, which Barb, a rabbi's daughter, was well equipped to handle. Piano was not a requirement for her duties, but Barb, peering at the liturgical songbook, was determined to make a go of it, if I survived her practice sessions.

I checked out the songbook while they were out running errands. Although the darkness in my left eye had yet to lift, my right eye did okay. By the time Barb sat down on the piano bench next to me, I had run through several of the melodies. A bit too much on minor keys for my taste, but easy enough.

"We could use your help," she said, which is how I became her accompanist on Saturday mornings.

The soldiers and civilian personnel seemed grateful for my presence, although I had yet to make it past single-word responses to any questions. Talking seemed not so much difficult as beside the point. I was alive, wasn't I? Didn't that rate as a cosmic joke, not warranting any additional comment?

Without conscious effort, I found myself standing next to Barb and Bev as they lit the candle on Friday nights. I tore off a piece of challah when it came around to me. I listened to their prayers on Saturday mornings, yet faith of any kind seemed so alien to me. I couldn't imagine praying to a God who would allow Mama and my brothers to die and let that terrible woman kill a kindhearted person like Miguel.

Bev seemed to divine what was going on with me. She tried to tell me about how Jews believe that God's mission for them is to heal the world. I thought, either the Jews have failed in their task, or God is nothing more than a cartoon fantasy.

One evening, she called us to say that something had come up on base and she would have to stay overnight. Overnight turned into several days. Although Barb told me not to worry, she spent a lot of time between Bev's infrequent phone calls finding new ways to use dates in her recipes. Her wheeling and dealing with a truck driver had landed us a case of dates. We were both beginning to regret that trade.

Next Saturday morning, Barb took us on base for services, taking advantage of her approved visit to take us by Bev's office. Bev wasn't there, but another staff member took us aside and told us what was happening.

One of the negatives, a young soldier grown restless in quarantine, arranged to be let outside for a date with a female soldier from another barracks. That wasn't the first time rules were bent for bored personnel, or even the tenth time, as it turned out. One of them got infected en route to the meeting place and passed VSF on to the other.

Fort Hood sprayed weekly around the barracks, Bev said, but nature beat the odds with a mosquito. I'd hiked over the years by the river and through woodlands in the area. Only a matter of time, then the time came. During the usual weekly blood tests, several soldiers in both of the main quarantine barracks tested positive. The flood began.

We went over to the chapel, where Barb led her group through the usual service with a longer than usual dose of prayers for the sick. Afterward, we found Bev in between trips to her clients. She was an athletic woman in her forties, but her weight loss over the past few months etched her cheekbones in sharp relief when she attempted to smile.

"What do you say to them?" I interrupted her conversation with Barb.

The number of words coming out of my mouth surprised all three of us.

"To the soldiers who are dying?" Bev said. "Not much, really. I listen, I listen a lot. There are ways they show what they want to hear. They tell me that they regret mistakes they made, they hope they didn't let down their fellow soldiers, and they want to be ready for whatever's ahead. I tell them what they need to hear, but mainly I listen."

Listening to the dead. I had been doing a lot of that lately. Daniel, my youngest nephew, that sweet toddler with the thick dark curls. I couldn't get his face out of my mind, or the giggles. He was laughing when my brother carried him into the garage. Laughing, not wheezing like the others. Had I been so exhausted by the death rattles of my family that I couldn't hear its absence?

On the way back to the house, Barb knew something was wrong. She couldn't help but reach over and pat my arm as she drove.

"It's hard, isn't it, Dora, knowing that those young men and women are dying, and there's nothing that can be done to stop it."

"I let Mark kill my nephew. Daniel hadn't been coughing. I just assumed…"

The stinging in my bad eye told me I was crying.

"You didn't know. End of story. You didn't know."

"I should have."

We had arrived in their driveway. Barb kept her face pointing forward, not moving from behind the wheel.

"I killed my parents," she said flatly. "They had plenty of food, the neighborhood security company was still on the job, but Dad's hip was bothering him. I said, come down from Plano and stay with us. This was before the roads got bad, before we knew we were immune.

"I was so glad to see them." Her voice was beginning to fracture. "And when they started getting sick, Bev said, 'You need to be careful. You don't want to catch it.' But I wasn't going to wear some damn mask and make my mother feel even worse. I thought I was making such a sacrifice, but I killed them."

Now I was the one doing the arm patting.

After a few minutes, Barb looked at me, her customary warmth returning. "So, we're a couple of screw-ups?"

I shrugged.

"Come on. I found a date roll recipe online we haven't tried yet. Cressy Mungia has another new foster child. Let's foist it on them for a change."

# Chapter 8

*Debra Shanrahan*

That skinny young reporter with the tousled hair had moved on from Florida. He was now reporting for CNN in Atlanta, traveling with a DOD truck through the alleys of east Atlanta. DOD was now popularly defined as Dead on Delivery.

A prized partner on the route was each truck's sniffer dog. The crew, heavily armed and flak-jacketed per form, responded to each hit by the dog with a bullhorn announcement of their intentions. If there was no response from the residence, the crew rammed the door, quickly body-bagged corpses, then scurried back to the truck. The dog, wearing its own jacket, was carried back to the truck. He was too valuable to risk during the operation.

The reporter, James Ayers, told the camera that this crew had the fastest recorded time on pick-ups, which seemed to be a source of pride to all concerned. I suppose it meant they were less likely to get shot at by the neighbors.

On this run, the crew found a baby in the living room, crying feebly in a blood-spattered crib. Ayers, tossing his microphone to someone behind the camera, gathered the child into his arms.

Immediately, the scene shifted back to the studio. Ayers said that the child was being treated for dehydration at Children's Healthcare Pediatric Hospital. All individuals in the home had been dead at least three days, meaning that the infant most likely was IA. Good. The younger, the better. Who knew when mothers could safely bear more children?

The newsreader then announced something that I'd heard on the grapevine for days. Fulton County officials were on the verge of declaring metropolitan Atlanta an IA zone, with the not unrelated news that water rationing had been ended. A pair of light rains had lightened the heat of May, which was such a strange notion to me, that whilst not enough in itself to break the drought, gave them the nerve to state what was bloody obvious. Fewer people meant less water usage.

Only a few neighborhoods, located in east Atlanta, remained uncleared of bodies, and even the most diehard sensitives had boarded buses for safe towns up north.

It counted as lovely news for someone, but the news closer to home, not so rich. Somehow, someone on the CDC sensitives floor broke containment. They cracked a window for a breath of air, smuggled in fruit, or failed to spray a fresh supply of packaged goods. Something happened, I don't know what. There were only four of them left, restricted to an isolation room. And then there were three.

I didn't know the tall, spare man walking into her office, but Bao-Zhai freaked upon seeing him. She scrambled through her desk drawers looking for a mask.

Dr. Muhammed Nazir sat down in her visitor's chair.

"Put me to work. And I want a delivery pizza. I can't take another Lean Cuisine."

"But you're in danger right now." Bao-Zhai pulled on her mask as she spoke.

Dr. Nazir reached across her desk and gently took off her mask.

"I intend to die as a free man, applying my skills as I've been trained to do. I believe I am doing the will of Allah."

Bao-Zhai was crying as he spoke, something I hadn't seen her do since we met. I learned later that the two of them had been partners on a project together, and now they were partners again.

Over the next few days, Dr. Nazir reported to his station, working diligently well into the night. In the short time allotted him, he made no breakthroughs in curing the disease that killed him, but he got his wish.

*Wylie Halverson*

Some genius decided to program Turner Classic Movies with every bad-news science fiction film ever made. Selma said they were trying to make us feel better.

See how hard a time Charlton Heston is having against those apes. Guess how many vampires Will Smith can handle. I considered it in bad taste, but at least they seemed to have some sense of the gravity of the situation, unlike other people in Hollywood.

There were films ready to be shown, shot before all this happened. Apparently, they felt it important to premiere their films in a movie theater, so CNN had coverage of a weekend film festival in downtown Los Angeles.

With so many of the stars dead or in hiding, only a handful of them showed up, but there were, believe it or not, fans present for the occasion. Even a couple of photographers. It looks to me, if you cram enough people together in front of a camera, you can create the illusion of a crowd. The movies then went straight to television. Once we saw them, I can't say the movies were all that special, on the whole, but my kids loved the animated one. Perhaps it's the spirit of the enterprise that matters more than the actual result.

I've never been a great TV fan because I used to prefer Netflixing series, but there we were, watching TV every night. There was a reality show where they stuck cameras inside one of those safe towns, I believe somewhere in northern Wyoming. The idea, of course, being to see who was going to die first. The producers said it showed the triumph of the human spirit. Nonsense.

What we watched was NBC. They came up with the idea of making certain nights of programs exactly the way it was for a particular year. One night might be the Seinfeld years, another Will and Grace. They'd run the same commercials, everything the same, but with actors, writers and directors, those few who were still around, that is, introducing each program and telling little anecdotes.

Since we were already living in one, I had no interest in watching disaster movies. As for those poor souls in Wyoming, I thought that was the worst form of voyeurism, a kind of death pornography.

Father Jerzy was good about checking to make sure all the families were getting along okay. He gave me the news one evening when he came by to check on the kids. He said that most of the shut-ins we sent upstate were dying, despite all the spraying, and the fact that they were as far north as they could be and not be in Canada proper. From what we heard, the Canadians weren't doing any better, at least not the ones closer to the border.

The weather had been turning balmier over the past few years. We couldn't stop summer from coming on. Terribly upsetting. These were our neighbors, and so many of them had been my students. By and large, most of our people were well behaved.

The local access channel showed graduation exercises from last year, along with old games and concerts. I couldn't wrap my mind around the fact that most of the people I saw on every channel were either dead or about to be dead.

Selma and I talked when the children weren't around about what we would do if the virus started attacking us. She said she couldn't commit suicide because it would be a mortal sin. I reminded her about how all those years the Church condemned us for our sexuality, so what's one more sin? Perhaps I used a bit too flippant a tone, but I meant it. If there was no cure in sight, if our children were suffering, then I felt we had a moral duty to end their pain. If that, and loving Selma, put me in Purgatory or worse, then punch my ticket now.

*Dreya Underhill*

I shouldn't have been surprised, really. My sister was young, in love, and ready to follow Lanasha anywhere. But to Martinez, California? They were both working at the Shell oil refinery. Leesa said she didn't mind the stink and she loved the excitement. I don't know about excitement, but she was in a place where she could be useful.

As for me, I had a problem: Susan wanted me back at the nursery, but I was considering an offer to manage a produce company there in Salinas. The owners had died, and since they couldn't find an heir, Union Bank went in with Monterey County on hiring us to get crops in the ground. To think I had been hired as crew boss because some people saw me at Market Square, hawking those tomatoes. I had a good bunch that worked hard for me, so I give them all the credit.

I drove through the fog one morning and ended up at the house the bank had lined up for me. Four bedrooms, two baths, nice yard, a Jacuzzi. I was thinking to myself if only Rita could see me now. If only I could see Rita.

I had to be honest with myself. As much as I liked Susan, I couldn't let this chance go by. The company was offering me a two-year contract with a third-year option, a no-rent house, and a company pickup. If they picked up my option after the third year, the house was mine, free and clear. I'd be working the land, feeding thousands of people, maybe more, and calling the shots.

I called Susan and told her the situation. She was real upset over it. So was I. Even though we hadn't known each other long, we'd been relying on each other so much, texting like breathing.

Coming back down Route 183, I saw a pickup off to the side of the road. It had been a while since a bug bomb had gone off. Most of the straights had died or been cleared out by then, headed east somewhere or into the bubble towns.

I had a rifle for protection, so I slowed down to see what was going on. Going by, I saw a woman at the wheel. I decided to check on whether she needed help. When I got out, I kept my rifle handy, but she turned out to be a girl with a headdress on. Not the Muslim kind, but the Mennonite kind. They're like the Amish, but not so stuck on wearing black. Hanky heads is what Pops called them.

You might think a country girl would freak seeing someone like me coming at them with a gun in hand, but I kept the rifle pointed down and a smile on my face. Girl didn't flinch. She told me she hit the brakes hard to avoid a dog and the car died. I got her car started, and after first trying to blow me off, she agreed to follow me into town.

I knew some of the locals had gotten together to turn a private Christian school into an orphanage, although I'm sure they called it something nicer than that. I think they had in mind eventually placing as many kids as possible with families, but to start out by creating a safe, stable situation for them.

Elizabeth, that was the girl's name, looked to be about twelve or thirteen. Why push her about what happened? I already knew the basics.

No way could I take the kid in. I didn't have a wife, and even if Leesa came back, I wouldn't trust her to be responsible, so all I could do was drop by after work every day to check on things. She kept the hanky on her head, but she didn't pitch a fit over wearing jeans and kicks. One day, I took her out to the field with me. She had a blast.

It turned out Elizabeth's people had grown their own food out in the country. She didn't say much, but I put it together. They were some of the straights that refused to leave for the bubble towns, although I'm betting they weren't the ones building bombs. They just didn't like modern ways, period, and it didn't matter if we were gay or straight or Martians.

Elizabeth liked digging in the soil, so it got to where she would stay at the school during the week and with me on the weekends.

One afternoon, I was out in the field checking where a blight had been trying to get established. I saw Susan, of all people, walking toward me. She was wearing a fluorescent pink top that made her stand out bright as a video game against the rows of lettuce. Her partner had come back. Susan couldn't stand to be there running the nursery with her, dealing with all that crap.

This time I held her without losing my mind. I kissed her and let the rest of it slip away. She felt… alive. Alive, like me.

I hadn't felt like I deserved Susan, not the happiness part, not the love and patience. I don't know that Rita and I were meant to last. She had her ways, and I had mine, but the walking fever took whatever future we could have had together. I had this woman in front of me, willing to make a go of it, and I knew now that I could.

It's true we hadn't known each other long, but we understood each other, which matters more in the long run.

*Analyn Orante*
A video map in the Sit Room showed all the safe towns and cordoned-off counties in green, the Infected/Asymptomatic areas in yellow. Unlike the old red state-blue state days, you couldn't have a mix in colors. Everyday, the map lost more and more green, while the yellows remained constant. The yellows were mostly in urban areas.

President Budin believed that viral negative citizens, now officially called sensitives, needed to feel we weren't using this as an opportunity to push them out of entire regions of the country. That's why IA relocations were almost all to the urban centers, leaving the suburbs and exurbs alone.

We participated in a daydream, a pleasant fiction, that someday we would all live close by each other, that a cure would be found, and soon.

During a morning meeting at the Sit Room, Secretary of Commerce Fujita came right out and said what was on everyone's mind. "It's time, Madam President. It's time for the endgame."

Dr. Tofill chimed in on the video hookup. He pointed out the obvious: most of our safe towns had lost containment, plus the rural resistance had picked up steam in recent weeks.

They were shooting from trees, setting fires, and leaving bombs. The FBI kept finding bodies of these people out in the woods, people who were fighting us down to their last feverish breath.

Little known fact: we never talked about how many citizens had died that week. It was there in black and white in our folder. You couldn't comprehend such a number. A confirmed sixty million Americans dead during the first three months. That alone was a terrible statistic, a human tragedy, but then they kept on dying. When I talked to my sources overseas, the numbers varied from country to country, but were uniformly bad.

Researchers estimated that upwards of one hundred million died worldwide of the Spanish flu. This worked out to around five percent of the total population. The Spanish Flu easily fit the definition of a Category 5 pandemic, just like the Black Death.

We didn't have a Category 6. We didn't have the language for a ninety-percent fatality rate, let alone know what to call something that simply would not quit killing us.

Over half of our fellow Americans were now dead, at minimum. We knew the numbers were much higher than that because we lacked the resources to retake Florida. In many parts of the country, particularly the south and southwest, authorities were overwhelmed by the scope of the problem.

I remember one mayor called the governor of Arkansas asking for permission to burn bodies. It hadn't rained there in months, so permission was denied. The mayor did it anyway, and she wasn't the only one. What else could they do?

So, when Secretary Fujita made his point, we understood that it had come down to this moment. We were losing the fight. Unless we transported our remaining negatives to the newly designated Barrow Base in northern Alaska, it was game over.

We were already sending groups up on ships. The Canadians were giving us trouble about road access and about our running ferries up from Puget Sound.

The Canadians weren't saying much for public consumption. My sources told me that they were no better than we were at containing VSF. They had experienced their warmest winter on record, followed by the warmest spring, and now all of North America was going through its warmest summer, again, on record.

The Canadians had several thousand sensitives living as far north as could be sustainable. They couldn't stick any more people up there. It outstretched their capacity to maintain them, to airdrop filters and pesticides, medical supplies, and food. It tires me out thinking of that logistical nightmare, combined with the inevitability of vectors thriving in warmer temperatures. It's no wonder Canada didn't want any more refugees.

President Budin thanked Secretary Fujita for his input, then she turned to us and said that it was time for Berlin.

It was code-named for the airlift campaign during the Cold War. We intended to fly as many sensitives as we could to northern Alaska. FitzGerald's soldiers and elements of the Army Corps of Engineers had performed brilliantly in expanding Point Barrow and other northern communities. We knew the dangers in shipping so many people over long distances to be considerable. Even with all our protective measures, there was still a significant danger of contagion.

Just as with the mayors building funeral pyres, what else could we do?

*Dora Navarro*

The way Bev explained it to me was that an entire platoon refused to board the flight to Alaska. The command sergeant happened to be one of Bev's clients, so she went and talked to him. It turned out he had another mission in mind.

Sheriff's deputies were trying to track down the river rats. Isolated houses were still getting attacked, bodies found floating in the river. No wonder I kept watch at night.

Bev said the sergeant and his men understood what it meant, but they knew odds were they would die anyway. This way, they would be doing something they had trained to do.

The sergeant told her, "I don't want ya'll thinking that's all people like us were about—killing and being angry." It worried him that someday they might all be gone, and then what would we remember them for?

The entire operation took about a week. Helicopters with heat-sensing equipment found the targets. Bev said there were some very surprised deer caught up in this. Then the helicopter crews told the soldiers and deputies where to go. They killed fourteen or fifteen river rats in all, a lot less than we thought there would be. They were called the dead-enders, and now they, and the troops who killed them, were dead. I was sorry about the soldiers, but the others? It was better for everyone concerned that they got taken down.

I felt a little safer, and once I had the special rearview mirrors installed on my Subaru, I was ready to drive. Although Barb had an appointment lined up for me in Austin with an eye specialist, I couldn't imagine driving there, even in a convoy.

For my first trip alone, I went into nearby Salado to the dry cleaners to pick up Mama's quilt. The man there, who was training a girl in how to run the press, said the place had belonged to his brother. He hoped to go to regular hours once his property assumption was approved.

With so many people dying, so many services disrupted, who needed a dry cleaners? If you wanted a new winter coat, grab one out of a store window. People were still doing that, even though deputies had the authority to shoot looters on sight. Or, you could do some trading at one of the swap meets you saw on practically every corner.

But what if you were really attached to your old coat, your jacket, or your mother's quilt? Maybe you needed to get a pair of slacks altered because you had lost weight due to stress and poor diet. Life goes on for the dry cleaners, too.

The man in charge, Scott Bayard, was friendly. He didn't know when he would be able to stay open more than two days a week, but he sounded optimistic.

While he was talking, he checked me out. He was discreet about it, but he didn't mind me noticing. There were few of us around anymore. Some stuff you read online claimed that this disease proved bisexuals had been faking all along, which wasn't true, at least in my case.

When I returned home, I spread the quilt out on my bed so Barb could see Mama's work. She was so impressed, which anyone would be. Mama liked doing theme quilts. This one was about Texas history. There was a beautiful stained-glass effect on the border that looked like medieval bluebonnets.

As Barb admired the quilt, I pointed out the squares I had sewn. She immediately wanted me to get going on a project. I mean, we're talking high school the last time I did any sewing, but the more she talked about finding me a Singer sewing machine, the more I thought about how happy that would have made Mama, to see me take it up again.

"I'd love for you to show me how to quilt." Barb had a hopeful expression.

That evening on the news, they showed the latest fire in Colorado. The biggest one by far. Firefighters were still working on the one in New Mexico. They didn't think either of the fires was deliberately set, not that it mattered.

Barb had traded the rest of the dates for some jars of chipped beef. For supper, we ate it on couscous with a huge garden salad. Again. If not for Bev's occasional MREs, the main dishes would have gotten monotonous.

We were still harvesting peaches, which ended up in spiced and plain varieties for canning as well as for the freezer. I did a lot of the work on that. It worried me that I wasn't contributing enough to the household.

Over bowls of grilled peaches topped with homemade frozen yogurt, Barb remembered to tell me that one of Cressy Mungia's foster kids wanted to take piano lessons. A boy named D'Wayne Lloyd. That name sounded familiar.

"Oh, my God. That's Solomon's little brother." Solomon Lloyd, the piano student I had gone to see at the club where I was the only one wearing a mask.

"Of course, I'd love to take him on. I'd do it for free."

"I think not," Barb said. "Cressy had a ton of canned beans given to her. We can swing a deal here."

# Chapter 9

*Debra Shanrahan*

Regularly scheduled flights had resumed between Australia and the United States. No reason not to have them now, except that your average world citizen preferred Australians to leave the planet. The message came down from Personnel. Did I want to return home?

Apparently, someone up the food chain decided they didn't need me under their thumb anymore. Free to travel, if I wanted to. On the theory that most of the ones who hated me there were now dead, I thought it was safe to go back home. That would mean leaving Bao-Zhai. Not my jollies to be the staff flunky, but not much call for a large animal vet in Atlanta, is there?

Then the director of Fulton County Animal Services resigned and moved back wherever she came from. Board didn't want to promote from within, due to a personality clash, I'm thinking, so I put in for it. Mind you, I had yet to receive a proper passport, was as illegal an alien as you can get, but they hired me. In a perverse sort of way, it helped that I was semi-famous. They suspected I might have relevant job skills.

About Bao-Zhai's favorite drug: I found out at the store that the Coca-Cola cannery was importing raw materials from Cuba. Cuba had been hit as hard as anyone, but whoever was running the place now (the news said it was a collective) certainly knew how to turn a profit. Now, if I could find a bag of coffee that didn't cost both arms and legs. A brutal remark, I'm sure, but one would think with so many people gone, there'd be plenty of java to go around. You'd be far from spot on.

I desperately needed a caffeine infusion. Then in the news it said that the FBI had broken up a ring of hoarders. Some people saw the crisis as their main chance. They scarpered with warehouses of food, but more important, they took the coffee. Little poofters. FBI brought them up on charges. They returned the coffee to the rightful business owners.

All I cared about was that the Starbucks down by Emory had my favorite Guatemalan available again. The price? Still boldfaced robbery.

*Wylie Halverson*

Selma knew which cow to select: the lowest producer. That didn't make it any easier on the kids. There's no room for sentimentality on a farm, but they were townies. They had never looked a cow in the face and said, well, better you than me. We needed meat, both to eat and to trade for supplies.

The neighbors who came to help out brought some things we needed. Quid pro quo. Father Jerzy asked for the tongue. He had in mind a Polish recipe. I told him, you're welcome to it.

David Grakh, the florist, took me over to the side and told me that he was taking care of his dad's pigs. When the order came to slaughter the pigs, his dad refused, so when he died, David moved out to the farm to look after the animals. Pigs aren't particular about what ends up in the slop. I suspect we weren't the only stock owners who went foraging.

"Do you think we'd get in trouble if we had a pig day?" He had an anxious expression on his face.

"Oh, I think it'd be okay." I felt almost giddy from the thought of all that sausage. And pork roast. And ham steak. "So you think you can spare a pig then?"

"You betcha. I've got a couple of market hogs that have been topped off for ages. I'd say they're around two hundred pounds apiece. I could use help slaughtering them."

David Grakh is on the burly side. He's not anyone's idea of a fragile flower lover, but I understood the need for an extra pair of hands. I could not imagine the toll it took on Selma to keep the farm running before her instant family came along.

Two hundred pounds, each. Instantly, I felt guilty, thinking of what it meant. Those pigs could be covered from snout to tail in plague-infected ticks, but no one here had to worry about it now.

I hadn't heard yet how many, if any, of our shut-ins made it to Barrow Base in Alaska. On the radio it said that, according to the current census, there were only seven hundred residents left in the entire county.

According to the Feds, we should have expected up to ten percent to survive in any given place. That didn't take into account how many moved away when they graduated from high school. Then there were the children killed during the crisis by neglect, an unrelated illness, or by parents who thought they were sparing their children a much worse fate.

We filed papers on all six of our children, including Regina, when the district judge came through town. We realized that, whatever happened, they needed a formal foster care arrangement. It did worry me that they were being cared for by women on the far end of middle age.

When the radio announced that couples could now register their partnerships, even be married in a civil ceremony, I learned to my utter surprise Selma's true age. A life lived outdoors, and the decision not to dye her gray hair, gave Selma a distinguished appearance, but it didn't make her any older than her actual age of forty-two.

In those years I stayed away from Stevens Point, Selma and her brother matriculated from high school, and when I returned, she went into the Army for a six-year stint. Our kids had one parental unit with more gas in the tank. We weren't the only family made up of mismatched parts, but we all were trying to make the situation work.

Speaking of hard workers, Don Metzger must have worn down my resistance, because when he stood for the special mayoral election, I voted for him. I had to really think about it when the new school board met and offered me the superintendent position. I figured it was because I was the oldest faculty member remaining.

Selma said, "Do it, Wy. Those kids need you."

So much to work through before the fall semester began. How were we going to provide a school lunch? Even with Dave Grakh's pigs, and the sheriff's department cracking down on hoarders, there weren't enough food staples on hand, not enough to get us through the winter. Thank the Lord all our gardens were producing.

Metzger, excuse me, *Mayor* Metzger, announced that community canning sessions would be taking place every Saturday through the fall. Some boys in town were building an industrial dryer to make jerky and dried fruits.

I didn't want to look at the TV some nights. They had a channel just for stories about the dead called Obit. I believe it used to be a shopping channel. There was also a new FBI show about catching cheaters and hoarders.

The reality show in that safe town ended the way I thought it would. Every Sunday night, there was a variety show from Las Vegas, Los Angeles, or New York. Dancers or the dead, take your pick. As for me, I read a lot.

*Dreya Underhill*

Elizabeth shared her bedroom with her foster sister, Maria, a quiet twelve-year-old Elizabeth couldn't bear to leave behind at the orphanage. After a couple of weekends of what Susan called taking her for a spin, we decided that Elizabeth was right. We couldn't leave Maria behind, either, although as a family we were up against it trying to keep her supplied with all things mermaid. The girls couldn't stand the idea of having separate bedrooms, which was something I lusted after at their age.

At the produce company, Susan was a lifesaver since she had more business experience than I did. At one time, she had been a corporate hotshot. You wouldn't have figured her for a hard case, but when it came to dealing with the shippers, there was no one tougher.

"It's not my problem what fuel is costing you these days." She would bite off her words and throw them into the receiver for her unlucky caller to catch.

"We have the same shortages as you, the same labor problem, the same everything. If you want a shoulder to cry on, go see your boyfriend. In the meantime, I have the records right in front of me from last year. We're not changing a thing."

The State of California kept busy arresting gas gougers. It was hard enough for people to travel these days without emptying their wallet in some nowhere town. I didn't have time for TV, but one of my workers was crazy about a reality show where four fraternity brothers were driving across the country. One of the networks had a satellite truck with them, so it was real reality, you get what I'm saying.

When they broke down in Cleveland (all right, I did watch sometimes), they ended up at a wedding party. Make that, parties. People hooking up at some place called Johnny's. There were two men I can tell you right now weren't going to last a week together. I couldn't slam them for trying.

It's one thing to be for gay marriage when you're going against the rest of the world, but now, the straights, the ones who were left, couldn't do jack about it. That is, if they even cared.

It got me to thinking a little harder about what I needed to do. I went to a swap meet in downtown Salinas one Sunday where I picked up a couple of wedding rings. Leesa had Mom and Pops's rings. I figured, you never know. She might actually grow up someday.

That day, I barbecued some chicken, Susan made a big salad, and the girls showed off their tortillas. Kind of square looking, but they tasted okay.

I showed Susan the rings and said, "What do you think? Do you want to be street legal?" Real smooth, but she dug it.

Monday we went by the courthouse and filled out the paperwork. It worried Elizabeth that we didn't get married in a church, and Maria, little Miss Echo, had the same opinion. Susan had been raised sort-of Buddhist/sort-of Pentecostal. I wasn't much of anything, due to my parents' difference of opinion.

There was a church in town most people were attending. It had been one of those places where they raise their hands all the time, but now it was a mix: some Methodist, some Pentecostal, some New Age. I don't know if it all worked for me, but I liked the music, and the preachers didn't get on my nerves.

No satellite truck recorded the whole thing, but we did go ahead and have our ceremony at the church. We had a big turnout from my crew. Lots of people, tons of food.

One of the wedding presents was a half-case of Twinkies. Susan has this weakness, you see. She tries to be a granola girl, but when she saw the Twinkies, she broke down and cried. It made me think, I hope it's true what they say about those things, that they last forever.

*Analyn Orante*

The United Nations general session finally came to fruition with forty-two countries sending delegates. No one objected to the Australians.

We had special accommodations prepared for any sensitives, but it was the middle of summer in New York when we pulled the session together. No special rooms needed, unfortunately.

I had hoped our delegate would be able to introduce the proposed neutral borders treaty, which asked signatories to renounce violence against refugees and to not impede humanitarian shipments. It never came to a vote.

We did denounce North Korea's bombing of its border regions with China and South Korea, but since the attacks were restricted to its side of the border, the neighbors saw no need to respond. That was an insanely xenophobic response by anyone's standard, to kill your own people in order to sterilize, quote-unquote, your borders, but par for the course for North Korea those days.

New British Prime Minister Jane Bowsler came to the White House for a small reception. We didn't feel it appropriate to push the pomp and circumstance. President Budin went with her to New York. None of us wanted our President over the water anytime soon.

Congress had finally agreed to the President's choice to fill the Vice President vacancy. I thought Rawlings was an excellent choice: four-time U.S. Representative out of Arizona, turned Microsoft executive. He and his husband were in the process of adopting two foster children. The fact that he had been a Libertarian should not have been controversial, given the situation. President Budin believed in Rawlings, and in the end she got her man.

We had two years before the next presidential election, and hardly any time to prepare for the Congressionals.

On that account, my assistant, Bill Levine, said, "Expect a catastrophe. That way we'll be pleased with it only being a disaster."

President Budin said we wouldn't be able to redistrict in time for the fall elections, which meant some representatives would be elected from districts with approximately zero in the way of voters. Two hairdressers and a mountain goat? Just run it, accept the results, however undemocratic, and then plan for the next election.

Here's one thing that bothered me: some reporters had the idea that our country was being run by the B-team, or to be honest, the D-League. The legends had left the stage.

Obviously, we were going through what, by all rights, should have been a killing blow. Who could move on from that? But, you do. You do try to move on. My family, most of my friends, my peers, my idols, my cousins in the Philippines. If I stopped to think about it, I froze up. So I didn't stop to think.

I pointed out at a press conference that the number of survivors wasn't relevant to the task of leading our country. About the time of the American Revolution, the population of all the colonies combined was under two million, one-fourth being slaves who built this country but who had no political power.

I freely concede that our forefathers were an amazing group of individuals, but they were human beings, like us. They were forced to be better than they really were, I believe. They had no choice but to reach for greatness. George Washington made a lot of mistakes as a general, don't forget, but he had a knack for making the right decision at the right time. And the man was unbelievably lucky.

President Budin had managed not to get shot off her horse. We still had a country. We couldn't get a reliable estimate on how many sensitives were left since so many were in hiding or their bodies hadn't been discovered yet.

As far as IAs, gathering up all the state estimates gave us a figure somewhere between twenty to forty-five million, which was another way of stating that we didn't have a handle on the numbers. The fever was in us, but it hadn't killed us.

In some ways, the country as a whole was starting to get back on its feet. Essential services were running in all the yellow zones. Our Alaskan zone represented a huge drain of resources, but it was still hanging in there, plus the biodomes construction was getting off to a good start.

Florida? Who knew? According to satellite images, flyovers, and communications analysis, we believed that several thousand individuals were living in Florida, virtually all of them in the interior. They were hermits, basically, living as far apart from each other as possible. Probably most of them were IAs, but President Budin decided to leave that problem alone for a while. We needed to let nature do some of the detoxing for us before we went back in.

Although our oil refineries were running at a fraction of their previous volume, we still possessed significant reserves. The compact with Brazil, in which we mutually abandoned all trade restrictions, guaranteed we would not run out of fuel of any kind for the immediate future.

We had no choice but to write off all the Old World energy sources, and that included the North Sea. We couldn't risk stretching out our lines and making ourselves that vulnerable again. If we couldn't dig our fuel out of the Gulf, grow it in a field, or buy it from Brazil, forget it. Hybrid was the big buzzword, not to mention electric cars and natural gas.

All that was in the talking stages, identifying what was left in our industrial sector. In the meantime, we had more pressing needs, such as food shortages. Establishing a reliable chain of supply to those in need proved to be harder than we anticipated.

Guard and Reserve units had performed brilliantly in securing major shipping routes. Hijackings had largely been eliminated, or the main perpetrators had died of the fever, but a lot of people were still suffering from shortages.

Secretary of Commerce Fujita worked to create the Feed America consortium. That was where Wal-Mart, Target, Costco, and a half-dozen other food companies agreed to synchronize their stockpiles according to population levels in their area and what they still had available. It made no sense to have a ton of frozen fries in Boston, yet none in Des Moines or Tulsa.

I can't imagine how it would have been managed before the Internet, before the software era, when companies lacked flexibility in movement.

One solution to one problem. One down, a million to go.

It was decided that the Secretary of State should visit our partners overseas. This was a rather short list. England, France, and Germany, to be precise, with visits planned to South Korea and Japan in the fall.

Bill said that the King wanted to meet me, and I assure you, a more unlikely sentence I've never heard. Then he started telling me about an incident that happened off the coast of Maine involving a Coast Guard cutter and a yacht that had been out to sea for several months. The man on board had been eating fish and filtering his water, hoping to outlast the epidemic.

"Not to be melodramatic," Bill started to say. We both stared at each other and burst out into laughter. Perhaps the laughter verged on being hysterical on my part. If there ever was a proper time to be melodramatic, we were living in it.

*Dora Navarro*

Cressy Mungia was a round, determined woman who appeared decades older than I remembered from when I was giving her daughter, Benicia, piano lessons less than two years ago.

She and her husband, Luis, used to run a specialty meat shop in Belton with the help of their oldest son, but now Luis and all her children were gone.

Cressy still had the shop open, offering venison, chicken, various game, lamb, goat, and beef, glorious beef. She preferred cash, and a lot of it, but she enjoyed dickering, like with the rough-hewn man trying to trade his vintage Barbie collection for a rack of lamb.

I had a feeling the Barbies weren't his originally, and from the sound of it, he wasn't going home with the lamb unless he upped his offer.

"Thirty bucks and the dolls. Final offer," he said. "Don't forget, I brought you that deer."

"We already dealt on that. I need gas in my truck. Thirty bucks won't get it out of the driveway. Make it forty." Mungia spoke with a finality that told Frontier Barbie she wouldn't bend under pressure. He caved.

I admired the chorizo, glistening in its tray under the glass. That was definitely coming home with me.

Cressy treated me to a smile. "Miss Navarro, how did D'Wayne do this morning? You know, he's working hard."

"He's talented," I said, truthfully.

A large, withdrawn boy of fifteen, D'Wayne had been receiving lessons from his brother before the fever. I couldn't tell how he felt about the lessons, but he always came prepared. His silence pushed me to talk more, although I still was no one's idea of a sparkling conversationalist.

So far, I had been paid with a case of baked beans, a brisket, tamales, and five pounds of freshly ground top sirloin. In the meantime, word of mouth had landed me two other students, both of them foster children, and both of them, the parents felt, in need of self-expression.

Music as therapy. For them, perhaps. I didn't feel anything getting better. Not the permanent darkness in my left eye, nor the sleeplessness, nor a feeling that was hard to describe, but like static in an amplifier, an omnipresent buzz that wouldn't go away.

"Chorizo this time?" Cressy deftly snapped up four links as she spoke.

"You read my mind."

"I read your eye."

"How do you keep going?" I asked. Again with the weird questions, and when, tell me, when would that ever stop?

Cressy had the links wrapped, bagged, and in my hands in a matter of seconds. She leaned over the counter and pondered.

"Okay," she said. "Loaded question, I'll give you a loaded answer. God. God runs the show. All I do is try to keep up."

That's right, I remembered. She's a Mormon.

"How do you... how did you work out being gay and being married?"

"I got married at eighteen. I had feelings. I knew exactly who and what I was, but I also knew that I wanted to have a husband waiting for me in heaven. I wanted everything my sisters had. We have the option, you know, of being celibate, but I couldn't handle that, and I knew I wanted children. Luis was a good man and a wonderful father. He didn't ask from me what I was unable to give him. It wasn't his fault, it was mine," she said with the same manner that had deflated her previous customer.

"What was your fault, being gay?"

"No. Getting married and having children. That was my sin. If they'd never lived, they'd never have suffered the way they did. I know they're safe in heaven, but I had no right to put them through the hell that was that disease. Luis, he'd have died whether or not I was with him. It was a terrible thing I did."

Best to let that subject slide. "Are there other members here?"

"Oh, yes. More Latter Day Saints in Killeen than here, and we've found some members on base. We had eighteen at my house Monday night," she said with notably more enthusiasm. We both needed a change in topics.

"How are you going to keep it going? Since you can't get married, you can't have children."

It turned out that their church's president and other top leaders survived the early months of the fever by going into seclusion at a location in northern Utah or possibly Idaho. Cressy didn't know which. There, a quorum of seventy met, and there were twelve apostles, and everyone was an elder. They'd begun hammering out ideas, but then most of them started dying off.

I couldn't understand anything Cressy said after that, but then, the details of Mama's relatives' many feuds in Mississippi congealed long ago in my mind into "the Stantons don't talk to the MacBrides."

I took a stab at it. "Your president had a vision of the future where gays are included if they form a covenant consisting of two men and two women?"

"That's basically right, and our new church president was a member of the Presidency of the Seventy, which is an amazing blessing, when you think about it, that God installed him in that place, and the others in their places, as well."

Most of what she said flew over my head, but I did get the gist of it: a group faced with extinction found a way to go forward. I suppose having a leader who is allowed, in fact expected, to be a prophet turns out to be a plus.

Mama never worried about my salvation. She said that God would sort it out in the end. I was her only daughter, and God wouldn't keep her baby away from her, no matter what.

Driving home, I saw a U-Haul pull out of the driveway of a brick split-level house. A man in shorts was already applying his weed-eater to the wildly overgrown lawn. I had been in that house last year, the guest of my soon-to-be ex-boyfriend at his cousin's college graduation party.

Robert was dead. I knew that. His voice sounded breathy when he called me while I was in Odessa. I hadn't tried to look him up after I returned home. I had only recently gotten back to visiting with my friends. The last woman I dated most definitely was alive and living with her partner in a place near the river.

They survived the fever, survived the panic, survived the river rat attacks, with the damage limited to a bullet through the living room window and a car stolen. They were both now working for the electric company. They landed on their feet.

I felt as though I were still facedown on that highway. Maybe starting to get up on one knee, but blind and clueless.

Coming through the back door into the kitchen, I saw Barb sitting in the breakfast nook. She was watching an emaciated woman pile-drive a plate of tamales.

"Hello there, Dora," she said calmly. "We have a visitor. Linda Maselka, right?"

Linda Maselka said nothing as she continued to shovel her food. Clothed in a muddy work shirt and jeans, she might have been twenty, she might have been fifty. There was no way of knowing the age buried beneath her tangled blonde hair and the crevasses in her weathered skin.

Linda Maselka had a pistol lying next to her plate. Something went gray in me. I dropped the chorizo on the kitchen counter.

I went upstairs, grabbed the rifle by my bed, and came back to find Linda Maselka standing at the foot of the stairs, the pistol in her hand but pointed downward. Barb stood at the kitchen door, saying something no doubt relevant to the moment. Linda Maselka and I were too intrigued by each other to pay attention to her.

"I'm dead, in case you hadn't noticed already." Linda Maselka had a surprisingly strong baritone. "Been dead for a long time now. My brother died, his family. They're gone. I'm eating my food, just minding my business, so you mind yours. I'll be gone soon enough."

With that, Linda Maselka went back to the table where she finished up on the tamales. A plate of Spanish rice, salsa, and tortillas went down next, during which I sat on the stairs and watched her, unwilling and unable to lay down my rifle.

Then, clutching her canteen, which Barb filled for her from the faucet, Linda Maselka barely nodded to us and loped out the back door.

Barb asked if I wanted tamales for supper, acting as though nothing important had just occurred.

"Did you let her in?" I asked.

"Yes. I saw her come up the drive, big as Broadway." Barb examined the chorizo then placed it in the refrigerator. "She had that gun stuck in her belt, but she didn't threaten me with it. She was hungry."

"She's one of them, the river rats. Who knows what she'd have done if I hadn't come in."

"She might've held me up, but I don't think she would have killed me."

"You know how many people have died around here, maybe from her gun, so I don't get you at all."

I sat down in the breakfast nook, my rifle propped in the corner. Barb might not have been taking the threat seriously, but I did.

I heard the telltale sound of Bev's car coming up the driveway. Barb sat down across from me.

"Dora, I recognized her. Not her in particular, but her type. She said she worked at Federal Express for several years and then at the Workforce Commission processing claims. Her brother and his family moved into a camper—yes, by the river—and she came along to help protect the kids. She says she didn't participate in any raids on houses."

"Do you believe her?"

"No, I don't. I gave her a meal. I told her that the county's hiring, and I told her the Catholic church'll let her take a shower in the rectory, or so the rumor goes. I had no intention of letting her come any farther than the kitchen, Dora. I'm not a complete idiot."

She spoke with a sharp tone that would have made Cressy Mungia proud.

"I'm not saying you're stupid."

The grayness seeped out of me, and I could finally see Barb the way she really was: scared, yet regal. I finally remembered about the gun in the cookie jar. Linda Maselka wouldn't have stood a chance. Still, I didn't regret bringing out the rifle.

Bev came through the back door. "Please tell me you've made tamales." She must have seen the look on my face. "What happened?"

# Chapter 10

*Debra Shanrahan*

If any fact explained the impossibility of viral sensitives ever rejoining the rest of us, it was this: a tick found on the damned stray poodle carried VSF, but it was not one of the eleven mutations discovered thus far. According to lab results sent over to my office, this was a new version, fast and lethal. This made it harder to transmit and quicker to the kill, much like Ebola.

If the fever had gone zoonotic with this version, it might have been contained to the Moree Region and the district around the Chinese slaughterhouse. We would have knocked it down flat. Though it had rediscovered its roots, VSF had yet to map a course to our destruction. Even this stone cold killer couldn't raise a ruffle on the blood sample provided, which happened to be my own. I reckoned it was only a matter of time before IAs began carrying it, making us damned quick grim reapers for any luckless sensitive.

I sent a copy of the results, along with my thoughts on the matter, via courier to Bao-Zhai. As I watched the teenaged girl tear off on her scooter, I wondered, does she have a license to drive, and should I inquire about the gun she's wearing? It was best not to wonder about an underage girl's newly appropriate behavior.

In this universe, as the new director of Fulton County Animal Services, I had more pressing matters, such as investigating possible rabies in a raccoon. It had been brought into our office by an irate mother. She claimed said raccoon scratched her daughter. The creature had been bludgeoned with a shovel and stuffed into a fancy metal wastebasket.

The daughter, a sawed-off delinquent in a Hawks jersey, mutely pointed out for me the approximate region of her invisible scratch. I did a double take.

"Ma'am? Your daughter, is she really your daughter?"

"What do you mean? Of course she's my kid."

The mother fairly bristled with leftover raccoon-killing hostility.

I looked at one face, then to the other. Same freckles, same pale green eyes, same piss-poor bleach job. Perhaps not everything can be chalked up to genetics.

"I mean no disrespect. Surely you know that there are very few mother-daughter combos roaming about these days. A sight like this, it gives one hope."

A true enough statement, and it did mellow the old hatchet enough that she agreed to give her description of the raccoon's behavior before its demise. Poor thing was seen chewing on a Crispy Creme doughnut left on their lawn chair, and in my experience, that was probably not a strong indicator of rabies.

I sent them off with one of my assistants to finish the interview and take their information. I assumed they would want the trashcan back, sans raccoon.

I had my crews out, as I had every working day since I took the job, collecting strays for delivery to the holding facility. Techs searched the strays for ticks and drew blood for our ongoing comparative studies. Then came triage.

My predecessor couldn't stomach the logical method of dealing with such a massive number of unmastered animals. I didn't like it, either. We were all in the shit. It was well advertised locally that if you wanted to save your dog from the dogcatchers, then have it properly yarded, give it a collar, and why not make it look cared for.

Because, I'll tell anyone this, if you're not doing those three things, you don't have a pet, you have a notion of one. Too many dogs had gone feral. We rarely went after cats since rats needed killing. The dogs were our main concern.

Not enough of them had died in the early months, to be blunt on the subject. I fielded phone calls daily from people upset over our twenty-four-hour euthanizing policy, yet were they there to adopt all those diseased, starving beasts? Of course not. We had children over at the Emory University dorms waiting for foster parents. All I'm saying is, have a sense of priorities.

In the midst of starting my new position and Bao-Zhai receiving a promotion to assistant project director, we had moved into our house. It was a plush residence in an area situated roughly between the CDC campus and my office. We both worked long hours that allowed little time to spend together, yet Bao-Zhai never complained about my taking the position. We both have strong personalities. It made sense to give us breathing space.

It had taken awhile to process the previous owners' personal effects, hampered by the awkwardness of touching someone else's private life. I managed to boil it down to two boxes of what I thought a relative might someday want.

The federal government had a website where you could register the boxes and list the owners and whatever personal data that would help in identification. Then you downloaded copies, affixed one to each box, and delivered them to your community's designated storage center. There, trained curators stored the boxes in a climate-controlled facility, every step of the process documented.

Wishful thinking. Few communities possessed the space or manpower for that organized an effort. I had nothing from Mum, my sister, the whole lot of them. After numerous phone calls, I located a few friends still alive and somewhat kicking. One of them promised to go by Mum's house to see if there was anything worth salvaging.

She also said the newspaper was starting to use words like "hero" about me. A nice turn of opinion, but not enough to make me want to go back. Not yet.

While out on errands that took me over much of the sweaty, trash-infested downtown area, I swung by the warehouse to drop off the boxes. The security guard sat ensconced in his air-conditioned office playing Madden football. He maintained his grip on the game controller.

The former occupants of our house, a middle-aged couple with two college-aged children, had done some good in their lives. The husband served as a volunteer with the American Heart Association. The wife knew how to throw a beaut of a pot, to judge from the pieces we displayed throughout the house.

They might have been well-scrubbed predators, but I don't think so. Cleaning out their hidden corners revealed ordinary, blameless lives.

Under provisions of the federal property assumption act, cities and counties had the right to assign homes outright to individuals in vital professions and to lease them to others in less critical fields. Bao-Zhai and I were deemed vital enough to own Bill and Tracie Heaton's former space.

In a rare moment of sentiment, Bao-Zhai voiced the hope that the Heatons would have approved of us being there. Who knows? I think they would have preferred to be alive and living in a ditch if that's what it took, and as for Mum's house, I didn't care who might be living in it now. It didn't have Mum.

*Wylie Halverson*

"What do you mean, nonviable?" I asked over the phone. Yelled, to be more precise.

"Ms. Halverson." The woman began to explain. I didn't like her effort the second time, either.

She described herself as being head of the Wisconsin Department of Public Instruction. Her task was to figure out which communities had the ability to provide K-12 instruction for its students. She said that the Stevens Point area failed to meet the criteria.

"Criteria for what, survival? Our people are reasonably well fed these days. You should see what we're already harvesting out of our gardens."

"It's not about the food, Ms. Halverson. After you called about the teacher certification waivers, I checked with the governor's office. Your community is on the list of those moving to Wausau."

"Wausau? It's not any bigger than us."

I knew I was not being the least bit controlled on the subject, but here we had survived, at times done better than survive, with very little help from the government.

"Ms. Halverson, your community has one full-time physician left."

"We have doctors who visit."

"Visiting doctors, who are under incredible strain from covering such a wide area. All our services are stretched beyond the breaking point. Wausau has more of an industrial base, more available housing, and we've already aided the relocation of residents from several other communities to there.

"Ms. Halverson, I'm deeply proud of what you and others have done to keep our state afloat. North Dakota, I understand, can't even keep their electricity running.

"Sorry, that's beside the point. I'm recommending to the governor's office that your K-12 system be declared nonviable. This means that we are decertifying Stevens Point and allocating your funds to viable school systems."

"That is a serious mistake."

"It's the only possible solution. You have too many children and not enough support staff. You'll end up struggling in a one-horse town trying to keep your children well educated, well fed, and with appropriate access to health care. Before we begin spreading precious resources over every nook and cranny of the state, we have to be clear-eyed. We have to be honest about what every community has to offer."

She spoke with a wearied patience that began to sink into me.

"We're getting our businesses back up," I said, "and we've kept our dairy farms in operation. Cows don't milk themselves."

"Cows don't need children, and they don't need pediatricians." She sighed. "I have it on authority from the governor's office that our first phase is about to begin. Senior citizens and the disabled will be moved from nonviable to viable communities as soon as housing and transportation become available. We need it done as soon as possible."

I hung up the phone. Then I went outside to tell Selma the news.

"Wausau?" she said with a sputter. "Heck, if they want to jerk us around, then let's move people our way, like over from Rapids. State's treating us like checkers? Then let's just move the board."

*Dreya Underhill*

"Darwin, Darwin Fuller. I'm here about your opening."

I heard his raspy voice before I turned into the personnel office. He sounded street-toughened, yet uncertain. Fuller averted his eyes while our human services/bookkeeper/secretary rattled through her questions.

It took me a moment to figure him out. Fuller sported tattoos on both wrists, his locks needed some work, and his clothes looked second-hand at best, but he smelled clean, and he was in excellent shape.

"When did they let you out of the joint?"

He didn't act surprised by the question. "A few weeks ago. I went out to Oakland to check on things, then when I was coming through here, I heard y'all were hiring packers."

"Where were you headed?"

His eyes met mine. "I don't know. Had a friend in Whittier who ain't answering the phone, but I figured he'd still be around there somewhere."

My secretary flashed me a look that said, are you sure about this?

"Mr. Fuller, if we decide to hire you, we have some trailers behind the plant where we're housing single crew members. Two things we won't have going on: stealing people's stuff or dealing drugs. I know the government just legalized most of it, but bring it around here and I won't bother with the deputies, I'll take you out myself."

He nodded calmly. "My auntie was on the pipe. I got no feel for that."

Fuller turned out to be a hard worker. He was quiet and kept to himself at first. I wasn't surprised that he took up with Nando, an effeminate teenager with a beautiful face but no common sense.

The gay studs tend to be that way, I told Susan one night after we put the girls to bed. The quiet gave us a prime opportunity to put together the Little Mermaid makeup table I bought from a man at church.

"They barely associate with your average gay guys. Studs don't think they're gay, but as long as their lover puts on some lipstick, they're okay with it. And, speaking of makeup, I don't want Maria painted up when she's at school. The other parents will think I'm a chump."

"She just wants to pretend. I won't let her go to school looking that way. And how do studs think people like them survived VSF? Genes don't lie, Dreya." She finished with the last screw. "There. She's going to love it."

"Oh yeah. Right up her alley." I admired the completed table. "Maybe Fuller needs to justify it in his mind based on what he's been through."

I told her what I had learned from reading articles online, adding that on to what my packing shift chief found out for me.

Fuller had been a low-level Crips soldier in for drug activity. He managed to survive the first death waves and riots. Since most of the guards died or disappeared, he ended up on the body disposal detail, which at the penitentiary involved keeping a steady fire going at the pit.

Burning corpses. I couldn't imagine dealing with the smell, given what it was like being trapped in my apartment with the dying for weeks on end.

Outside the walls he could have escaped, or make that should have escaped, given the conditions, and yet he didn't. Who knows, maybe he felt the same sense of responsibility I did with Rita's relatives. I believed their disease was going to kill me, yet I refused to abandon my job.

Fuller knew he was needed, so he stayed.

In his old job, he probably killed or helped kill people. Born and raised middle-class Andreya Underhill, the woman I used to be, wouldn't have hired him in the first place, much less have kept him on.

Here and now, I needed a solid employee who wouldn't walk off the job. Maybe both he and I had changed.

*Analyn Orante*
While waiting for the television crew to finish setting up, I listened to Bill Levine whisper a last-minute reminder to smile. My attention drifted to the ceiling where a beautiful antique glass chandelier attempted to glow. It was overmatched by the glare from the camera lights.

"It's Waterford, I believe." His keen eyes as usual nailed my point of distraction.

"Why do they call it the White Drawing Room?" I whispered. "The ceiling is white, I'll grant you, but the walls are beige and the curtains are red. It's more like the Predominantly Pale Drawing Room."

"Should I file a protest with the Ministry?"

"I suppose not."

Prime Minister Jane Bowsler strode into the room with her assistants. Make that, assistant, along with the Secretary of State for Foreign and Commonwealth Affairs, a dewy-cheeked man easily mistaken for staff.

Tucking into the chair next to me, Prime Minister Bowsler clipped on her microphone, then shook my hand forthrightly.

After mutual health inquiries and my thoughts about the repairs at Heathrow in which I assured her "one can hardly spot where the damages occurred," the press warmer came off without a hitch.

Many weeks of preparation between our offices had arranged every phase of the visit, from the choir of schoolboys singing "God Bless America" at Westminster Abbey, to the Filipino professor invited to the reception (what Manilan diaspora accounted for him, I wondered), and now a thorough walloping by the press.

Forewarned, I maintained bland, Cream of Wheat thoughts. No, I had no comments regarding Eire's absorption of Northern Ireland that caused a flow of Protestant refugees to England, other than, "It is heartening to witness a great nation open its arms to those in need."

"Did this mean the United States viewed with displeasure France's decision to deny immigration from former dependencies, and what about France's alleged oppression of minorities?"

"That's a multi-part question which requires a longer answer than this format permits."

"France was removed from your itinerary. It has been reported that Presidents Budin and Martin recently had a shouting argument over the phone. Can you tell us the substance of the disagreement?"

"We hope to visit soon. France is a strong ally with historic ties to our nation. Our freedom in part derives from France's support during the American Revolution. It is our hope that France will draw upon its democratic institutions during this crisis. We stand ready to provide whatever assistance is appropriate."

More tossed brickbats concerned my next and final stop, Germany. Germany had issued a general invitation to all world citizens fluent in German, announcing that a home, a job, and a stable political climate awaited each one of them.

In the early weeks of the fever, Germany kicked out thousands of non-Germans. In recent months, it had gone through a change of heart caused by its massive population losses.

"Did Secretary of State Orante believe that natural fluency in a state's primary language should be required for immigrants?" Primed by Bill's seminar on Air Force Two, I knew that this was about Prime Minister Bowsler's call to increase immigration from India.

"I can only speak from my family's experience." I felt wearied by the questioners' code words. "English is spoken by many in the Philippines, but it is fair to say that the Filipino take on English is not universal, so when my parents moved to Georgia they had a problem making themselves understood. They spoke English well enough, but with a heavy accent. Some would have thought of them as nothing more than foreigners with dark skins, but my father served in the United States Marines and my mother made a mean mint julep."

What do Brits know about mint juleps? Focus, Ana.

"I'm a born and raised Georgian. I know where the battlefields are, I can sing the University of Georgia's fight song, and I have a portrait of President Carter in my office. I'm also a proud Filipino-American. Wherever people move, they carry a piece of home with them, but their descendants are more connected to the new home.

"The Germans have developed a strategy consistent with their principles and where they want to take their nation. I applaud their willingness to welcome people from many nations."

Prime Minister Bowsler smoothly took over from there, and soon enough, she and I were eating lunch together in a sunny, flower-laden room. There were flowers everywhere I was driven in London. Such a characteristically English touch. In some neighborhoods, that aroma failed to cover the stench.

England, like Japan, an island nation, suffered a higher percentage of fatalities during the first death waves than we did. Most of the losses occurred in urban areas lacking in large-scale potential burial grounds. When spring rains produced the inevitable grotesques, pits had to be deepened and bodies reburied.

We didn't discuss those gruesome details. Unlike President Budin, Bowsler had never married. The fever wrenched Bowsler from the middle ranks of her party into her current standing.

As I gazed at Bowsler, an attractive brunette, it again occurred to me that the new politics dictated that one should never say "but you don't look like a lesbian" to fellow survivors. Even before the fever, you saw feminine lesbians, but androgyny was more common. Now, you saw the usual range of pre-VSF types mixed in with many who would never have been identified as gay, Secretary of Defense Clayton FitzGerald being a classic example.

"So, what are your thoughts regarding Russia, vis-à-vis NATO?"

Bowsler appeared to be considering another helping of curried cauliflower. I'd made no sighting of Yorkshire pudding thus far on this trip, but at least the scone at breakfast met my expectations.

"Because of our energy compact with Brazil," I said, "and the new government in Venezuela, we're not as constrained as some members of NATO in responding to the Kremlin's internal policies regarding ethnic minorities. As you can well appreciate, our shortage in personnel hampers our ability to assist in international relief efforts."

"How is your Alaska project going?"

Hundreds of thousands of people were crammed into hastily constructed pods designed to seal off sections in case of suspected VSF. Air filters, packaged meals, video games, suicides. Biodome construction desperately needed finishing.

"We're looking at spring before the biodomes are fully operational," I said.

She updated me on her comparable situation. "Our two remaining island enclaves are still intact. Resupply is difficult, but our luck appears to be holding. The only bit of luck we've had thus far."

The British first moved sensitives to northern Scotland and the islands, including the Hebrides, Isle of Man, and Shetland; then the refuges failed, one by one.

By the time Bowsler moved into 10 Downing Street, the whole of northern Scotland was a killing zone, both from VSF and from warring sensitive factions wiping out entire villages to install their own groups, so her first task was pacification of the north. A bloody business all around. Margaret Thatcher would have been proud.

A year ago, I had been anticipating a planned vacation to Spain. That moveable feast of tapas, parties, and beautiful women I would see again in the spring, but not as a mere government functionary.

A public actor on a devastated stage, I found myself playing an unfamiliar role. Described in our press as the love child of Cory Aquino and Harry Truman, I found more inspiration in the words, if not always the life, of Churchill.

He didn't say, "Never, never, never, never give up." The actual speech, to some schoolboys in 1941, was, "Never, never, in nothing great or small, large or petty, never give in except to convictions of honour and good sense. Never yield to force; never yield to the apparently overwhelming might of the enemy."

Desperate to limit our losses, we had been forced to yield for too long. Somehow we had to find a way to quit retreating from the fever. If it ever found a way to kill IAs, where then could we hide?

Bowsler's own speech upon coming into office drew from Shakespeare's *Henry V*. She called her and her fellow survivors "we few, we happy few, we band of brothers and sisters." Happiness, she said, might be long in coming, but in the meantime, there would always be an England bound together by tradition and fraternal comradeship.

Servants brought in frosty dishes of strawberry kulfi. I allowed myself a moment to remember my parents. How proud they would have been to know their daughter was eating lunch with the Prime Minister of England. They had always been proud of me. They chose to ignore my sexuality, as did I, for the most part.

And now, in a world where I was a member of the majority, I had the right to fall in love with anyone I chose. If I had the time, which I didn't. I dropped the wool I had been gathering and tried to regain my focus.

Bowsler had been pointedly devoting her attention to the dish in front of her. She asked whether I wanted more dessert.

"Sorry," I said to her. "I was thinking of my parents and how they would have felt about this."

"Pleased and proud, one should hope," she said warmly.

"They were always completely supportive. Now, if you don't mind, I would like to discuss the VSF research initiative." I'm back on my game. Go, Dawgs.

"Yes, I certainly appreciate your kindness in allowing our scientists to participate in the project."

"We couldn't do it without them. President Budin is concerned about the embryonic program. She feels that, given the way VSF has been mutating, there's danger in concentrating too much of our human resources in one place."

"Her hesitance is understandable."

The British government had been making that very point for some time.

"We accept your offer to host further research into embryonic viability," I said.

Our only hope of surviving, not only as a nation but also as a people, necessitated a two-track race: one, to find a cure for all forms of VSF; the other, to save the next generation.

Fetal research had always been controversial in the United States. Even though pig fetuses had been the focus of our program, by necessity it would have to move on to humans at some point. That meant creating embryos, most of which would be killed by VSF.

In a sense, it wasn't abortion; we wanted them to live. But already in Congress, there was proposed legislation to ban all fetal research.

To create dozens or more of doomed embryos to every one survivor struck opponents as an immoral use of government resources. They wanted us to throw everything at curing VSF, and in the meantime let nature decide which women could carry to term.

I understood the tension between our two goals. We still didn't know why some gays died of VSF, let alone the majority of humanity. The key was in our genes, but beyond that, I wasn't equipped to speculate.

The pact with Britain meant going to war against VSF for the survival of our species, even if that struggle meant losing battles in the beginning.

President Budin told us that we would never give up. Never.

*Dora Navarro*

Anyone who has been to Austin knows all about the bridge. Once sunset comes around, so do the bats.

One night, back when I was waiting on Mama to die, I made the mistake of turning on the radio. I heard an evangelist yelling about vampires taking over the world. He sounded more like some guy you would hear on a corner in downtown Austin telling you how the world was going to end.

The world ended. At least, the evangelist's world ended, but I didn't see any vampires, just bats.

Before the sunset visit, Scott Bayard and I had a busy day driving around Austin. It looked battle-scarred by fires and vandalism and was still cluttered with piles of trash. You could see signs of life, though, in the form of "We're Still Open" signs and pedestrians.

Bev had been the one to call Scott to ask if he would drive me into Austin. She may have wanted to push along our slow steps toward dating. I'd been over to his brother's house where he stayed in Salado, and we had attended a charity benefit for foster families. I guess that could be called a date, even if the whole time I kept thinking about how Mama would have signed up for a dozen orphans. I'm sure Scott didn't find me to be a fun companion that evening.

On the way into Austin, he explained how his taking over the dry cleaning business had fulfilled a pledge to his brother.

"I've made sure the store is still in the family, but now that I have good people trained, I can move back home." He whipped us around a Mercedes Benz stalled on I-35.

The highway medians and roadsides rioted with native grasses and wildflowers. I wondered if the highway department planned to ever do upkeep again. I wondered if there was still a highway department.

This blue skies August morning felt more like a midnight ice storm. Cars and trucks were just random ghosts passing one another.

Recently hired at U-Haul, Scott planned to continue collecting abandoned company vehicles and trailers, then radically revise operations.

"Movers are going to be just one part of the customer base now. There are a lot of stores in this area that are cut off from their corporate owners, or the owners are there, but the money's not. They need inventory; they need to deliver products within their area. No one has an established business plan these days. They aren't able to pay, or don't necessarily need, long-haul truckers. We'll piggyback jobs, whether for business or for the movers, either way."

He didn't lack for confidence.

Our tour of his business was brief, but I did meet his office manager, a tattooed woman who gave off a nightclub bouncer vibe. I saw a worker busy installing security bars in the windows.

The trip to his house, located in northern Austin, took us through weedy, garbage-lined neighborhoods where every few blocks you might see a trimmed yard and still more window bars.

"The relocation board wants me to move, you know," Scott said glumly as he pulled into his driveway.

"Why?"

"Services. I see their point. They don't have enough people yet to maintain their heavy equipment. Then there're the fuel bills. That's why the board picked out neighborhoods that already have a higher concentration of residents. That's where it will deign to provide complete services. They'll hand a house over to you, furnishings included, if you agree to stay in the house for five years. They figure it's better for policing and for watching over the children. I see their point, but when I think of what all I put into this place, it makes me sick. I'll never be able to recoup it."

Stepping out on to his driveway, I caught the mingled aroma of magnolias and decomposing animals. Or humans.

He grimaced. "Yeah, it's bad, isn't it? Hang on, I'll be back out in a jiffy."

As I waited on him, I looked at the houses nearby. Scott had been an account executive with a phone company. He must have made good money, or he lived beyond his means, like so many did, chasing their version of the American dream.

I had been teaching students, playing gigs, and accompanying church services. Another couple of years of that, and then I'd go back to school for a degree in something tech-oriented. That had been my plan, fuzzy to say the least, but a plan of sorts. Now what?

Coming out of the front door, Scott called out, "I have a present for you."

Chugging along on his flip-flops, he tucked his flat-screen into the back of the SUV to the sound of my one-woman chorus of thanks. Then he put us back on the road toward downtown.

The new house boasted the then-latest HD flat-screen, so Scott gave me his old one. His smile faded as he looked at my face.

"You know, doctors can do a lot for eyes these days."

"It's not about that." I considered for a moment. "Well, maybe a little bit. Your neighborhood. It's so sad. I mean, they had such plans, thinking they had all the time in the world. Me, I lived in a little apartment, and I didn't worry about getting ahead."

"I wouldn't assume that they knew what all they wanted. You buy a house to make a future for yourself. A life investment. But this house, I saw it as a fixer-upper. Previous owner ruined the interior. I had no intention of living in it long-term, but I hate knowing I'm screwed, that we're all screwed. Just now, we've driven by a few million dollars in real estate, but that's old money. What's a house worth now? What's money worth now? Nobody knows."

Dr. Rajasthan's office was in a building with windows that sparkled in the afternoon sun. Much of downtown looked unusually tidy. I realized what was missing, besides thousands of extra cars, were the over-amped and under-medicated space hippies who gave Austin much of its offbeat flavor. Scott said rumor was the Austin City Council, frantic to present an orderly front, had the street people moved down south somewhere.

All I saw that warm afternoon were starched dress shirts and shoulder holsters, designer shades and nervous glances, telling me that Austin might be living up to its TV ads guaranteeing safety, but pedestrians didn't trust the publicity. I agreed with them on that.

A slender man with an up-all-night vibe, Dr. Rajasthan ran the tests on my eyes. Then he sat me down in his office. He first offered me a Snickers bar. I collected it to give later to Bev; then I prepared my face to hear the news. Who knew what nightmares he had seen as a physician during the past few months? I would be a grateful patient, regardless of the news.

"You must understand that your eye sustained serious damage as a result of the pesticide spray, the injuries from your fall, and, of course, the infection that followed."

He used a plastic model to illustrate his points.

"Considering such multiple traumas, you're fortunate that the antibiotics proved to be efficacious for your right eye, which has healed with minor scarring. But your left eye isn't so good a picture. You have a scarred cornea, and the retina is detached and deteriorating, resulting in the blindness that you're experiencing. I can try to reattach it, but I won't fully know the condition of the retina until I get in there. As for the cornea, I don't recommend taking steps to replace it until we know what's going on with the retina. The retina is everything."

He offered not a miracle, but a maybe. Now, to discuss another problem, one not fixable by surgery.

"I can pay for the visit today, but as far as your working on my eye, I don't have the money for that."

He raised his eyebrows. "My dear, you are not the only person to come into my office with a monetary problem. Speak to the lady at the desk. We have worked out many arrangements."

"I give piano lessons, so there is that."

The smile vanished, to be replaced by a wounded expression in his eyes.

"Ah, my dear, I wish it were still possible for you to give my daughter lessons. She took piano for six years. Yes, speak to my secretary. We shall work out the details. I want to get into your eye and see what can be done."

# Chapter 11

*Debra Shanrahan*

"I don't get it. Why put me in your commercial?" I asked the bearded young man sitting in my office.

A two-man camera crew operated behind him. Please dial down the lights a few megawatts.

He blinked nervously. "When the office called, you said you would agree to appear."

Yes, and I would do anything to please Immigration, the divine arbiter of my continued stay with Bao-Zhai. Purely voluntary, the woman on the phone said. Right.

"Not that I want to be crusty about it, but what makes you think Australians will line up to move to America, based on my recommendation? And why move now? In case you haven't noticed, crews are still shifting loads of corpses, and the only reason we're not in a bloody remix of the Great Depression is because the President refuses to let the stock exchanges open back up. Mind you, I like the fact that we're living in a metaphorical bubble and not the real one they're building in Alaska."

The interviewer ramped up his intensity.

"Now is the time for our New Ellis Island campaign, before Congress puts on the brakes, before our stronger companies freeze out potential competitors, before houses and office buildings begin crumbling from lack of maintenance, before we let our fear of foreigners turn us into a neo-Victorian, status quo boutique shop."

The lad should have kept his camera running as I doubt I could have generated his volume.

"So, this isn't really about compassion for the downtrodden, is it? Good. Much more straightforward to hang out your help-wanted sign. Loads of people might want to move here. Why aren't you talking to a Japanese expat?"

"That's on our next stop. We have interviews planned with a Japanese couple, a Czech artist, and an Israeli plumber."

"No Nigerians, no Egyptians, no Pakis?"

He signaled for his crew to stop recording.

"I know you're quite busy with your work, so you may not have seen reports about Nigeria. It's split into several parts, and all of them agree that the West is to blame. They're not the only ones saying that in the developing world. Any Nigerian saying he or she wants to move to America is asking for trouble. Botswana and Namibia are stable, so we're advertising in their local media. The problem there is getting people out without having to make stopovers in countries that, frankly, hate our guts. About Egypt..."

"They're claiming their survivors aren't gay."

The Ikhwân al-Safà, or Brethren of Purity, movement had sprung up seemingly overnight in many Arab countries. Their women, still without rights, were supposed to make babies, but couldn't, of course. You had gay men blaming lesbians for miscarrying.

The Saudis and several other Arab states were using that tactic, but in Dubai and Jordan, those in charge were offering themselves as stable trading partners.

"What do you want me to say?"

"Just what you think are the advantages of living in the United States, and the disadvantages."

He signaled his crew to resume shooting.

If your country hadn't rerouted our plane, would I now be encouraging my countrymen to move to Canada? Possibly. But that's a different turn of the cards, isn't it?

"All right then. Anyone living in Atlanta knows that the trash is piled up to your knickers in many of the neighborhoods, but those are places where no one's living right now. It makes sense to leave off on upkeep. You move in, they'll move out the trash, I guarantee. Bao-Zhai and I live in a good neighborhood. Power hasn't gone off for weeks.

"Another couple recently moved in across the street. They're black fellows. Really nice. I wouldn't be concerned about black people. They get quite the bad rap in the media. Most of the worries I've had have been from rednecks and guppies not wanting to manage their pets. If you lot move in, we'll party hard and give the rednecks hell."

The man's face looked as though he had swallowed a treble hook.

*Wylie Halverson*

Wynette, my older sister, lived for forty years in the same house with the same husband. They raised two girls and a boy; the three of them produced five grandchildren.

During that bad spell I experienced in my thirties, when I didn't feel like pretending anymore, Wynette graciously invited me to stay with her in Milwaukee while I recovered from a failed romance. I say romance, although the amour was mostly on my part. The other woman, despite her ardent cuddling and pledges of undying love, dumped me the moment her estranged husband came back into the picture.

Milwaukee, where I taught middle school for several years, served as a much-needed respite. Then, lonely for home, and needed to help care for Mother, whose bones even then were cratering from a form of arthritis, I returned to Stevens Point.

Wynette wasn't the kind of person who brooked personal revelations. Willetta, my younger sister, knew before I knew. She never stinted in granting me a permanent place setting in her life, however often her husbands and stepchildren changed from decade to decade. One so sensible, the other so mercurial, and both now gone.

Their houses, however, had both ended up with me, as per federal inheritance laws passed during the spring. The laws extended automatic property assumptions to brothers/sisters, aunts/uncles, and nieces/nephews, in that order, but not cousins. That probably would have been harder to prove.

One morning, leaving the milking to the older girls and the school in equally capable hands, Selma and I traveled to Milwaukee to pick up sets of house keys from a bank officer. Wynette's house had piqued the interest of the city's urban reclamation board.

It was situated within an area chock-a-block with gays, not that I had ever noticed any in the Third Ward during my stay so many years ago. Patterns change.

Wynette's house had been broken into, but all that appeared missing were the contents of the pantry. While Selma cut pieces of cardboard to tape over the broken windows, I swept up the fragments. We had already dropped by Willetta's place, pristine in outward appearance, but with my sister's usual slapdash clutter within. In both homes, although bodies had been cleared, evidence of the plague streaked their bedrooms and clotted their hallways.

Everyone could tell we were sisters. The same fair complexion, the same Norwegian features, the same penetrating voice. Only one important difference among us. And now, would there be strangers moving in, strangers to admire or make fun of Wynette's red and green Christmas afghan that she displayed year-round?

According to the rules of urban reclamation we'd downloaded off the Internet, once the respondent was notified of a property assumption, he or she had six months to file a claim. After that time, property taxes would accumulate. If that didn't concentrate the mind, nothing would.

"What do you think?" Selma sat down beside me on the davenport and handed over the thermos. We took turns sipping coffee as we talked over the options.

Stevens Point was melting away, and not in a grand decades-long decline worthy of the Ambersons. Mayor Metzger's relocation effort failed to attract residents from nearby communities. Was it the state's ad campaign, or was it the knowledge that economic assistance would flow to favored cities, ignoring places like Stevens Point? Was it simply the fear of being abandoned if another disaster hit?

Our city council voted to accept the state's recommendation; then phase one began. Trucks moved older residents, the disabled, and foster parents with large broods to Wausau.

I expected 'Pointers in their twenties to welcome the comparatively brighter lights of Wausau. It shocked me how many others seemed not to mind the prospect of reducing our town to the level of a pit stop for cars and milk trucks, leaving only cow-minders and people who wouldn't move, no matter what.

According to the state's relocation website, those who left wouldn't be required to pay taxes on property left behind, but would be paid by future buyers fifty percent of its original market value. "Future buyers" sounded like a pipe dream. Almost all of my merchant friends were leaving, taking with them whatever the trucks could carry. In some cases, empty buildings were promised to them. For others, the promise was free storage and a leg up on opening new storefronts.

The big dairy operation north of town had recently offered to buy out Selma. She hadn't turned them down yet.

"Would it bother you, leaving your farm behind?"

"Not really. My brother didn't have the world's best work ethic. Once our parents retired, if we were going to keep the Steicher name on the gate, I knew who was going to do it: me. As far as I'm concerned, we tried to make a go of it, you know?"

Just in case one of the houses appeared to be in fairly good condition, and more important, if Selma turned out to be as resigned as I was to the situation, I had brought along my résumé and copies of my various certifications. I had already submitted an application over the Internet.

We drove over to the school district office on West Vliet. An elderly woman, crowned with an impressive hair bun, glanced at my papers. She shuttled me in to see the hiring director, a wisp of a girl who might have been out of her teens, but you couldn't have convinced me of that.

"You can start right away, but I understand you have to move so we can certainly push that to the middle of next week, but if you can start sooner than that, we'd love to see you, and I see on your résumé that you're fostering six children. Is that right?"

She allowed a nanosecond for my nod.

"Wonderful. That gives you an extra six points. The State Foster Parenting Act awards incentive points for positions with any state, county, city, or public education entity covered previous to VSF under existing pension and taxation schedules. And I see you're certified in several subjects and you even worked previously in Milwaukee. I see that you applied for history or English, but where we need you immediately is a principal's position at Community High School."

"I can start Wednesday," I said when she took a breath.

Less than an hour after walking in the building, I came out with a job, an assigned parking space, and an ID tag. Over slices of pepperoni pizza at a restaurant down the street, Selma chuckled at my impression of the speed talker.

"I guess we should have added a few more kids if we'd known you'd get points for it."

I hadn't bothered with haggling over salary. I was going to take the job, regardless, and who knew if anyone was going to get paid on a regular basis.

Schools could tax however they wanted, but most properties these days were owned by dead people, occupied by squatters, or going through assumptions by companies and relatives such as myself. Good luck on creating a steady cash flow out of that. Maybe in a couple of years, some eagle-eyed government bookkeepers would straighten out that particular kerfuffle.

I never had reason to imagine what the end of the world might look like, but who would have dreamed that there would still be the evening news, Meals on Wheels, and parent-teacher meetings?

There were terrible situations elsewhere, and frankly I didn't see the Feds ever getting control of Florida, but in our little spot, we'd survived what I prayed was the worst of it.

The sensitives died so quickly, leaving houses essentially untouched and a mountain of possessions behind. It felt at times as though they had all gone on vacation.

Until you came across the bodies, decaying reminders that there had been many places to try to hide from the plague, to hide from us. Everyday, there were incidents involving sensitives afraid to risk the offered flights to Alaska. How hard a life that had to be for them, to be terrified of the very air they breathed.

So for me, it didn't matter how many carrots and sticks Madison and Washington D.C. used with us, or how many corporate partnerships and sweetheart deals they cut in order to maintain vital services and, most likely, line someone's pocket.

We all could still end up dying of the plague. I saw my family, friends, and hometown destroyed because of it. I didn't intend to forget that fact just because I was supposed to be a model citizen and go where they wanted me to go.

*Dreya Underhill*

The fuel crunch was easing, something for which Leesa took full credit in her textings. My sister had been promoted to control panel operator on her shift at the refinery. Because of the lack of qualified personnel, anyone showing potential went into a trainee program, which is why her girlfriend, Lanasha, now worked as an apprentice gauger, whatever that meant.

Leesa kept trying to talk me into moving to Martinez. I was doing the same thing in reverse, but neither of us budged, proving that we were carbon copies of Pops. Stone stubborn.

My job was going great. We were sending out trucks of produce constantly, including nights and weekends, which meant us burning through assistants until hiring one that stuck. She proved to be both good at her work and reliable. Not an easy combination to find.

One afternoon, an older man wearing a maple leaf sweater came into my office. He announced that he was from British Columbia. Would I like to move to Canada? Free house, guaranteed job, bring the wife and kids. He offered fast-tracked permanent residency and a shortened citizenship process. No pressure, but would I like to see these brand new brochures?

I knew there were black people in Canada because I had seen hockey players on TV, but to see one in the flesh felt kind of special in this day and age. There weren't as many Canadians as us, so not as many gays, which added up to how many gay black Canadians?

"I estimate several thousand in our province alone," Gus Chamberlain answered. "Many newcomers of all backgrounds have moved to British Columbia over the past few months. Vancouver has always been a cosmopolitan city and, I might add, quite lovely this time of year. If you're interested in attending a job fair, I have plane tickets and a voucher for hotel rooms. They're going quickly."

Susan came in while he was talking. He and I brought her up to speed, but she looked as overwhelmed as I felt.

"I don't know. We've been in a whirlwind these past few months, to tell the truth," she said.

"I understand. It's scary thinking about moving, especially these days, but I'd like you to consider the fact that gays and lesbians have possessed full equality in Canada for years. When you think about it, our sensitives showed foresight even before the Moree Fever hit. It makes me proud to know that we're doing our best to take care of the ones we have left. We've had our problems. Still do. I'm not asking you to move to paradise sight unseen, but simply to pay us a visit."

Moree. I hadn't heard that name for the walking fever. Susan invited Gus over for dinner.

A few days later, we were in Vancouver for a dream vacation. It felt almost literally like a dream, because whatever had happened to the city during the walking fever, I didn't notice any signs of it, except that a bunch of businesses were still closed. There were no piles of trash along the Millennium skytrain line, no stench of dead bodies, and no people toting guns on the street, except for their police officers.

But one thing Canadians had in common with us was The Look, as Susan called it. A haunted way of seeing you and seeing through you at the same time. We stayed at a bed and breakfast off Commercial Drive, which our guide, a feisty older woman named Reiko, said had been a lesbian mecca before the fever.

The girls couldn't have cared less about grownup things. They were more impressed by snacks in the mini-fridge. Elizabeth thought for sure that a previous guest had left them. We told them, "They're not free, but you can help yourself." Not that they needed the encouragement.

Our first morning, we joined other prospects on a bus trip out to north of town where we walked on the Capilano Suspension Bridge hundreds of feet above the forest floor. A crisp feel to the air that early October told me I would be investing in heavy socks if I lived in Vancouver, global warming or not. There, breathing in cool jade, I strolled with Susan through the evergreens—tall ones below, giants above. The girls, made timid by the dizzying heights, tucked close to our heels.

It made me remember growing up in San Diego, where I often visited my trees in Balboa Park, and then my years spent sweet-talking plants into taking root in arid soil. In British Columbia, I would be hard-pressed to slow them down.

I breathed in the smell of the cedar planks on which we were standing, breathed out, and just stood there, not looking down at the river and not looking up at the sky.

Rita. I had been working my ass off growing produce, taking care of my sudden family, then having a great time on this trip, and I couldn't stop thinking. Why Rita? Why Susan's family? Why Elizabeth's three younger siblings? Why not me?

The urge came over me to climb over the rail, to crash myself into the rocks, to make my body, for that one instant before I died, feel the pain she endured those last days. There were times in church where I could lose myself for a while. I'd join in singing an old Marvin Sapp song, "In His Presence," until I heard prayers for those who had passed. I'd see some old man with tears flowing down his face, and it got too much for me sometimes. To be honest, it was too much for me constantly. I just pretended that I had it all together.

"Baby?" Susan stood close by, concern etched into her eyes.

"I don't deserve this," I might have said.

My fingers traced the flight path of the birds we could see weaving through the branches below.

She eased herself into my arms and said quietly, "Reiko says we'll be meeting with the job recruiters at two. Oh, and how big a house the city gives us depends on which companies hire us. There's a pecking order."

"Susan?" Elizabeth called out. "Can we go to the gift shop? I want to buy a magnet."

Surrounded by a view Photoshop could only dream of faking, and all she's thinking is that there's still an empty spot on the fridge back home.

Leesa would get a kick out of the girls. If I took the long view, a year or two more at the refinery might give my sister enough work experience to score a job up here.

If I took the short view, my body might bounce once or twice when it hit bottom.

Definitely flipping out. I felt my body shaking, shaking until it sank into me that, for however long, Susan had been slowly rubbing my arms.

"Just breathe, Dreya. Just breathe. You're having a panic attack. You've been long overdue for an existentialist crisis, so why not have it two hundred feet in the air."

She spoke with a deliberate air of calm.

Somehow, Susan putting a name to it made my heart quit racing. After a few minutes, I felt recovered enough to catch up to our tour group at the gift shop. Elizabeth narrowed down her magnet choices to three definites and five maybes, while Maria, unable to find any mermaids, rejoiced in finding a treasure trove of pink princess decals.

Back on the bus we went. We ended up at a restaurant down on Robson Street where we ate Japanese tapas, which was a first for me. Then we walked over to the hotel to meet individually with recruiters. Our girls were ushered off with other kids in the group for younger-flavored entertainment.

In the interviews, each company seemed to have been given the same report on me, with Gus Chamberlain the likely source. The highlights included starting my own business at the age of seventeen, my market initiative in San Francisco (I knew it was just tomatoes, but oh well), and the produce company. I sounded like a good prospect. Hell, I was a good prospect, and crazy, going by how I acted on the bridge.

During the break, Susan and I shared what we thought about the interviews, and then we checked in on the girls. Our shy little Maria was kicking everyone's butt in Wii bowling, while in a complete role reversal, Elizabeth was sitting on a beanbag reading a Cheetah Girls book.

Back at the meeting room, we learned that Susan had been tendered a management-level position at the Vancouver Port Authority. I had follow-up interviews scheduled with Cintas Canada, which made uniforms, as well as with an organic food company. We came back to the bed and breakfast that night with me still not knowing if I had been hired.

"It's okay," I told her honestly. "If you get hired and I don't, we'll come up here anyway, and I'm sure I'll find work."

"Don't be such a saint. Those companies are probably wrestling each other over who gets to hire you." She gave her pillow a forearm shiver and sidearm shake. With Susan, a pillow stayed fluffed.

"We don't have to do this, you know. I know you weren't feeling it originally. It'd be okay if we moved back to San Francisco."

"It's definitely not okay with me," she said. "And it's not because of my ex."

Her brow crinkled in thought. "Maybe it's partly because of her. But there's not as many good homes left there now. They said on the news that over fifty thousand people have moved to the Bay area since March, and I'm not fighting with her over the house. The way I see it, the Canadians have put together a good package. There's hardly any crime rate. Even in Salinas, stuff's still happening. You know that. So, if we come here, the girls attend quality schools, and we can make a life for ourselves. No baby steps this time. We really start fresh."

The call came as we were sitting down to a breakfast of Eggs Benedict with Canadian bacon, naturally, and I learned I would now be a company liaison to growers in the field. I'd be a troubleshooter, with my own vehicle and a travel allowance.

Susan and I qualified for a four-bedroom residence in a neighborhood the recruiter assured me was high class.

Amidst the celebrating, the thought came to me that, while I looked forward to my new ride, I wasn't getting rid of the van. Who knew when it might come in handy again?

*Analyn Orante*

Two years previously, I had attended an international pandemic preparedness conference in Osaka, Japan. At the time, I noticed how people there sausaged themselves into trains and wormed their way through urban crowds. That was a commonplace observation, not worth mentioning to my hosts.

There didn't appear to be enough breathing space, it looked to me, but people can get used to just about anything, including the vast changes that had occurred since then.

Our first stop on the Pacific Rim was Seoul. While there, I attended a packed church service, then appeared in a live broadcast where selected citizens questioned me about my country's trade policies and my impressions of their home. After that, I visited a seafood market, again in a live feed. Viewers at home and I were reminded that South Korea, unlike some of its neighbors, had not embarked on a ruinous pesticide spraying campaign of its cities, countryside, and beaches.

On a specially prepared outdoor grill at the market, a chef prepared nakji bokkeum—stir-fried octopus—for the American ambassador, a Korean pop star, and me. There were too many onions for my taste, but flavorful, although I didn't much like the camera flashes every time I took a swallow.

Avoiding a mass chemical assault turned out to be the right move. Chemical spraying, no matter how extensive, at best delays catastrophe. Total environmental containment is the only real solution for sensitives. This also happens to be beyond the capacity of any nation to achieve for more than a fraction of its affected population.

The Koreans' reason for not spraying came not from environmental concerns, but from the misguided belief of their late health minister that the focus should be on shipping IAs to the coast. They thought the further inland, the safer.

Once the gay connection was discovered, many governments attempted round-ups of known and suspected IAs, with a goal of transporting them to isolated areas.

This was an effort attempted, not achieved, except during the earliest stages. The death toll rose too rapidly through all major cities, spreading panic and VSF in equal measures.

It had been a bad time to be different or to look different.

In South Korea, a brave, quixotic campaign to filter the air of entire city blocks failed, in part due to the lack of properly shielded workers to maintain the great swaths of plastic sheeting used. In the Philippines, they quickly ran out of supplies of gloves and masks. My relatives died in rapid order, but at least they didn't starve.

Hokkaido, Japan's northernmost island, played an unwilling host to IA refugees. By early spring, the lower islands had been devastated by the one-two punch of VSF and toxic sprays. Hunger forced the IAs first into a largely depopulated Sapporo. From there, they traveled through the underwater Seikan Tunnel that connected Hokkaido to the main island of Honshu.

Surviving sensitives were hiding out anywhere they could create personal sealed spaces, however flimsy, however unlikely the designs downloaded from Internet websites.

An exiled IA general named Nagai Ezo led his ad-hoc army in their initial goal of destroying the automated sprayers, many of which were being directed via remote control.

This effort quickly morphed (and many wondered if it may have been intended from the start) into establishing an organized, disciplined IA presence throughout the islands. If that meant relocating every one of the remaining uncontained sensitives, and killing those who resisted, General Ezo believed the strategy to be critical to the survival of Japan.

My government advocated a less violent approach to the problem. Reality dictated that we also recognize the situation on the ground.

I could see the damage from the air as we flew into Narita International Airport. There were gray, dead patches in the countryside and blackened ruins amongst standing buildings.

When I walked through the air terminal to our waiting limousine buses, the officials looked no different from those I met with in Osaka two years earlier. I saw the same trendy haircuts, tailored suits, and businesslike smiles of men and women eager to make a good impression.

On the drive into Tokyo, I saw very few children on the street. Masks were a commonplace. Some people even carried small oxygen bottles. We were taken to a scrupulously clean underground parking garage. You'd have never known a car ever stayed there. It was there that I accepted what appeared to be a designer version of a mask and goggles set.

"You will not need it in this building, but it may become necessary while traveling outdoors. Our scientists tell us that several more rainstorms should neutralize the worst effects of chemicals lingering in the air, although the soil, of course, entails a lengthier process."

The chief trade attaché possessed flawless English.

She was young and atypically tall. She stuck to her talking points with a genial smile, and admitted without hesitation that her government was still routing out what she called rogues.

"Those who agree to move to Hokkaido peacefully are treated in a proper manner, as you know from visits by officials from the Red Cross. Like your country, we experienced problems in ensuring public safety before our new government was well established. In that time, there were abuses of trust on both sides.

"We offer so much to our allies: our technology, advanced cars, medical knowledge, and for that, we need much in return. It will be years before the poison is cleansed from our soil and rivers. It will be years before the memories of atrocities fade. Among the nations, we have done better than many, worse than some."

She spoke as though the events happened long ago. We were only into early October, mere months at most since the events we were discussing.

From our sources, Ezo understood what his role should be in national politics. Elections were being allowed to go forward on the local level, which is always a positive sign.

The next morning, our hosts took us down the aisles of a store called Natural Lawson, where the proprietor, a rugged-looking woman in her fifties, offered me a cinnamon bun.

"It's good for you." She plopped the bun in my hand.

There might have been toxins in the air, but I just about inhaled the bun, it was that fresh tasting. My stomach, despite my reliance on motion sickness remedies, is not a happy traveler, so I hadn't eaten much since the previous night.

Who knew to what lengths my host country had gone to feed me? Sources told me that the new government kept uncovering caches of food in caves, tunnels, sealed buildings, and temples, often next to decaying bodies.

We had not been exiled to a wintry hell, unlike President Ezo's compatriots, who found themselves reduced to eating bark. However, some of our sensitives would have gladly marched us into the sea, or perhaps burned us to a crisp, to judge by how many fires had been set.

Fresh memories of near-starvation probably had much to do with why the new Japanese government seized non-IA properties. On the surface, the approach might have sounded similar to ours, but crucial details differed. In Japan, decisions on properties were made by the national government-corporate compact, rather than by local governments. They also chose not to recognize the property inheritance rights of surviving relatives.

While morally problematic, it was, arguably, internal politics and not a core issue for our delegation.

Until I was attacked by Minoru Takeaki.

Only nineteen years old, he was the nephew of a software billionaire. After somehow surviving a nightmarish bus ride to Hokkaido, he weathered conditions made even harsher by the fact that his famous uncle made no effort to protect him.

Since liberation, Minoru had worked for the train system. No problems had been reported, but in the investigation afterward, coworkers described his collection of army rifles, knives, and ceremonial swords.

When I stepped out of the store, I knew none of that. With my own Secret Service attachment plus Japanese security guards providing protection, I had no cause for concern. To create a positive impression, my hosts had selected a clean, well-kept boulevard in a quiet area of Tokyo.

I was starting to ask the attaché a question on some topic I don't recall, when out of nowhere, a man drove a Toyota Aristo directly at our party.

The attaché and Adam Neubarger, my head of security, pushed me behind a media van parked closest to where we were standing. During the barrage of small arms fire, what went through my mind was that, after all we had been through, the death threats and disruptions, the first serious assassination attempt occurs in Japan?

I flashed on an image of Uma Thurman in her Bruce Lee action suit while I was squashed on the ground under my protectors.

I heard the car crash into something nearby, that something being our limousine. It took a hit to the bumper but was still drivable.

This proved to be a piece of luck. As guards were dragging the driver's bullet-ridden body from the Toyota and Adam helped me to my feet, I heard a shouted warning, then felt something sharp enter my back. This time, no one let me touch the ground. I found myself being almost hurled into the limousine and then rushed to the hospital.

"I'm breathing just fine," I told Adam, who applied pressure to the wound.

He and another Secret Service officer carried on cross-current-earpiece barks about safe routes to the nearest hospital and setting perimeters. These were subjects about which I had no useful input to give, being that it was out of my area of expertise, and being that I was about to pass out.

I woke up that evening in a heavily guarded hospital room. I had a monumental ache in my back and tubes sticking out of me, but I was alive.

Relying on the distraction caused by his accomplice, Minoru ran at me with a sword. This drew fire from the guards, but the force of his dying thrust carried the sword forward enough to enter my back. The blade punctured my left lung and barely missed my heart. I don't recall whether, as the media reported, he shouted out any stock samurai phrases as he lay dying on the ground. The less romance we attach to assassins, the better.

The next evening, President Ezo came to my room. According to Bill Levine, who stayed behind on this trip, the media showed hundreds of young women keeping vigil outside my hospital. Many of them clutched posters of songbirds.

In the reporting of my actions during the early phases of the fever, the media decided to dub me "The Canary," modeled after the coal-mine bird that warns of danger. I was their idol of the moment.

Speaking of the real thing, the singer I ate octopus with in Seoul released overnight a song called "God's Little Songbird" in my honor. I imagine it had already been in the works before the assassination attempt.

President Ezo brought neither tunes nor canaries to my room. Instead, he brought a deal that cut through the weeks of negotiations our respective teams had been slogging through before my arrival.

He told me that a shipment of hybrid vehicles would be sailing for Seattle that week, and would I please accept his personal apology.

He also presented me with a set of first editions by Yukio Mishima. That seemed somehow appropriate. Negotiators would work out actual terms before the auto shipment reached port, but Ezo's move displayed political astuteness.

He was a middle-aged, hawk-nosed man with an unaffected style. He didn't come off as a potential dictator, but only time would tell about that. Terrified citizens gladly give away their rights, a lesson we Americans learned time and time again through previous crises.

I thought to myself, I survived. The rest is gravy. President Budin called me often, seeking my opinion on various matters. We spent more time talking about hobbies we hadn't been able to pursue, mutual acquaintances long gone, and personal lives that had gone out the window.

"Maybe you should round me up a would-be ninja while you're there," she said. "I haven't had eight hours uninterrupted sleep since this whole thing started."

I told her to shut her mouth and not ask for a latter-day Booth.

"Okay," she said. "But just come back home, would you? We need you. Heck, I need you."

*Dora Navarro*

The seventy-two hours enforced bed rest had ended. I sat on the side of the hospital bed, dressed and trying not to fidget while I waited on Barb and Bev to collect me.

The surgery, after all the waiting, after all the hope, came to nothing. Dr. Rajasthan tried to piece together a functioning retina, but all he found to work with were threads, so fragile that his touching them splintered them further.

When I awoke afterward, I could tell by his tone of voice that the news would be bad. He said he would see whether I qualified for an experimental procedure that could insert an artificial retina.

"There's already a waiting list of patients who have significant deficits in both eyes." The words may have been blunt, but his voice sounded gentle.

I told him not to bother, to let the blind have their chances. I had one good eye remaining. I had my health and my friends. I needed to move on, literally.

Although Scott offered me his place to stay, complete "with very few strings attached," he assured me with a smile, I knew that it was time to strike out on my own.

With the help of one of Bev's friends, I had already interviewed at Solectron, owned by Flextronics, for a spot in their new apprentice program. Apprentice was a word much in vogue now, taking over for such words as "intern" and "almost free labor."

Solectron ran an apartment complex not far from its campus in Austin. I would be moving there sometime late fall. I had no clue in what program I would be placed. The interviewer mentioned that the company, in partnership with a Japanese company, planned to ramp up its production of Self-Service Automation (SSA) systems. The new generation of machines would allow customers to test blood and urine samples, pick from dozens of insurance providers, and purchase anything from grilled steaks to margaritas mixed on the spot.

"Why should humans have to stand around at a check-out desk doing menial labor?" the interviewer said. "We have these machines for a reason."

It occurred to me during her talk that my role in this heroic enterprise would involve a lot of menial labor, but who knew what I might end up doing if I stuck to it.

Teaching piano was fine for old Dora in the Neverland of last year where I had plenty of students, some gigs on the side, and the loyal Methodists of Belton to keep me in rent money. I would miss my students, D'Wayne, in particular, but I needed to find a steady job.

Bev, our resident prophet of doom, said there was no way we could avoid having a Great Depression. Me, I was tired of my little depression. It was time to take my one-eyed pirate act into a new phase.

# Chapter 12

*Debra Shanrahan*

I predicted to Bao-Zhai that Dr. Tofill would be neither surprised nor amused by his birthday party. We drank our cups of punch and waited with the rest of the guests for him to come through the door. And waited.

Unlike most of us house-rich/cash-poor newbies, the mayor actually owned his digs before the fever, and pronounced himself thrilled to host the affair. Waiters in white uniforms swanned about carrying trays of punch and champagne. The only jarring note to the affair was all the trash lining the avenue in front of the estate.

That, and the fact a storm the previous night had knocked out power in much of the area. Electricity had been restored in the mayor's neighborhood. No coincidence, I figured. We were swathed in comfort, and we were well lit, in both meanings of the phrase.

"You did say you saw him getting out of his car?" Dr. Hari Bose, a tall, elegant man, had recently taken over as Tofill's chief assistant.

Bao-Zhai groaned. "I'm not blind, Hari. I did see the man."

Tofill burst through the door, tossed his jacket up to the butler's waiting arms, and headed for the buffet table that, in deference to the guest of honor, featured a step stool. He loaded his plate, accepted a glass of champagne, and sat in a modest-sized chair, with the apparent aim of enduring the occasion as best he could.

"What bee flew into his bonnet?" Dr. Bose and I shuffled along a buffet line heavy on summer sausage, cheese, and green salads. A small, precious dish of olives had been finished off by the time our turn came around, damn it.

"What? Oh, another module went down in Barrow," Dr. Bose said. "DoomGrrl—I think that's her name—anyhow, her website is running live updates. James is pretty upset about it."

DoomGrrl, the teenaged daughter of a business executive, fled with her family to northern Canada the previous winter, then trekked over to Barrow Base. They had to take the last few, brutal miles on foot when their truck broke down.

She was one of many there blogging or podcasting. At first, she voiced a spiritual bent. God's will, God's justice, God's grace. Next came an array of self-destructive behaviors, including one in which she and her friends went on a legendary multi-pod bender, followed by anger. The final stage of acceptance, I judged unlikely to come, from what I had read. My staff loved DoomGrrl's rants, but then, they weren't much older than she.

"I didn't know Tofill read that stuff."

I sopped a chunk of bread with drippings from the empty olive bowl. Hoarders and scavengers and delays on shipments from Spain and Italy. I didn't care what excuse the store used. I wanted my olives, and I wanted them now.

"Someone on his staff sent him the link. He, uh, he started writing her about the vaccine trials and all that." Dr. Bose looked around cautiously.

"I already know how the trials have been going. Terribly."

"James feels that people up there aren't being told the truth, but the government is afraid the situation will get even worse in Barrow if they learn how far away we are from finding a cure or treatment."

"Instead of the Pollyanna rah-rah, he tells her, basically you're screwed. Hope you survive until the biodomes are finished."

My words might have been sarcastic, but my mood certainly wasn't. I liked DoomGrrl. She reminded me of my sister, Bettina, what with her Tori Amos hair and venomous remarks. I had progressed to where I could think about Bettina and not kick a hole in a nearby wall. That marked progress, of a sort.

There had already been a mini-exodus from Barrow Base of sensitives electing to leave the pods. They thought they stood a better chance living in isolated villages throughout the North Slope rather than jammed, cheek-to-jowl, waiting for a cock-up. I didn't blame them, really.

I pulled up an ottoman and sat by Tofill.

He slapped his glass down on the side table and glared at me. "What?"

"Aren't you little Miss Mary Sunshine."

Tofill set aside his plate of spinach salad and cocked his finger at a passing waiter for another dose of champagne.

"I like you," he said, drawing out the phrase. "You are so far on the other side of couth, you're actually quite bearable."

"Go on." I reached over to claim his plate.

"No, that's it. Did you hear who they elected to Congress downstate?" he said, apropos of nothing.

"I'm more a victim of domestic politics than a practitioner, thank you very much."

"Maybe you should pay attention. I imagine you're being speed-raced to citizenship. Let me enlighten you: both parties planted ringers in districts where feet are few on the ground. That's how Mike Tocker goes to Washington."

"And precisely who is Mr. Tocker?"

"Football hero at the University of Georgia. He spent twenty years in the oil industry and the last thirty days in Valdosta. We're eating borrowed food and playing politics. In the meantime, our fellow citizens continue to drop like flies, and according to CNN, which occasionally notices the rest of the world, there's a famine throughout most of Africa."

"Excuse me, but Africans can plant veg as well as anyone. And why are you jonesing for Africa in particular? The whole bleeding planet is in trouble."

Tofill told me about river blindness, a preventable health problem in a sub-Saharan African country where he had run an NGO—non-governmental organization—before returning to the States. Tofill's contact told him that the clinic, the program, the entire region was in a state of collapse.

In some parts of the continent, access to food continued to be a problem as well, due to banditry that made our worries seem like nothing.

He told me, "Tanzania, Mali, Botswana, some places are hanging in there, but most of the continent, from Tunis down to Cape Town, is screwed. I hope you're not planning on a nice cup of cocoa anytime soon. Ivory Coast is having a problem bringing in the beans these days."

That worried me. I liked my chocolate oranges. "That's a load of rot. Cocoa came from America. Even I know that."

"Currently, from South America and the Dominican Republic, from what the article said. There's hope for African cocoa, if not for Africans. Hershey and Mars signed a truce and are deciding on which prince to pay off in Ghana."

"I thought you said Ivory Coast."

"Yes, I said Ivory Coast. If I told you Ivory soap came from there, would you believe me?"

"Excuse me, I'm Australian. Our schools care about geography."

The mask slipped, revealing a man in pain.

"You might think they're just a bunch of faggots like us. But wouldn't you know it? Give us a sniff of power, and we out-butch General Patton. And what asshole thought of serving me caviar with a side of guilt? Oh yes, our lovely mayor. Say happy birthday, Debs."

*Wylie Halverson*

An old biddy of a custodian—older than me, at any rate—told me about the warehouse after I wasted three days in phone calls that bounced me around what was left of the Milwaukee school bureaucracy.

Strine Dent, a melancholic math teacher, told me on the way to the warehouse district that he knew I was a keeper on my first day as principal. That's when I tossed out three students for various offenses and likewise tossed a teacher for sleeping on the job. I was on to Strine, too. The gentleman talked a sour game, yet his kids paid attention, and some real teaching was going on in his classroom.

Chelsea and Regina seemed to be enjoying high school, even though dressed in jeans and Stevens Point letter jackets, they looked dowdy compared to their high-fashion classmates.

Chelsea's good cheer derived from the fact that Milwaukee schools planned a full basketball schedule, even if it meant teams had to play each other several times during the course of the season. Both she and Regina walked on to practices at Community High School, easily earning spots.

Selma said that all Chelsea needed was a place to work out her frustrations, and if that meant fouling out by halftime, so be it.

Some of my students stayed in group homes, others had found parents of a sort, but most of the older kids were living in their old homes or in new apartments. A local judge had let it be known he could help them file emancipation papers in the absence of parents. Sixteen-year-old kids were making critical decisions and not always the best ones.

Based on their appearance, you wouldn't have known whether they had been rich or poor in their previous lives. Virtually all of them had scavenged through houses and stolen from stores. They had whatever they wanted by way of possessions. In high school, though, beauty and charisma still trump everything.

In my old Stevens Point of a year ago, there had been a few problems in school with violence and drugs. Past the death waves, past neighborhood quarantines and martial law, past the utter destruction of their lives, Milwaukee's young couldn't be bothered to battle one another. Fights were few, overdoses far too many.

These wizened children, these faux adults, needed more than drug counseling; they needed a way to act out. That's why I decreed that there be pep squads at all volleyball and basketball games. Pep squad leaders, drill teams, even cheerleaders.

I saw to it that kids received time to practice routines, and everyone got picked for a squad, without exception. There were four squads altogether at our high school. One of them had a live band, while the others used deejays. Kids used all kinds of costumes and props. It could get very elaborate.

The idea spread to the other two remaining high schools in Milwaukee and eventually to Waukesha, Racine, and elsewhere.

I didn't know my experiment would turn out to be influential. I simply wanted these kids to yell and throw things around, instead of holding their sorrows inward.

Dixon hated the move initially. Since he was a pocket version of his coach father, he had been looking forward to basketball season. Stuck riding the bench at his new school, he gave the coach much unsolicited advice until we convinced him to tamp it down. I had the sense that school at Stevens Point had been hard on him, socially speaking, but it was all he knew back then. Better the bullies you know than the ones you don't.

His new school was hardly trauma-free, not with everything that had happened and was continuing to happen to these children. Dixon, however, blossomed in Milwaukee. He was popular with the kids, even if not with his new coach, and new friends kept coming over to play video games with him. Reha still was painfully shy around others, but we hoped in time that would improve.

November blurred past nonstop. I was grateful that Selma stayed home to take care of our younger children. Make that, mostly at home. She became a one-woman anti-crime wave, not so much joining the neighborhood watch as embodying it.

Dixon helped her install motion lighting and security cameras to scare away vandals and thieves. Our neighbors were so appreciative. They sent gifts of food and toys for the kids.

Strine Dent complained nonstop about the school cafeteria. He would have griped even if a cordon bleu chef had been slinging hash. After one too many emails, I tossed the problem in his lap. I had enough to deal with.

A furnace that kept breaking down, a depressed workforce, and paychecks, what paychecks? Never mind a school board bitterly at odds over how to revamp everything at once. All the while, I read about the latest coups in countries such as Kazakhstan, Bolivia, and Indonesia. In the news, speculation ran rampant that we IAs would soon start showing symptoms of the plague. I switched channels whenever talk turned to that subject. Don't whistle past a graveyard.

I began hearing about a local man named Pratchett, who owned a medical supply company before the plague hit. He was rumored to be in possession of several warehouses full of food, consumer items, and his previous stock in trade.

According to Strine Dent, Pratchett relied on security guards armed with guns. The police were reluctant to go after him because the hospitals needed what he had, even if the prices were disgraceful.

Strine was always dressed in a succession of sharp, funereal black suits. He made it clear to me that there was no percentage in fighting whatever passed for City Hall these days. Don't bother asking the politicians for help. If we wanted something, we would have to pull strings and steal the whole ball, if we had to.

That's why I decided not to ask where the new cooks came from. They were a pair of Asian youths whose lack of English told me volumes about their green card status. I also did not explore how they latched on to fresh vegetables.

I felt as though I had dropped into an apocalyptic film noir. All we needed was a gumshoe detective and Barbara Stanwyck to finish off the scene. I missed home, but home had up and moved away from me.

I wondered what the future held for our younger kids. Dixon, Chelsea, and Regina knew what it was like to live in the pre-plague world with all those people and the inbred assumptions.

Our middle child, Reha, who turned eight in November, what would she recall? She was the daughter of an Iranian father who taught at UW-Stevens Point and his American wife.

Her hearing problem didn't get detected until she was in pre-school, probably because of a sickly younger brother who swallowed her parents' attention. That had been another reason for us to move to Milwaukee. Here, we found a speech therapist, but she already needed to be fitted for a new pair of hearing aids. Selma was working on that problem; I had no doubt she would find a solution.

Our youngest two, Jarrod and Felicity, were absolute joys. Felicity, a rambunctious tomboy whose apparent goal was to climb every mountain she imagined there being in our house, and Jarrod, a dreamy-eyed one-year-old who only wanted to crawl in Selma's wake. Maybe someday, scientists would cure the plague. For our children, this was their known world.

I knew from watching the news that Wisconsin wasn't the only state rushing to concentrate survivors in urban areas. Reluctantly, I had come to agree with the general principle: kids needed to be near other kids, and near doctors, reliable power grids, factories, colleges, and everything else we used to take for granted.

But, in practicality, things were a mess. We didn't have near enough police and firefighters, nor enough certified plumbers and mechanics. We had plenty of industrial engineers, social workers, IT techs, and realtors. We also had a regiment's worth of health-care professionals, so none of us were in danger of missing regular check-ups.

Our governor said on a call-in show that the state was recruiting high-quality immigrants from across the globe. She stressed that they would be English-speaking and educated. Thankfully, one caller brought up the point I wanted to make.

"I don't care if they finished high school. Can they fix the plumbing in my bathroom?"

Strine Dent told me there were reports of bears found hibernating in garages out in the suburbs. Wolves roved through the same emptied areas. Pratchett, the King Hoarder, was an urban predator who needed to be dealt with by the authorities.

There were no guards in front of the school supply warehouse we visited. Strine didn't even have to use his crowbar. The keys we'd located in the district office worked fine. We packed my pickup to the gills with books, paper, printer cartridges, and anything else that looked like it might come in handy.

Our flush of success chilled when, two blocks away, we saw Hummers with tinted windows parked in front of a large gray building.

"I believe we have been duly noted," Strine said as we drove by.

*Dreya Underhill*

A sturdy white woman, dressed in overalls, walked me through a Prince George processing facility. She didn't seem to notice the November chill, which was more than I could say for myself, despite layers of clothing.

The company didn't see Prince George as a primary source. It was situated too far north for intensive cultivation, but the area had a reputation for wild berries of all kinds.

She told me that the main refrigeration unit was about worn out, and that they could use a new sprayer. They had plenty of trucks for what the field crews brought in, but what they needed, more than anything, were more hands for next season.

"How many?" I asked her.

"For the peak time, a dozen more for crews and that many in processors."

I couldn't place her accent. In my weeks of travel, mainly around market gardens and dairies in the Fraser River delta region, I had not yet learned to place regional accents. I had been surprised by the variety of people claiming to be native Canadians.

That was the least confusing part of living in another country. We hosted a party one night where a bitter argument broke out between two of my coworkers about ridings. It had something to do with politics. Susan and I caught ourselves wearing the same fake smile. Okay, whatever, and how about some more dip? I knew I might someday decide on citizenship. Then, I'd have to figure out this ridings business, but in the meantime, call me a guest worker with a company pickup and full benefits.

Speaking of guest workers. "I can get you some people for next season, but the catch is that we need to place them now. If there's work for them to do when they're not in the brambles, I can hook you up."

The woman fired back with her strange, English-kind-of-German accent. "Hook us up. The *Citizen* has pages online of businesses needing help, and I know for damned sure the plywood company's bitching about needing workers."

"Do you mind kids?"

The woman, name of Brenda, popped me in the arm. Playfully, I thought.

"You shitting me? Kids? We've been talking about signing up for an orphan flight from back east. We have couples dying to adopt, but the government's up to its tits already in problems. Bring us some kids, and your company has a contract with the whole town, for Chrissake, not just my little patch."

"Okay. Here's the deal. The workers came off a freighter from Thailand. They're ethnic Chinese. Is that going to be a problem?"

She kept her eyes square upon me. She told me she had moved to Oregon from South Africa over twenty years ago. She'd go back sometimes for visits, which is how she met a woman named Cornelia, who moved to Oregon to be with her. Immigration wouldn't approve Cornelia for a green card.

"We couldn't get past that three-times-divorced bastard who kept turning down her application. I would have returned to South Africa with her, but she said, 'No, Brenda. Stay where you are. I'll find my way back.' Cue the bloody violins. Dead, dead, dead. Happened in the big fire.

"There're some Chinese who don't mind freezing their asses off? Get them here, get them now. We have a shit-load of cold weather gear on hand for them to wear and big, warm houses."

I called Susan that night from my hotel. I brightened her day with my news about where to place some of her refugees. Susan's position at the Port Authority put her in a prime spot to know about who and what the ships were trying to bring in these days.

Once upon a time, the Chinese that came in were illegal immigrants who had paid small fortunes to smugglers for low-wage jobs in North America. Now, although smugglers still brought some clients by way of China, most of the traffic came from countries where Chinese minorities had gone from being disliked to being targets for attacks.

I don't know who to blame for the walking fever, Chinese techies messing around with death in a bottle, or, according to the rumors, the Americans who gave it to them in the first place, but I do know that those scared souls coming off the freighters had nothing to do with what happened.

Susan promised me a home-cooked meal when I got back. Despite that, I still was looking forward to getting back, antacids and all. The next morning, I drove south down Route 97. I didn't stop until I reached Williams Lake, a town located in an area known for ranching and forestry, according to my BlackBerry.

At the gas station, a man told me about a gay couple new to the area, who were said to be mushroom pickers. Morels were on my list of contract gets, since the company had purchased a pair of Vancouver restaurants. Wild mushroom pickers are highly secretive, from what I'm told, and when most of them had died, they took with them their knowledge of locations.

A light snow dropped in wisps over the highway. I debated whether to push on to Kamloops, where I needed to meet with a new ginseng cooperative. Morels. There were three stars next to the word. That made up my mind.

Following directions from the man at the gas station, I ended up in a deeply wooded area. About the time I thought I was lost, I wasn't. I saw before me the prime riverside view, the large home, and the gay couple standing on their front porch. They fed me pasta dressed with a tasty mushroom sauce. They admitted to knowing something about morels.

It didn't take long to arrive at a deal since I happen to like my plant life tamed by yours truly, not tangled up with snakes, bears, and possibly poisonous fungi. They could keep their secrets as long as they delivered the mushrooms, please.

While driving away from their property, I saw a sign about a nature sanctuary and decided to follow it. I thought this might be a place to take Susan and the girls sometime. A couple of turns, a mile along a narrow road, then no farther. A barbed wire barrier blocked access to the bridge. A sign read that the sanctuary was closed. No date posted as to when it would reopen.

I started to back up the pickup when a metallic flash caught my eye. I saw in the distance a large, windowless, aluminum storage building.

In spring and summer, foliage would provide plenty of cover. Winter, the barricade would stop all but the most dedicated nature lovers. But on that late fall day, many of the trees were bare, and snow had yet to apply a thick coating. If you kept your eye trained, you could see it clearly. In the place of the building's entrance stood a corrugated steel hut the size of a one-car garage. A clear, reddish plastic bubble covered the door.

That was a strange touch. Someone must still be worried about catching the walking fever, or had been worried before they died or fled farther north. The building was grounded on all sides by long slabs of concrete. The building, the concrete, the bubble—all of it looked new.

I sat in my company pickup, stunned. Straights. Here.

Its builders should have erected a privacy fence, should have made the place as invisible as possible. Why weren't they up in the Yukon? Or maybe I was wrong.

I figured out the trick to the barricade. There was a well-disguised latch that unloosed a section. I climbed through, closed the latch, and walked over the bridge onto a trail lined with white birch trees.

As the snowfall began to take on serious weight, I cursed the weather and my curiosity. Then I heard a bear growl. Since the growl came with a touch of audio distortion, my nerves held steady. I looked around and found the motion detector patch on a nearby tree. If I had been a deer or a rookie hiker, that sound would have sent me running. When I came closer to the building, I saw that the red bubble was more like an igloo, with its roots buried in the ground. You'd have to stoop a bit to get in, but you'd get in. That is, if the door opened.

A weatherproof bag hung on a hook by the door. I unzipped it to find a walkie-talkie.

"Hello? You need anything?" I couldn't think of anything else to say.

There was no response.

"Your security sucks. Whoever's taking care of you needs to block the view better than this. I'm just saying."

Still no response, but then the door to the converted garage rolled open. I walked in a hunched-over position down the short plastic corridor through the door. It closed behind me. Instantly, I was hammered by a blast of freezing air that, in a few seconds, went down a couple of notches. Maybe to less than a wind tunnel.

A female voice came out of a nearby speaker. "Don't come any farther. The fans are intended to keep you, and anything you might have brought in, from infecting us."

A spotlight pinned me in its halo as a door swung open in the far wall. A woman appeared in the entrance but came no farther.

"Have you been seeking us?" Her voice, disembodied, came through the speaker.

"No. I'm on a business trip. I thought I'd check out the nature sanctuary. It's on the map, you know. Once I saw the building…"

A moment of darkness, then an overhead light came on. I could see the woman clearly now. She was young and white, maybe in her early twenties, with long, brown hair.

Back behind her, there were at least two other women, one of whom was clutching a long black tube. A weapon of some kind, I assumed. If I tried to run now, they'd use it, and the door was probably locked anyway. Curiosity kills Dreya.

I thought it felt nippy walking up the trail. Sadly, I was wrong. I now had a new definition for freezing: as in-a-meat-locker-captured-by-a-serial-killer cold.

"You have questions." The woman didn't pause for a response. "We are a contemplative community. A religious order, but two of us have renounced our vows, myself included."

"So you're nuns."

They would pray over my icicled corpse, if it came to that.

"Yes. Elsewhere, we once had a retreat. People came for visits. It was quite restful for them."

This seemed to be the moment to say something, but what? Pops had been old-school AME, my mother a Catholic, but they never cut a deal on how my sister and I should be raised. We went to churches everywhere, even Unitarian for a time. I remember liking Baptist potlucks the best. That tells you how deep my church training went.

"What's your name?"

"Lauren."

Her face was tired and drawn. She didn't look rested or like she had meditated lately.

"So why are you here, if you're not doing the nun thing?"

"I'm not praying anymore, if that's what you mean. I serve God by serving my sisters."

"God has no use for us anymore. Sorry. I'm just quoting my father. I don't know if he was right."

The women behind her stirred but didn't speak. What was it like to live there? Did they have cameras to record their surroundings, or were they totally cut off?

She asked my name, and I gave it; then the door behind me opened. "Would you wait outside ten minutes?" Lauren asked.

Ten stretched to fifteen and then to twenty. During my pacing in front of the place, I noticed one camera, pegged from the side of the garage. There was a satellite dish on the roof and what looked like a garbage bin along the side of the building. Maybe it was accessible from the inside, or maybe they left their trash in the ice room for someone to collect.

How many women lived inside? Comfortably, the place could fit a dozen. From what I'd read, nuns like keeping it close to the bone, no frills for them, so figure twenty, tops.

I couldn't have done it. I couldn't keep my elbows in, my attitude godly, 24/7. How did they?

I heard footsteps behind me crunching down on the gravel. I turned around to find Lauren, lugging a bag. She advanced. I backed up.

"Is that bag something you need delivering? I can do it for you."

She wouldn't stop coming toward me. My foot slipped, and by the time I had righted myself, she stood in front of me.

"I need to bum a ride."

"I'm infected. I'll kill you. I won't mean to, but you know that's what'll happen. What, are you tired of being stuck in there? Do you have someone I can call? Maybe they can move you to another place."

Swiftly, she took one more step and kissed me on the lips.

"There," she said with grim satisfaction. "Now, I can't go back in."

I turned around and stomped back to the pickup, too upset to speak. Before I knew I had the disease, I killed six of Rita's relatives. They were faithful Catholics, so before they lost their minds, several of them begged for last rites. Online, I found the name of a priest making house calls for that purpose, but I could never get past his voice mail.

All I could do was read prayers I printed out from a website. All I could do was recite phrases that had little meaning to me, and now I had an ex-nun with a death wish dogging my heels.

Option One: I could use my cell to locate the nearest emergency responder, give them the location, and be on my way.

Option Two: I could go back to the walkie-talkie and explain the situation to the nuns. Someone was taking care of them. Someone else could deal with the woman.

"We—they—aren't in hiding," Lauren said. "The Church is establishing retreats to remind you that we still exist. Several communities have already agreed to be hosts. Think of it as a modern-day monastery. The project hasn't been formally announced yet, so we're not quite ready for visitors."

I took my first good look at her. She was older than my original estimate, but not by much. Maybe late twenties.

"Your kissing me, that wasn't fair. A lot of us tried to help the ones who were sick. We didn't know at first we were spreading it. And now, you've…"

She gazed at me, her body trembling with emotion. Correction: trembling with cold. I noticed that she was wearing jeans and a plaid shirt. Even in my heavy weather gear, I was freezing. That decided me.

We barely spoke on the drive into Williams Lake, just enough to determine she wasn't having Williams Lake, so on we went to Kamloops. The weather and our mood began to warm up slightly.

She was an American from Idaho, a former schoolteacher who took her vows less than a year before the walking fever. She claimed to not have a death wish.

"I think I might be immune. Back when it hit, I helped out at the hospital and never developed so much as a sniffle."

"Did you wear protective clothing?"

"Yes, but many people took precautions and still died."

"Some of them didn't. They're with the others living up north."

I didn't have a mask to offer her. "It's none of my business, but why did you stop praying? I can understand why you would give up on it, but then you decided to ride down here with the nuns, anyway."

"I believe in the project. You people can't just focus on building biodomes and converting military bases to house us over some far horizon, giving you license to forget about us. In the old days, monasteries preserved knowledge for generations to come. Now, the St. Benedict Refuges will serve as living reminders to you people of the lives lost and the lives needing to be saved."

"Benedict?" That phrase "you people" was starting to irritate me.

"He's the patron saint for those with fever and for the dying, also for those who are in religious orders. He was a hermit for a while. Pope Adrian VII picked him, in part, because so many came to him for guidance, even when he was a hermit living off the beaten path."

Option Three: I decided to drop her off at a clinic in Kamloops. The kiss barely took a second, and now, even with the heater going full blast, the pickup was still on the cool side. She might not be infected. The clinic could place her in isolation and test her blood. Best outcome: she'd be on a mercy flight to Yukon. I didn't want to think about the worst outcome.

I drove Lauren directly to the clinic, where they drew blood to test it for sensitivity. They agreed to keep her in their isolation ward, which the RN said had been empty for months. In twenty-four hours, they'd know whether she would fly or die.

"You can't make me go in there."

Her words were pure defiance. Her expression? Scared shitless. I knew the law: we can't be around them without everyone wearing protection.

I broke that law driving her unmasked to Kamloops, a point that did not impress her one bit.

Fine. We could both dig in our heels. "Did you get bored in there? If you don't want to live in the sealed settlements, there are villages up north where they have to wear safety suits to go outside, but they do get to be out in nature. They die a lot faster than the sealed ones, but it's their decision to make. Here, you're dragging me into the situation, and that's not right."

"I didn't mean to. You're not to blame, whatever happens, but I'm not going in there without a fight."

Given the fire in her expression, I figured that for a prediction.

The nurse's head had been bobbing back and forth watching our argument. She stepped in.

"Ma'am, it's not up to you whether you stay or not. You have to be admitted. I've already called our security guard, so he'll be suited up properly."

"What if I'm… what if I'm homosexual?" Both the nurse and I stared at her. "I think I could be."

"My late partner identified as being gay, and she died of the fever." That was still so hard for me to say. "Let the nurse take care of you for a couple of days until you know what's up. You've been serving your sisters, so why not chill for a while and let someone else take a run at it?"

That finally convinced her, or at least got her to walk down the hall with the nurse, who I heard delivering a complicated explanation of what to expect.

Lauren took her own sweet time coming out. Not even the ultimate disaster had tempted her until now. Call it mind over flesh, faith over truth, I guess, but to me she was just being stubborn.

Back on schedule, I drove over to the ginseng company's office where a young man showed me his business plan. He was the son of the original owner, who had partnered with my company to produce energy drinks before the disaster hit.

A willowy, nervous man, he griped about the road leading to their farm. Potholes had developed that no one in charge seemed able, or willing, to fix.

"I told them we'd pay for the repairs, but they said that wasn't the problem. They don't have enough workers to cover the area. At this rate, the whole province is going down the chute. All that money being spent on the Yukoners going, and in the meantime, our roads are turning to crap, and the government still won't adopt the U.S. plan."

"U.S. plan?"

He explained that cities in the U.S. had to meet a certain mark in population or be on a vital route in order to keep getting services.

Prince George probably didn't look necessary to him, but the people there were committed to keeping the town alive, and with the help of Chinese refugees, they would.

When I finished at the ginseng office, I called Susan, who told me there was a new freighter of refugees in the harbor.

"We're doing intake on them now. You won't believe where they came from. Argentina."

"I thought that situation had gotten straightened out." Hadn't there been a coup and then a counter-coup? Or was that Chile?

"They're claiming status as religious refugees. Dreya, they're Jews. Apparently, the new government is blaming Jewish scientists for what happened. They weren't letting their Jewish citizens fly out of the country, so these people hired a ship, kept it on the down low, and escaped. I'm not sure why they didn't dock at Los Angeles, but their rabbi said a few of them are pretty old. He was concerned that they would be sent back. He thought Canada might be more open."

She told me there were over four hundred passengers, with a sister ship due in any day. The ship was so packed, some of those on board had to be taken directly to the hospital due to exhaustion and non-fever illnesses. I asked her to find out if any of them had mechanical experience.

"I'm pretty sure I can place them immediately in Kamloops. I could place a lot of them here, whether or not they can hold a hammer."

The next day, I visited with city leaders, who seemed as thrilled as the woman in Prince George at the idea of bringing healthy prospects to town. I may have exaggerated the blue-collar cred of Susan's Argentineans. Anyhow, my simple job of lining up contracts for next year had morphed into a mission my company might not have been thrilled to know was taking so much of my time.

It did work out for my bosses in one way. Through a local, I learned about a large greenhouse known for its exotic vegetables and herbs. It turned out to be a good get for the Vancouver restaurants. The greenhouse was being run by a post-fever family new to things green. I spent an enjoyable afternoon giving them pointers on correcting soil acidity. Nuts and bolts only a gardener gets off on. By that evening, I had a do-gooder buzz I knew would be gone the moment I stepped into the clinic.

The nurse was smiling when I arrived. Lauren's blood samples turned out to be non-reactive, meaning she was gay, hadn't been infected, and wasn't going to die if she did catch the walking fever.

That was good news all around, but she didn't take it that way. She sat in the waiting room, sipping on a Starbucks coffee. She did not look at all happy about escaping death.

I sat in a rickety chair next to her.

"If you can get your praying problem worked out, I bet there's still a need for nuns. And if not, you could go back to teaching."

"Do you pray, do any of you people pray?"

Again with that phrase. "When I'm in church with our daughters, I do. They're young. They still believe."

"But you don't. Believe."

Rita destroyed in a river of blood, my parents dead. A year ago, terrible things had been happening, but the people I loved still looked healthy.

"I believe that if you put a seed in the ground and give it your best care and attention, it'll come up, nine times out of ten. I don't believe a tree is God. I'm not that mystical, but I don't think it's an accident that the Adam and Eve story took place in a garden. I know many of us do pray. And the phrase 'you people' describes yourself, too."

Her jaw unclenched, the shoulders loosened, and after a few minutes, she came to her feet.

"Can you give me a ride?"

"Vancouver okay?"

"Sure. Just another stop on the road to Purgatory."

*Analyn Orante*

Bauxite. I don't go to bed dreaming of aluminum, but the executives at Alcoa wanted our help in reestablishing their operations in Guinea. They claimed that the Russians had paid off the government there to tie up the supply. Even if that was true, I didn't view that as a critical issue. We had ample supplies on hand, according to our experts. We produced many tons of it a year, and in terms of recyclables, we were sitting on a mountain's worth. Let's prioritize.

President Budin voiced a different opinion on the matter. Our partners in Japan needed aluminum for the cars they were producing, for one thing. And for another, she was unwilling to concede major parts of the global economy to other players. Since she had her hands full dealing with Wall Street's opening bell, which was scheduled the next morning, I knew she had given me my marching orders. Go out and make a difference.

Before I left the office, we made plans to meet that evening for dinner. I insisted on setting a specific time. If I didn't, she would work past midnight and never notice missing a meal.

On my way back to the State Department, Bill Levine called me. There had been another incident along the Mexican border with California. A group of Americans went across the border and claimed a number of unoccupied businesses and even a ranch. We knew there was more to the situation than political theater.

Our Border Patrol had been stretched beyond its limits, but in recent months had rebounded, due to our recruitment program. Although our open borders deal with Canada relieved some of the stress, it only made the problem with Mexico that much more flammable.

Our governments couldn't agree to terms for discussion, which meant we had quite a ways to go in working out what to do about Mexican and Central American nationals who had relocated to our border states in the past year.

Mexico City said they were refugees. We said they're illegal aliens. Back and forth it went. Congress had repealed most legislation having to do with illicit drugs, and that move had ruined what was left of the drug cartels. There were plenty of jobs here, regardless of one's legal status, just like before the fever. The problem really boiled down to land and who owned it.

San Diego County alone had over two thousand disputed property and business assumptions. These were battles between the county and the squatters, who weren't all foreign nationals. City and county governments across the country wanted to control the process so there'd be a paper trail, essentially. Tax revenues, budget planning, health services. They needed to know who was where.

In some cases, foreign nationals had moved into homes or taken over businesses for which the governing authority had located a qualifying relative. The approach was clear-cut: evict the current occupants. The actual eviction might be ugly, but legally valid.

But what did you do in situations where no relatives came forth? A legal resident could file for property assumption. If the legal resident passed background checks, then evict the squatters. Legals first.

Where the sticky part came was that in the past few months, the squatters who were illegal aliens had been playing a vital role in our nation's recovery. They repaired power lines, they filled a vast and visible number of blue-collar jobs, and even though there were many professionals among them, the popular perception was otherwise.

This explained the occasional property assumption where the governing authority decided in favor of the illegal alien, rather than the legal resident. Typically, the foreign national worked in a vital role, while the legal resident had an arrest record a mile long.

The law works case by case. It doesn't always look like justice. It doesn't always look fair. That's what led to the land grab south of Tijuana, which was only the latest in several border incidents.

The San Diego consortium did their homework: all of the properties lacked original ownership and attracted no heirs. The Mexican government had all it could do to handle problems in its capital. It possessed little or no authority elsewhere, particularly in the north.

I don't know if the Californians had a long-term plan to establish homes and businesses in Mexico, but they started something of a land rush along the border. Maybe that's too strong a phrase. These weren't Sooners lined up to race across Indian Territory. But entrepreneurs on both sides of the border were willing to hire stand-ins to file for property assumptions.

Border security couldn't contain the situation. I'm not alone in blaming the land disputes as a factor in the collapse of the ruling political party in Mexico. It also explained why Northern Mexico began its path toward independence.

I had come to some conclusions of my own. Although I was trained in the subtle art of diplomacy, I'm better at knocking heads together. In the year since our country came under viral attack, I had used or supported robust tactics that were necessary to keep our ship afloat, but now we had entered complicated waters.

Americans were still dying of VSF. Up north, our crews were working in horrendous conditions on the biodome project. That said, many parts of the world were doing much worse than we were.

In contrast, Norway barely skipped a beat. Their northern sealed settlement, a model of safety and comfort, housed over a hundred thousand sensitives. The country had long made a strong commitment to renewable energy sources. They hadn't had much of a refugee problem compared to some of their neighbors. According to the Norwegian ambassador, citizens were voting on how to memorialize the dead.

The Norwegians weren't living in paradise, but you couldn't have convinced your average Albanian of that fact. New leaders, new governments kept springing up everywhere, and I, for one, felt I didn't possess a broad enough skill set.

The assassination attempt had no bearing on my decision to resign. Bill Levine already knew my job inside out. I knew of others equally as capable to step into my shoes.

There were also more personal reasons.

Over a late-night dinner of pasta and salad, I revealed my plans to President Budin. She tried to talk me out of it, but she needed a Secretary of State who wouldn't be perceived as being too close to the President.

"Do you think we're too close?" she asked.

"No, ma'am."

A smile curled her lips. "I could take that in a number of ways, Ana."

"Yes, you could."

With that, we returned to the previous conversation about international reaction to the consolidation of our stock markets and new controlling mechanisms designed to prevent a crash. Small talk only a pair of policy wonks would enjoy. Afterward, we made plans for dinner the next night.

*Dora Navarro*

I had my suspicions. The way Scott acted around me in public, like Mr. We're-Just-Friends, ticked me off, especially since he would be so romantic when we were alone. Talk about being closeted.

Finally, I confronted him about it. He didn't want to say it, so I said it for him. He didn't like people looking at us.

Everywhere we went, we saw gay or lesbian couples, almost no mixed couples. Scott, I think, had always been conscious of the status quo and fitting in. He was a nail that wanted to get hammered down, even when there wasn't a hammer around. I didn't think the looks were hostile. More compassionate, almost like nostalgic.

He said he didn't want his TV back. As if all we had to resolve was who had what. We hadn't moved in together, hadn't gotten past being friends with benefits, if you can call it a benefit.

Anyhow. Move on.

Austin was starting to look better. Most of the trash had been picked up. If you kept out of certain parts of town, you didn't have to see all those empty rows of houses with broken windows and overgrown yards. I hated to think of what they'd look like by next summer when the grass would be up past the windows. The city kept bragging about how many people had moved to the area.

I wondered how Odessa was holding up, but I couldn't stand the idea of trying to drive back there, not after what had happened.

My job at Solectron turned out to be something of a bait and switch, but in a good way. I thought I was going to be testing and assembling electronics for their self-serve machines, but after two weeks, they slotted me for training in project management.

They claimed I had good communication skills. They wouldn't have thought that a few months ago when I couldn't even say my own name. But to be honest, close work like that was hard on my eye, doing it eight hours straight, so I was glad to get picked for a different assignment.

Barb and Bev invited me to Friday evening services at an Austin synagogue. They drove down from Salado and picked me up. They were doing okay. Bev had her hands full with new psych clients at Fort Hood. What with all the base closures, and surviving personnel being transferred in, the place was jumping. Barb was thinking seriously about becoming a rabbi, but Bev said just give her twenty minutes and she'd move on to something else.

While sitting with them during the service, I realized I had been missing the music. At one point, I looked down. My fingers were working out an arrangement. There's a place in the service for silent meditation, and for the life of me I couldn't think of anything to say to Him. God, that is. So many of the prayers were praising Him, and for what? Killing Mama? Letting Miguel's killers escape justice? It seemed to me we were stroking His ego, and for what purpose?

I mean, I understood that humans had warped the virus to where it would kill us, and humans spread it around. God was in the picture, too. God made us with the ability to do harm to others, then God set deadly things among us. If you place a box of matches next to a child, are you surprised if he burns down the house?

The service went into the remembrance of the dead part. That's where they say Kaddish, and the rabbi asks everyone to say the names of those they lost.

As she slowly moved her arm from one side to the other, I heard so many names said aloud. Everyone spoke, even me. I said

Mama's name, then the names of my brothers, my nephews, my stepdad, and Miguel. I couldn't go on after that. It hurt too much.

I hadn't even begun to add up my cousins, my aunts and uncles, my straight friends, my piano students, all those lovely members at the Methodist church, that elderly couple who lived next door to me, musicians I'd played with, my ex-boyfriend. There wasn't enough time in the service to get them all in.

I decided that in order to do it right, I'd have to go to services on a regular basis. That's how I worked it out in my head. Every Friday night, I would come to this place and say aloud the names of people I knew had died.

I wanted to remind God. That is, if He cared, which I doubted very much. I cared. That was enough for me.

Afterward, we met up with some friends of Barb's and Bev's at a home nearby, where I was introduced to a singer named Stasia Millner. She had recently moved to Austin from Concord, Massachusetts. She told me she was looking for an accompanist, which didn't interest me much at the time, but she gave me a CD she had recorded. Over the next few days, I listened to the songs and was impressed by her style. It sounded like a blend of Rufus Wainwright and Imogen Heap, if that makes sense. I had lost her phone number, but at the next Friday service, I saw her again.

We sat together, and then we hung out afterward at her apartment playing songs and talking. This turned into something of a habit. I'd attend service and recite my reminders to God. Then, I'd spend the rest of the night kicking around some tunes with Stasia.

We were about the same age and had gone through some of the same experiences with our families. Someone might describe Stasia as medium—average height, average build, average attitude— except when she sings. That's when you know she's extraordinary.

We kind of worked our way into dating. My history of being with men didn't bother her. Maybe she knew that wasn't going to be much of an issue anymore. We were taking it slow. We'd both been through so much. Who needed more drama?

Stasia's day job consisted of boxing the personal effects of people who had died and cataloging their estates. City officials wanted to make sure the process was documented, so that if any relatives came along, they would find their family pictures in the right box in the right warehouse.

But there were other issues. You had to remove chemicals that might leak over time, empty refrigerators, make sure the gas and electricity were turned off, and destroy meds to prevent some idiot burglar from overdosing on heart pills. Stasia found all kinds of interesting items, like a huge carved ivory collection, a disassembled Yamaha motorcycle in some guy's den. She even found a dialysis machine.

Most of it she left in place. The Dora of a year ago would have thought she had a creepy job, but now I understood. There's nothing morbid about it. You're honoring their lives by making sure the things they left behind are treated in a respectful manner.

On the news, you'd hear cheerleaders (that's what I called them) saying we'd weathered the worst of the virus, been knocked down and gotten up again, sunny skies ahead. I had a job. Most everyone I knew was hanging in there, but sunny skies?

The President said the Alaskans were continuing to die of the virus, although those were mainly the ones who decided to live out in the settlements. The ones at the base were stuck in Alaska in the middle of winter, sealed in, sure, but afraid that a diseased bug or one of us might get in. Sunny skies. Right.

I did read where companies were setting up tech support centers to go inside the Dome when it was ready. You couldn't expect those people to sit inside and wait who knew how long for a vaccine or a cure and not have something to do in the meantime.

They had religious leaders in the base claiming that the Rapture had just now happened. I guess that meant the heterosexuals left behind were chock full of sin, even babies. I'm no religious expert, but even I know that can't be true.

Their leaders didn't say it was our fault for having a genetic glitch, I guess you'd call it, that didn't get discovered by the virus's makers. They didn't say let's kill the faggots. How could they? We were keeping them alive and literally dropping dead ourselves in accidents while building the Dome. Beyond that, what could they do except shout religion and complain we weren't doing enough?

According to CNN, there weren't that many of us left to do everything that needed doing. They had just come out with census figures that I thought were wishful thinking. In Texas, we had half a million survivors, or three quarters of a million, or tons more, if you included the Norteños. How could anyone really know until things settled down?

They did know there were forty-two thousand sensitives left in Barrow Base and the surrounding area. New York City was still big, around four hundred thousand, CNN said, and more moving in everyday.

Metro Austin had fattened up to eighty thousand, supposedly, but there were people who flat out refused to move to the living zones, even when their water got cut off.

Everyday there'd be someone on TV, worrying about maintaining the water-treatment plant or keeping the airport runways repaired, but you know what? The work was getting done. Maybe not by someone with a certificate after his or her name, but the water tasted fine, and planes were taking off and landing everyday.

I was here. That's all I knew.

# Chapter 13

*Debra Shanrahan*

I thought it was a bad idea, thoroughly. The Brits were the ones conducting embryonic research, not us. Bao-Zhai wanted to have a baby. I tell her, we'll adopt. There are plenty of kiddies needing a home. Why put yourself through the fertility treatments? She said if I wanted to adopt, we could do that, too, but she really, really wanted to bring a baby to term.

So far, the Brits had determined that during week five of a pregnancy is the make-or-break for a fetus. If it's still alive after that, even after exposure to VSF, then we know it's one of ours. Whatever makes us asymptomatic—makes us poofters, for that matter—happens then.

The Brits had also figured out that hormonal fluctuations at the proper time were important in fetal development, but they hadn't figured out the exactitudes. It seemed to vary from case to case. Hormones, though, were one key to the solution.

*In vitro* fertilization has to take place early for it to work at all, so there's no way to check for VSF sensitivity beforehand. Bao-Zhai went *in vitro* twice, and both times miscarried in the fifth week. I put my foot down, as if that ever did any good with her, and said she needed to look after her health.

You can't really spot a pregnant woman right off, not that early in the running, but I remember lying in bed with her and feeling the curve of her body. It's like everything about her was getting deeper, richer—yeah, that early. Anticipation does that to you. The second time she miscarried, I cried as much as she did. I didn't know I had such maternal ambitions until I wifed up with Bao.

She had done everything right. She did the shots, the stay in the clinic, everything. It wasn't her fault.

Ironically, the Domers were starting to have babies left and right. They needed some good news because, all in all, it had been an awful spring. The virus got loose in the north everywhere. It was carried up there by birds, ticks, the wind, who knows what all.

Spring came early, due to global warming, which gave the virus that much more time to reestablish itself. That is, if it ever left the north in the first place. All over the world, the island sanctuaries and so-called safe towns began falling apart. Now it was up to the Domes to help sensitives get through this thing.

There was a terrible fire in Montana, set by safe townies who had been resisting going north. I don't blame them for wanting to stay there. The odds weren't much better north unless you got your ticket punched for the Domes. But the fire, that was wrong. It spread into Yellowstone Park and made evacuation of survivors tough. The burners died by their own hands, I reckon.

It made me think again about home. Americans just think they've seen fires. We've had some real beauts. At least my friends back home hadn't had to deal with one of those lately. I'd been getting emails from them and phone calls from the government in Canberra. They wanted me back.

I'd become a symbol. Of what, I asked. Survival, they said. I'm like the rest of you lot, I told them. We're the winners of a genetic lottery none of us had ever thought would pay off triple jackpot.

I knew Bao-Zhai loved her work, but her citizenship application had hit a major snag. The Chinese were starting to cooperate since their new government came into power. Outsiders now would be granted access to the viral research center that started the whole mess. The Americans wanted her to fly there and find out more about the roots of the virus.

The Chinese got wind of that and said they had revoked her travel papers. They claimed she had to return to Beijing. Ludicrous, that, since she had lived in the States since she was a teenager. Owned a green card for eons. The Americans were making a show of taking them seriously. Too much of a show, I thought.

Dr. Tofill said he'd personally order a missile attack if the Chinese snatched her. It looked to me like, one way or the other, Bao-Zhai was headed to China, and she might never come back.

Bao-Zhai was pissed about the entire affair. She went to the trouble of locating other researchers who could go instead of her, but I guess she'd become a symbol, too.

We talked over what to do, batted it back and forth, and then decided on a plan of action. I got permission to travel with her as far as Seattle so we could have a last weekend together before she flew on to Beijing. We checked into the hotel, rented a car, and went out to see the sights. I couldn't tell if we were being watched, but she thought the Chinese had an agent following us. I don't know about that, but I did my best Mad Max impression just in case, dumped the car, and got us to the ferry. We tried to blend in with the other passengers.

Canada, O Canada. A couple of days later, we flew to Australia out of Vancouver. I'm dead cert that the Canadians weren't thrilled to have an international incident on their hands, but they were nice to us and made sure we got on the flight without any worries.

At the Melbourne airport, there was such a crowd I thought there had to be a movie star on board.

Bao-Zhai laughed at me. "Silly girl. They're here for you."

What a shocker. The government had gone all out to make me feel welcome. They rounded up my friends. They even brought in a man I went mud-bogging with years ago. I don't remember much about the interviews except being grateful they didn't go on too long.

In the meantime, the Canberra crew handed Bao-Zhai permanent residency papers and said they had a directorship lined up for her at a research institute there in Melbourne. Me, I had my choice of positions, but top on my agenda was getting us out of the terminal.

They drove us to our new home in a secluded area of the city. I thought the Atlanta digs were a stately manse, but this took several cakes. The neighborhood appeared as though nothing untoward had happened to it since circa 1954. But even though they laid out a spread with enough olives to choke a camel, noted I, we gave the festivities a regulation hour and had the whole lot clear out. We needed to decompress.

We sprawled on the sofa, traded off on a bottle of Chardonnay, and watched a rerun of *Blue Heelers* I hadn't seen before.

I couldn't risk taking a suspicious amount of luggage, and Bao-Zhai spent more time organizing her slides and files than packing. Melbourne can be a trifle brisk in June.

"I didn't bring any sweaters," I told Bao-Zhai. "Guess we'll both be hitting the stores."

"That's fine by me. I need to shop for baby clothes."

I stared at her. Her face had the classic butter-wouldn't-melt. Sometimes that woman just drives me spare.

"Bao, I don't want you to go through it again. It's not safe."

"I checked with Ralph in London. They've found a new combination of shots that's helping."

"They're shots for pigs, for Chrissake. They haven't tried anything with humans yet."

"Not officially."

Somehow that didn't surprise me. The Brits were as desperate as anyone to reduce their miscarriage rate.

"Even so, you're deliberately risking your health."

"We have to try, Debs. We can't sit around and wait. Did you know the Domers won't let their doctors take blood samples from the babies?"

"Why's that? Those tykes don't have VSF."

"The Domers are afraid we'll steal babies who are like us."

"We wouldn't do that."

"Oh yes, we would, if enough time goes by, their population's booming, and we're not able to replace ourselves. We'd have to. They're inside, we're out. None of the Domes will be self-supporting, not for a long time. You've heard the same stories I have. Women are already doing what I'm doing, and some of them are pretty far along now."

"Law of averages, love. Enough paint, enough wall, something will stick." Bad metaphor, Debs. "Some women have a higher incidence of homosexuality in their gene pool."

"Maybe they received the shots at the right time. Please support me on this, Debs. I'll know when it's time to stop trying."

I wasn't convinced of that, but I also knew better than to try and change Bao-Zhai's mind when she had it thoroughly in the cement.

Lying in bed that night, I listened to Bao's even breathing, her pace steady as ever. You could set a clock by it, find comfort in her solidity, but not at that moment.

Here I was, finally, back home where I was wanted, appreciated, and needed.

I found myself sitting in the backyard, staring up at the night sky, and saying hello to my old friend Hercules, that old rascal, always looking for trouble. Look, there's Scorpius wagging his tail. Twelve o'clock and all's well, except for the suds soaker in the lawn chair. Tsk, tsk, Debs. Shouldn't be mixing beer and wine like that.

Getting drunk, though, ranked as a free-will decision, one of the few I could claim as my own since checking on Ducket's prize boar. Virtually every step since then had been preordained by some authority or made to seem somehow the right, rational thing to do. Even coming back home had been a fallback plan to satisfy someone else. Bao-Zhai wanted the freedom to come and go as she wished. Here in Australia, she had it.

What did I want now? Not life as a symbol, that's for damned sure. I may have yelled that, because Bao appeared at my elbow directly, sitting in her own lawn chair and sipping sensibly on a can of Pub Squash. She handed me a can of Waterfords mineral water. So somebody thought it important to keep up the Waterfords. How civilized of them, or more likely, my countrymen had yet to drink up the supply left over from before VSF hit. I refused to call it the Moree Plague.

The latest Oz guesstimate had us at 1.2 million total population. That struck me as insanely optimistic. When the sealed settlements in bush began failing, the government flew several groups of sensitives to Heard and McDonald Islands, which are well qualified as sub-arctic versions of hell.

Resupply had been a bitch, but finally the Tasmanian Dome was completed. Our sensies, all nine thousand of them, were relocated to the new facility. Even the Kiwis had done better than us. They stuck their sensies up some mountain until they completed their Dome. They had upwards of twelve thousand in their facility, the overachieving buggers.

"The sky is beautiful here." Bao squeezed my hand.

"Right you are, love."

England. We could have, should have gone to England. That's where the reproductive research was going on, Bao's contact Ralph, the human subjects, and all the rest of it. She followed me, not the other way around. I'm the selfish wanker.

Before I could get too soppy with my apology, she cut me off.

"That's what the Internet's for, Debs. Whatever Ralph comes up with is just as easy to try here as in England and simpler to pull off because I'll have complete control of my own laboratory and staff.

"The Americans and the Chinese both think VSF is kind of like influenza. All we'll have to do, once vaccines are approved for the now-twenty variants out there, is to get everyone vaccinated first go-round. Then we'd manufacture new shots whenever a new variant comes along. They think it'll be a containable death toll with the shots. They're wrong.

"The vaccine trials have all failed so far because VSF isn't one virus. It's two. We know the virion is a variant of African swine fever, with a highly segmented genome, but the viral envelope itself, and its glycoproteins, I believe are from another virus. I haven't identified it yet, but it's similar to HIV, which means it has elements of a retrovirus."

"Bloody hell." I knew what that meant. You can treat HIV, but you can't cure it. Which meant... I didn't know what it meant.

"Are you saying we'll all develop active VSF eventually? That we'll all die? The sensies, those poor bastards, just happened to topple over first."

"I don't know yet. Our blood samples don't yet show any changes. They don't show anything except the presence of the virus. I do know that the drugs we use to fight HIV do nothing against VSF."

Babies. She wants babies who have immunity from the start, babies who, genetically speaking, will have an advantage on the rest of us. "You think the babies are the key to the whole thing. Stem cells and all that lot."

"If we can get enough of their stem cells to work with, we might be able to replicate the cells in the lab."

She gave me a confident smile then looked down, frowning, at her can.

"Don't worry, love. I saw some Cokes in the back of the fridge."

*Wylie Halverson*

The last of the reporters called at nine in the evening, and although I tried to be pleasant, I'm sure my level of effort had to be showing. My answers were strictly canned.

Yes, I said to the man, I was pleased to hear that the judge assessed a five-year sentence on Devlin Pratchett. Interesting to learn the rest of his name. He'd be serving it in the now-usual practice of picking up dead bodies and doing grunt work for the county.

No one spent time loafing in jail cells anymore, except those so violent the authorities felt that electronic cuffs and surveillance weren't enough of a security measure. The state had also gone to imbedding microchips in a convict's arm for better tracking.

The reporter wanted me to take credit for Pratchett's arrest, but I refused. All I contributed to the crime-stopping was the happenstance of being Selma's partner.

It all started back in January when I sent my secretary and a helper over to the warehouse to pick up more supplies. She found a large padlock on the gate. One of Pratchett's goons stopped them driving out of the warehouse district and told my secretary that all requests would have to be routed through his office. The goon even gave her a business card, the number on which I called the moment she returned.

I gave Pratchett several pieces of my mind. That evening, the man himself paid a visit to our house. The kids were in a buzz over the Hummer parked in front of our steps. I didn't like the looks of them—the flabby, pale bureaucrat at my door claiming to be Pratchett and the stupid-faced beefcake standing behind him.

This was the new-style Mafioso and his enforcer? I knew the beefcake was armed. I realized Pratchett, for all his bluster, had the means to cause us problems, but after everything that had happened up to now, I couldn't for the life of me take him seriously.

I laughed at him. I admit it. I laughed, even though he swore at me and said my school would never get so much as a pencil from his warehouse. I laughed again. Selma and the older kids watched the entire exchange. Within the hour, the whole family trooped over with me to the local police station to file a complaint.

Selma and the police commander had formed a warm partnership, based in equal parts on snacks and shared intelligence on thieves, so we were all on a first-name basis.

That was the end of it, I thought. The police would begin a minuet with Pratchett, starting with filing a complaint with his lawyer. Maybe a year later, the padlock would be taken off the school's warehouse. I thought old-style law and politics would dictate the pace of justice. Not anymore.

Selma colluded with our older kids and their friends on their own private war. They set up disguised security cameras in the warehouse district, ran spy kids on skateboards past Pratchett Enterprises, even hacked into his computers (and broke into his office after business hours, but I'm not supposed to know that), and used the information to identify the locations of all his squirreling.

One day after school, upwards of a hundred of my students staged what nowadays is called a Witness. That's where everyone arranges to meet at a place to shoot live-transmitted images of wrongdoing, whether of hoarding, price gouging, or some other offense *du jour*.

In this case, they went to one of the largest warehouses, broke the lock, and went inside, cameras running the whole time and the media invited to attend. Selma's police commander was happy to take advantage of the publicity to go against his boss's express orders. His cops arrested everyone at Pratchett Enterprises, including the head, for criminal hoarding and extortion.

New-style judges don't believe in slow, stately proceedings, nor do most grand juries. Did Pratchett rat out all he had bribed in city government and law enforcement? Indeed. Did those bribed resign? Of course.

The eventual disposition of the warehouse goods was more complicated than the criminal case. Eventually, the City of Milwaukee had to step in to resolve the dispute. It distributed what was confiscated among local schools and hospitals. A portion of the goods ended up back with the affected merchants. Wal-Mart and Target thought they should have received their entire heisted inventory.

No one was altogether happy with the outcome, except Selma's police commander, who ended up with a promotion.

If not for Pratchett's heart attack, the case would have been wrapped up months ago, but the judge waited for doctors to certify that he had completed cardio rehab. Once that came through, then came the sentencing. And the reporters.

Was I happy, the last caller of the night inquired. Not hearing a response, he repeated the question.

Was I happy? I declined to answer and got off the phone.

Father Jerzy poked his head out the dining room door. "The inquisition over with?"

"I'm not answering the phone anymore, if that's what you mean."

"Dixon is doing a good job with your cards."

"Thank God for big favors."

I sat next to Dixon and took back my cards. Chelsea had been in the lead on Texas Hold 'Em before I left, but Regina and Reha, playing as a team, had taken over the top spot.

Selma and Father Jerzy, who had been reassigned to Milwaukee earlier in the spring, were seated at the end of the table drinking coffee and acting conspiratorial. The little ones had been packed off to bed. I figured on at least one of them making a protest march before the evening ended.

Regina had decided to accept an academic scholarship offer from UW-Milwaukee's College of Engineering. She wanted to be a materials engineer. Ordinarily on the quiet side, she could be quite rhapsodic about the uses of titanium. She told me that back home she liked studying science, but would never have thought about making it a career before the plague. Before, she figured on becoming a nurse like her mother or perhaps choosing a career in the Army.

During the past few months, she blossomed in the classroom of a retired industrial scientist who volunteered to teach at my high school. I had no doubt that he was the ultimate source of the scholarship, as well as the reason why Regina was scheduled to spend her summer working at Johnson Controls here in Milwaukee.

Dixon wanted to go into the NBA. There were now eight teams back in action, complete with play-offs and statistics Dixon could quote verbatim. We didn't take his plans for a pro career altogether seriously, being that he had yet to finish middle school, and that he had already trumpeted career plans in video-game design, competitive rock climbing, and, in homage to Regina, materials engineering.

In regards to Chelsea, I never expected her to remain with us past her eighteenth birthday. We celebrated it back in March. Surprisingly, she hadn't joined so many of her classmates in visiting the emancipation judge. She rarely discussed her family, but the pictures of her brothers on the walls of the girls' room spoke volumes about how she felt.

Sullen didn't describe her behavior anymore. She did her chores and completed her homework with the same diligent yet remote manner. She reserved her emotions for the basketball court, where she led her team to a city championship and then to the state finals. Since universities were struggling to find their footing, not to mention their financing, most athletic scholarships had fallen by the wayside. Even so, several offers had come her way, including one from the University of Tennessee.

Imagine our surprise when she signed with UW-Milwaukee. Selma tried to point out that Tennessee was offering a full four-year scholarship. UW-Milwaukee could only guarantee athletes one year at a time, due to the funding crisis.

Regina was explaining to Reha again about the river in Texas Hold 'Em when Felicity appeared in the doorway.

"Mama Wy? Jarrod got more pie than me for dessert." At age two and a half, Felicity's vocabulary shot up whenever there was a prospect for sweets.

"That's because he finished his vegetables."

Felicity came up to Selma, who the kids called Smah. This was a contraction Reha had invented in the early months before her diction improved. Felicity raised her arms and received a lift into Selma's lap. She must have been disappointed by her view of the table. No pie anywhere. Only soft drinks and coffee.

The game continued with no further interruptions until a knock came on the back door. This would be Sybil, the foster daughter of our neighbors, who was dating Regina. Sybil is a pretty girl, if perhaps a bit high-strung. She seemed too fast for our Regina, but sometimes in life you have to take a few laps and risk the speeding ticket.

Chelsea rolled her eyes at how quickly Regina abandoned the game to loll on the back porch with Sybil. Father Jerzy, who snuck a piece of candy into Felicity's chubby hands, elected to sit with Reha.

The game eventually worked its way down to two contenders: Chelsea and myself. Mulish versus obstinate. We were evenly matched and disinclined to overplay our hands.

After a while, Dixon gathered up Felicity and, followed by Reha, led them to their bedrooms.

"Guess what," Selma said after they left.

"I know something's up. You and Father Jerzy have been conspiring all night."

"I've decided to file for the special election." Our alderman had been indicted on charges related to the Pratchett scandal.

"Finally," Chelsea said. "My friends keep asking me when you're going to run for mayor. I told them, you never know about Smah. She might take on the governor, the rate she's going."

Smah. Around the younger kids, Chelsea used our nicknames but never to our faces. I decided to let the breakthrough occur without comment.

"UW says they'll give me a job on campus," Chelsea said. She had me in deep trouble since I only had a pair of threes.

"I'm glad to hear that. A little pocket money should come in handy." The next round of cards was not helpful.

"Now I'll be able to pay rent."

I looked up from my cards. The girl was serious. When was she ever not serious?

"No, you won't."

"I need to do my share. The school's barely paying you anything, and I know Mr. Dent's been sending food from the cafeteria home with you."

"That's nothing for you to worry about. The government's about to increase the stipend. Things'll be getting better on that front. Anyhow, you should concentrate on your schooling."

"I'm an adult now. I'm living under this roof. I need to contribute."

"You're right," Selma said. "You've been helping with the kids all along. It's only fair we should start paying you."

Chelsea threw down her cards. A full house. The girl needed to go to Vegas, which only nuclear Armageddon would ever put out of business.

"You're not going to pay me for babysitting. This isn't good ol' Stevens Point, and we're all happy little townies going to Homecoming, and hoorah, everyone. You've been supporting me since day one. It's time I did something to help."

There were tears running down her face and down my own.

"No, there's no way you're paying a penny. It wouldn't be right. Look, none of us are in the family we started with, and God knows I wish you still had yours. Your parents were nice people."

"No, they weren't. Dad was a real asshole, always griping about something. That's why my brothers left after high school. They never came back, even for holidays. I don't know why my mom didn't—"

The chips went flying as Chelsea stormed into the living room. We ended up on the front porch.

"I'm grateful for you taking me in, but this is your house, not mine. I need to start paying in. It's only fair."

"But this is your house. Selma and I filed papers with the city to make sure the house goes to you kids if we should die."

She whirled around and stared at me. "What if I don't want it?"

"Then you and the others can decide on whether to sell it or rent it out."

She went down the stairs then came back up again. I waited her out. Everyone in the house who was still awake stood peeking through the door, Regina and Sybil included, waiting to see what would happen next. I had no clue myself.

"Dad said you were a dyke. Everybody knew, but no one made a big deal out of it, because you were a good teacher. He thought you set a bad example, but I didn't believe him. I thought you were a hard ass, but fair."

"I can't argue with the truth."

"Regina and Dixon and I have been talking about going commercial with the cheese curds. We still have our business contacts, and Smah says she can hook us up with a dairy." Her words came out in a rush.

Regina's voice came from behind me. "Sybil says her foster dad has an in with Metro Market."

"Awesome." Chelsea's face displayed more emotion than I had seen in ages. "Don't worry, we'll still do the school thing. What do you think, Mama Wy?"

"I think it's awesome, too."

The reporter should have called back. I now had an answer to the happiness question.

*Dreya Underhill*

Wei-Chow wanted to be called Charlie. I think he chose that name because the first Canadian he ever met when he came off the ship was a young Port Authority worker with that name.

This, according to Elizabeth, who had made it her life mission to turn our newest family member into a fluent, donut-loving North American, and Susan's efforts at steaming dim sum be damned.

After only four months of exposure to English, his accent strangled much of what he said, but I doubt I could have done as well at the age of eight, thrown into an alien place after losing everyone and everything he'd ever known.

Maria was thrilled to have someone she could boss for a change. Me, I hadn't welcomed the idea of adding a new member so soon, but this Chinese twin to Eric Cartman grew on me even as I felt the pressure to add a child by a more traditional way.

Leesa, my maturing, but still verbally-out-there sister, was to blame. All the dating sites online, and just about every other woman in the world, wanted to know how many gays were or are in your family. Until scientists came up with a foolproof baby-making scheme, a couple's best bet was to up the odds as much as possible.

Families with gay relatives tend to keep producing gay relatives, but a tendency is a football field away from being a guarantee. Before the fever, gays made up as much as ten percent of the population, but that doesn't mean a woman can have nine miscarriages and the tenth one goes the distance. You might succeed on the first one, or never. Who can tolerate losing baby after baby like that?

We knew Pops's oldest sister was a lesbian. She had been dead for years, but in her prime, a notorious bulldagger. On our mother's side, we knew of two first cousins for sure who were gay. The family lost track of them, or vice-versa, over the years. Who knew if they were still alive, but when Leesa and Lanasha visited an obstetrician in San Francisco, you would have thought she won the lottery. Your sister is gay, too? Let's throw in a parade, why don't we?

Doctors were trying wanna-be mothers on what people in England called the Nappy Cocktail. Everybody knew the recipe included hormone shots and a couple of drugs that were supposed to improve the odds if you took them at exactly the right times. The clinics' commercials showed couples and quadruples, the mothers looking well along.

Rumors claimed that not only was vaginal warmth important, you also had to be careful about the temperature in which the egg was fertilized. Yeah, right, and babies are delivered by UPS. Too much hope and not enough facts going around.

I couldn't imagine betting my pregnancy on what worked for a pig, but parents were doing anything to get past week five, including paying surrogate mothers who claimed to have a few percentage points more advantage.

Gay men were just as eager, going by what I heard. One TV show profiled a man with a family history even gayer than mine. Both parents and an older sister were gay and still alive, believe it or not. He and his partner had teamed up with a lesbian couple to start a family.

Leesa gave the obstetrician my name and personal information. I don't blame the callers, but I'm no fan of having my downtime interrupted. Our girls got wind of it and started begging me for a baby, as if I could pop one out on demand.

Susan never pushed me on the subject, which made me ask one day, what did she want? She said she couldn't put someone through that kind of trauma. That to me was a non-answer, so we explored the question further. Her ex-partner, it turned out, never wanted children; Susan did. Rita and I talked about having kids, but she never acted enthusiastic about the idea.

When Leesa and Lanasha came up for a visit in May, they were thinking about trying again. Their first try had resulted in a miscarriage.

I liked Lanasha. She looked like a banger stud, but her insides were pure marshmallow, proof of which being the tenderness she showed toward my sister, who still seemed fragile. Losing our parents, losing our entire universe, didn't seem to shake Leesa near as much as going through her failed pregnancy. She and her partner were determined to give it another go.

After they left Sunday morning, Susan and I took the kids to church. Wei-Chow/Charlie came from a Buddhist background, so at first we had left him behind with friends during church events. He wasn't having that one bit, so we started taking him to services with us, but Susan also insisted he receive instruction from a friend of hers who is a practicing Buddhist. What can I say? We were trying to balance it all out.

Susan had been raised some kind of half-Buddhist, half-Pentecostal. Maria was Catholic, Elizabeth was a Mennonite, and I wasn't anything in particular, which is why we attended the Church of the Christian Revival. Like the church in Salinas, it's a catchall.

I wondered what Pops would make of it? His oldest daughter co-parenting a family of five, and his little girl all grown up and fiercely determined to bring a new life into the world. Maybe God didn't have any use for us, but our kids needed God or some kind of Divine Placeholder. We'd pray to the Whatever until the Real Thing showed up.

I happened to see Lauren, the ex-nun, at the service. We spoke afterward. Susan was curious to meet the woman who kissed me as a death wish. Lauren was teaching English at a newcomer class and living in an apartment complex for singles.

I didn't ask her whether she planned to re-nun anytime soon. Maybe it's enough that she attended church. She mentioned in a fake-casual way that she was still celibate. I'm guessing that she hadn't worked out what she was supposed to do, God-wise. People-wise, it seemed clear enough to me: take care of the living; bury the dead.

Corpses were still being pulled from so-called sealed villages and other places up in the Yukon and Alaska. That couldn't have made the Domers feel too secure. You didn't have to go that far to find bodies, though. Hikers came across an entire camp of decaying remains outside of Ulkatcho, which is only a few hours north of Vancouver. On my business trips, I heard plenty of tales about bodies being found in attics, garages, or a hundred other places the straights had tried to hide. And some gays, I should say. We weren't all immune.

I tried once to explain how many had died to Elizabeth, who had grown up in a farming community with no access to TV and computers. What she knew of Salinas had mostly been limited to the library.

"So, you're saying Vancouver used to have a lot more people." She had a dubious look on her face.

"If you count the suburbs, there were a couple of million, from what I've been told."

"I don't see how that's possible. There's not enough room. Besides, my bus goes by a cemetery everyday. There's still a lot of room there."

"Most of the ones that died, they had to dig big holes outside of town to bury them in. It happened so fast, babe."

"If you say so. Maria says that most of them are hiding up north. You know, the Domers."

She said the last word with a spooked expression, as though they were ghosts.

In a way, they were, since we could only see the straights in TV programs and online. Even though several of the St. Benedict Refuges had gone public, their host communities were not being overrun by people wanting to pray at the visitor centers.

Our fear was still too strong. Too many of us had infected and killed those we loved to want to risk doing it again. Why bury more victims?

Elizabeth had a hard time understanding the enormous losses we had just experienced. The explanation for some problems, like HIV, would have to wait until she was more mature.

The Mounties busted a ring of smugglers who were shipping stolen medicine down to the States, mostly for HIV patients. HIV hadn't gone away, even though the media and government were now a lot more aggressive about prevention and treatment.

These days, addicts got what they wanted when they wanted once they registered, but the drugs came by prescription, not over the counter like with marijuana. In either case, customers paid the going rate.

Needles were free, unlike down in the States, but like with our southern neighbors, Canadians were tough on anyone who knowingly spread HIV. People had been convicted before the walking fever for not telling sexual partners of their HIV status. Now it was a major crime. We already had VSF. Who knew what the long-term consequences of that would be for anyone already dealing with HIV?

China and Iran hanged people who spread HIV. From the news reports, it didn't sound like they split hairs as to whether you knew you were doing it or not. In North America, you earned yourself a vacation behind bars. Some states even denied those prisoners medication for HIV. That might not have been death by hanging, but it ended the same way.

The thinking on abortion had also turned hard-core. Abortion was still technically legal to the third month in some places, but by law, if you wanted an abortion, they put your name in the paper and online. You had to see a counselor and be visited by an adoption agency. In some states, it could be grounds for losing your job—and your house if you had received it through a property assumption.

Before the third month, you had to prove the procedure was medically necessary. Down syndrome was a protected fetal condition now. That's one law I completely agree with. After the third month, abortions were essentially illegal, being that certificates were scarce to come by.

Susan said that there were limits to reproductive freedom; everybody needed to understand that. I thought about how hard women had fought to own their bodies, but that right, along with everything else in the world, had changed. When I saw the tears in my sister's eyes, I understood how complicated the situation had become.

I thought about having a baby before the walking fever. But now, with the government offering subsidies to mothers and incentives to higher-odds fathers, getting pregnant felt less like an expression of my and Susan's love for one another and more like a giant rainbow flag pin. And yet I did want to try, even though the possibility of failing the first, the second, who knew how many times, scared me.

When we got back home after eating potluck at the church, the answering machine was lit up with calls. Definitely time to change our phone number again.

Or, we could change the message to, "Baby-Making in Progress. Please Try Elsewhere."

"So, when do women start the shots?" I asked Susan.

She was flipping through her translation guide for words to explain to Wei-Chow/Charlie about using the dishwasher.

"The first set has to be done before fertilization and then in week three. The last sets are in weeks four and five, but since they have to be done at the clinic, they have to keep you..." Her head jerked around and she looked at me, her face disbelieving. "Don't tell me."

"You want me to write it down instead?"

The book, lucky for me a paperback, landed on my chest. Susan landed there moments later.

*Analyn Orante*
   *"El artista de la pintura, es él Velázquez?"*
   "Yes, it is. Do you like the painting?"

He was a docent, perhaps, or a government official. His exact role in my private tour of the Museo Nacional del Prado was unclear to me. An elderly Spaniard with an aquiline nose and a monkish fringe of white hair, Señor Saavedra-López continued to ignore my efforts at speaking his native language.

Did I like *Las Meninas*? "Like" seemed too trite a word. Every figure in the painting looked posed to the nth degree, particularly one of the maids, who wore a bustle large enough to park a silver tea service. The only individual appearing relaxed was the bull mastiff in the foreground, this despite some bratty kid's foot resting on his haunch. So much was going on in this work. Were there subliminal messages in the play of light and shadow, and what was the story behind the female dwarf? Was she a court jester, or a respected Dr. Tofill of her time?

If not for the fact I was due to speak in the auditorium to an international conference in less than twenty minutes, if not for that minor matter, I could pull up a chair and allow Señor Saavedra-López to continue to display his erudition in English.

In all my years of living in my nation's capital, I had visited the National Gallery precisely one time. Madrid had a different philosophy, it appeared, about where art belonged. Maybe more museums needed in-house conference centers, and vice-versa.

Reluctantly, I turned away. The United Nations Special Ambassador for Minority Rights was expected elsewhere.

I checked my BlackBerry for messages before entering the room. Rebecca had left a text message.

"Eat some tapas for me."

Gladly. But first, two hundred government and corporate flacks from the developed and developing world wanted to tell me how we should slice and dice international borders.

After every major war, lines get redrawn. Even though VSF had yet to claim its final victim, and even though it had been a deadly spring for any sensitive not living in a Dome, some of us were ready to turn mapmaking into a growth industry.

The entire continent of Africa needed a do-over, according to a faction within the United Nations. They proposed that all formal national lines be abolished in favor of historically established tribal regions. A political assembly of delegates from across the continent would then establish joint commercial zones and enact mutual defense treaties.

Humans were so sparse on the ground now. It made no sense to enforce a theoretical Gambia, Guinea, Mali, and Sierra Leone if from the post-VSF wreckage one could create a singular Mandinka homeland. This was the case pled by faction leader Mamady Keita, a Malian diplomat.

Bill Levine, my successor at the State Department, had previously shared his concerns with me about erasing Africa's hard drive. The plan necessitated whole-scale movements of people, in many cases, over thousands of miles. Why do it now, when conditions were so precarious?

Why not now, I heard from the conferees. They gave me statistics purporting to show that the die-off of sensitives had resulted in a sharp decline in mob actions and border wars. They claimed any large-scale relocations wouldn't be as traumatic as, for instance, the 1940s Indian partition.

The Mandinka delegation wasn't the only one making the case that gays were less prone to violence. Our own Justice Department had conducted a survey of police departments that, if one corrected for the massive population loss, showed a sharp drop in violent crime.

I had a hard time trusting that statistic. Rapists and boxers, serial killers and military heroes. We gays have proven ourselves capable of taking an axe and giving someone forty whacks, or in the case of my would-be assassin, wielding a samurai sword with deadly intent.

Maybe there were fewer per capita murders being committed these days, but only an idiot would leave her front door unlocked. A steep rise in theft was the other finding of the Justice Department. One would think that with millions of homes being unoccupied these days, and smaller towns virtually empty, there would be no reason to steal.

I happened to catch an episode of a news program that visited a gas station owner named Geronimo Trevino. He had the entire town of Lordsburg, New Mexico, to himself. It didn't appear to have been much more than a village to begin with. He must have been a talented handyman, because he had routed electricity to go solely to the places he needed. This included his home, which was still a modest trailer.

The interviewer asked why he hadn't moved into one of the bigger houses. Trevino said he liked his trailer and saw "no need to crowd the dead. They need their space, same as we do."

In contrast to Trevino, many footloose, traumatized youths, some of them no more than children, lived where they wanted and took what they needed, even from the living.

Rebecca felt it critical to give as much support as possible to foster families, particularly those who would take in teenagers. That's why the federal government issued tax credits and urged local and state governments to favor such families when issuing property assumptions.

Finally, she succeeded in getting Congress to pass the Public Works Program, which took its inspiration from Depression-era projects. Thousands of young people were recruited (or routed by police departments) into the program, given uniforms, discipline from retired military personnel, and trained to work where they were needed.

Just the upkeep alone on mass burial sites, sometimes involving digs and relocation, might have served as catharsis or the stuff of nightmares. But whether they repaired bridges, worked on farms, or cleaned city streets, PWP Youth Corps members were a visible sign of the Administration's determination to control the crime rate and give our citizens a sense of security.

We weren't the only country struggling for equilibrium, which was why, as I fielded questions at the Madrid conference, I wondered how many of my questioners had fully considered what the future might hold.

My job title with the United Nations told our public that the Canary (try as I might, I couldn't get the media to quit using that phrase) cared about the meek, the mild, and the overlooked, whether they be Jews in South America, Christians in Indonesia, or Muslims in France.

Basques were demonstrating outside the museum even as I spoke, voicing their demand for formal statehood status. Decidedly not meek and mild were they.

Lines were being redrawn on maps, and policies were debated around polished tables. Yet, even if scientists fixed the pregnancy problem, we would, for centuries to come, be like children, rattling around in our parents' giant shoes.

One of the speakers thought this was a wonderful idea. The United Nations had passed a worldwide ban on production of conventional petrol cars. We were going green with abandon. Air pollution in Los Angeles was a thing of the past.

The fishing industry was ecstatic about the hauls these days. Overfished species appeared to already be rebounding. Scientists even thought that global warming might slow down, due to our significantly smaller carbon footprint. Now we'd be able to relocate populations affected by persistent drought, so hooray for our near mass extinction.

Michael, my beloved and achingly missed little brother, had wanted to work in eco-commerce after graduation from the University of Texas.

While I sat there at the conference, having delivered my share of answers or non-answers to the conferees, what ran through my mind was that, sure, Michael might have added to the carbon footprint. Given his taste for classic Corvettes that he rebuilt himself, he probably added a minor percentage point in air pollution. Even so, he was more than an eater of cod, certainly more than a faceless fiction of the past.

Rebecca's late husband, Noah, also deserved more than a footnote in a future history book. The media already was asking us to set a date. It was too soon to discuss marriage, in my view, since she had never been granted any time to grieve the loss of her husband and child.

We were trying to know each other better in the midst of the most challenging period in our nation's history since the Revolution. This made one simple, quiet evening at home a rare, hard-won achievement.

Our man at the CDC, Dr. Tofill, told us that VSF might manifest itself someday in our bodies, perhaps in the same way that chickenpox reemerges decades later as shingles. Maybe VSF would return as something infinitely worse. Then again, we might remain symptom-free. Some viruses we carry cause no problems for healthy individuals.

These confident men and women describing the shape of a largely human-free world seemed unconcerned that we might not survive long-term. In that case, where would our Dome residents go? To the Moon? Talk of that, so prevalent on the Internet, was both premature and foolhardy. We had to prove that we could keep our sensitives safe and healthy here on Earth before indulging in ruinously expensive rocket launches. It was all we could do, in tandem with the Russians, to keep the Space Station in orbit.

I came to my feet and asked if I might deliver a few more remarks. With hardly any more set-up than that, I began.

"Before we return to the no doubt fascinating topic of territorial dispute resolution, let us consider how we intend to honor our friends and relatives who have died. We'll join them someday, whether because of some unknown outcome of the disease, or due to the simple passing of time. We will see them again. And when we do, what will we say to our mothers, to our fathers? That we cared more about old-growth forests than the bodies buried beneath them?

"I've been asked to advocate for those who lack majority status in their home countries. This I'm glad to do, but let me be presumptuous and speak for the dead, as well. I agree with you that throughout history, they started the wars and dropped the bombs. Maybe you can prove to me that they cornered the market in organized aggression. But when it was possible to hide our nature, we joined them on the front lines. We weren't gentle little lambs. Far from it.

"Did they slaughter our people, shackle us in institutions, and treat us as monsters with human faces? Yes, they did. But there were also many among them who treated us humanely. They may not have understood us, but they loved us. And we loved them. Even during the terrible times we've just experienced, there were voices of reason among them. Don't forget that fact. Remake the world, if you must, but I ask that you find some way to honor their achievements and mourn their passing."

*Dora Navarro*

"I don't hear you say much in class, Dora. Are you getting from it what you need?" Rabbi Claudia Weiss, a dark-haired woman with sympathetic eyes, made a point of shutting off her BlackBerry.

Her office was more than a bit cluttered, stacked as it was to the ceiling with boxes. The synagogue library was similarly cramped. In the kitchen, I had seen cupboards full of seder plates and cases of Jewish food items. No one would run short of gefilte fish for quite some time to come. Thousands of Jews had died in the Austin area, leaving behind items that ended up at the synagogue.

There were forty-eight students in my Thursday night Introduction to Judaism class, even more in the Monday night group.

Rabbi Weiss, who had been an associate rabbi when the epidemic hit, periodically scheduled one-on-one visits with students. I don't know how she managed to run the classes, train members to assist in service, and do everything else involved in her position. There didn't seem to be enough hours in the day. To judge by the dark circles under her eyes, she didn't get much sleep.

I thought back to a conversation I'd had with my girlfriend, Stasia Millner. She'd heard there had been hundreds who applied for the first post-epidemic classes. Even after paring away messianic types and the unstable, over a hundred had finished the class. Most of them underwent formal conversion, taking with them what amounted to being starter kits, built from the estates of those who had died.

Stasia's theory was that the students recalled stories in the media about how Jews had endured the Holocaust, been destroyed so many times before, and yet still came through faithful and strong.

"Goys think we have what it takes to go the distance, that we have a special knowledge," Stasia said.

"Do you?"

"I'm no expert. I understand the Hindu temple here has quadrupled its membership. I would almost bet that in India, Christians are getting great business these days. I think whatever faith people started with has either gotten stronger or gotten dumped."

For me, the class was a way of grounding myself. There were times I didn't quite believe in the reality of any given moment. Too much had happened. I missed Mama so desperately sometimes it felt like a physical pain, like a cancer in my chest. I don't remember her praying as she lay dying. She was more concerned about my comfort and about my plans. So typical of her. I shook off my mental wanderings.

Rabbi Weiss sat there with a tired, yet patient expression on her face. She had taken time out of her busy schedule to talk to me.

I needed to give her some kind of response to her question regarding how I felt about the class. "I've been keeping up on the Hebrew lessons. I'm pretty strong on the prayers now."

"That's good. I'm glad you're making progress, but what I'm asking about is you. Are you getting what you need?"

"I don't know. What am I supposed to be doing now? I'm not sure. It all seems so pointless."

"Going to services, or life in general?"

"I'm doing what they want me to do at my job. I'm figuring out problems and fixing them, but all we're doing is making automated self-services work better. Fewer humans, more machines. That's all my job is."

"It still sounds like useful work, but if it's not fullfilling, you could find something else to do. I've heard you and Stasia perform together."

"I have to make a living, Rabbi. No one's getting by on music these days."

"That's what I'd like to talk to you about. Our accompanist is moving back to New Jersey with his partner, so there is an opening.

We can't pay you much, but there's a nice house involved, and many of our families would welcome a familiar face as their child's piano teacher. About the house, our board filed property assumptions on several of our late members. The property I'm thinking about is fairly close by."

"*Tikkun olam.* Healing the world. You said that's the Jews' mission. Isn't that God's job? Is he pushing it off on us because he sucks at it?"

I should be accepting the job instead of turning weird on her.

She smiled at me. "Good. Being Jewish isn't about being a perfect little soldier for the cause. We're expected to have opinions. Healing the world? God does that when we're not preventing it. Water gets cleaner, air becomes more breathable, a forest grows up tall and strong. But, you and I, we can step in when there are floods and fires and—"

"Killer diseases. I know that some crazy people made swine fever. I get that, I do, so I'm not blaming God, not exactly."

"But God let it happen."

"Yes."

"You've told me a little bit about what you've been through. Would you say you're a stronger person, a more caring person now?"

"Maybe."

I thought about her question some more. Taking care of my dying family, staggering down a Texas highway nearly blind after the attack, then enduring all those months of struggle afterward.

"Yes," I said. "I'm a stronger, more caring person."

"I lost my entire family," Rabbi Weiss said, "and most of my congregation, and yet I consider myself to be fortunate. I have my work and my friends. I still have opportunities. To me, what gives my life meaning happens every day. Every day I'm given the chance to help others. My faith and life don't rest on how many prayers I know or on how much I've studied Talmud.

"There's a story in a book I've read several times. It's probably in that stack over by the door. A man named Victor Frankl was in a concentration camp during World War II. He remembered talking to a young woman who was about to die. She told him that her closest friend there was a tree that she could see through a window. Actually, all she could see was just one branch of the tree."

"A tree," I said. "That was her only friend." Well, it was a concentration camp. Any touch of beauty had to be an improvement.

"The woman told Frankl that she had lived a spoiled, self-centered life, but once she entered the camp, she found her spiritual core. The tree represented life to her, eternal life. I am here, I am here, it said.

"Dora, if I have any advice to give you, it's not about whether you should convert to Judaism. I ask that you find what gives your life meaning, and then live it. There, you'll find comfort. It's there that you'll find your strength."

I didn't know what to say to that. I got up and left her office. I drove back to my apartment, did my usual routine of laying out clothes for the next day, then took a shower.

As I stood under the stream, I thought about what Rabbi Weiss had said.

I didn't quite get all she was trying to say, but the part about seeking opportunities every day made sense.

I called Rabbi Weiss and accepted the job. I turned in my resignation at Solectron the next day and began moving into my new house.

Stasia joined me soon after.

One Friday evening during Kaddish, I realized that I had finished reciting all the names of everyone I had lost to the epidemic.

When Rabbi Weiss moved her arm across the congregation, I kept silent and listened to the others.

"Michael Orante," a blonde girl in front of me said.

Others chimed in with their names.

I am here, I am here, the voices said.

I am here.

Author Kelly Sinclair                    Photo Credit: Amy Spencer

# About the Author

**Kelly Sinclair** lives in Temple, Texas, but is a transplant from the South Plains. She has been a reporter, a rock singer-songwriter, and is currently a librarian. One of her poems appeared in the *Texas Observer* political magazine, and her computer-derived prints are featured in art galleries.

Sinclair has worked with an experimental art-rock ensemble, written country songs for such Texas acts as the Maines Brothers, and sung backup for funk bands and bluegrass performers. In her writing, she follows a similar path of exploring her creative boundaries, writing scripts, plays, and musical song-cycles.

# Also Available from Blue Feather Books:

## Accidental Rebels, by Kelly Sinclair

It's the summer of 1989, and in the small Texas town of Tantona, to be openly gay is to be notorious. But three closeted women are about to shake things up.

Mandy, a young reporter, is hung up on God and women. Librarian Tina is eager to ditch old personal dramas, and rocker Cat is struggling to get her band off the ground.

Unanticipated connections bring the women together... and then there's Sherron, a reckless blonde who becomes the talk of the town.

When secrets come doused in Texas barbecue sauce, all the ingredients are present for a surprising and spicy mix.

## Detours, by Jane Vollbrecht

It should have been a typical day of trimming shrubbery and edging lawns, but Gretchen VanStantvoordt—known to everyone as "Ellis"—first gets caught in a traffic jam and then lands in the emergency room with a badly sprained ankle. Mary Moss, a newfound friend who was caught in the same traffic jam, convinces Ellis that trying to tend to her dog and negotiate the stairs at her walk-up apartment while she's on crutches isn't such a good idea. Without friends or family in the vicinity, Ellis accepts Mary's offer for assistance.

When Ellis meets Natalie, Mary's nine-year-old daughter, she's ready to make tracks away from Mary as quickly as possible, but her bum ankle makes that impossible. Ellis stays with Mary and Natalie while she recovers. Little by little, Ellis develops a fondness for young Natalie... and develops something much deeper for Mary.

Ellis and Mary work out a plan for building a future—and a family—together. Destiny, it seems, has other plans and throws major roadblocks in their path. Ellis is forced to reconsider everything she thought she knew about where she wanted to go in life, and Mary learns that even with the perfect traveling companion, not all journeys are joyous.

No GPS can help them navigate the new road they're on. Come make the trip with Ellis and Mary as they discover that when life sends you on a detour, the wise traveler finds a way to enjoy the scenery.

# Playing for First, by Chris Paynter

Lisa Collins feels she has it all as an Indianapolis sportswriter covering the city's minor league baseball team and as a freelancer for the newspaper. Her best friend, bar owner Frankie Dunkin, helps keep her grounded and sane. Her life is uncomplicated-that is until Amy Perry enters her world.

Amy, the all-star first baseman for a professional women's baseball team, dreams the dream most boys do-to play in the major leagues. The Cincinnati Reds are about to give her that chance.

While covering Amy's ascent through the minor league system, out-and-proud Lisa finds herself falling for the closeted first baseman. But as they begin a relationship, something unexpected happens: Lisa realizes her feelings for Frankie Dunkin run much deeper than friendship.

With Amy facing harassment from her male teammates in her quest to break through the gender barrier, Lisa is torn between supporting her and exploring her feelings toward Frankie. Frankie has her own demons to face as painful physical and emotional scars from her past haunt her.

Despite the myriad conflicting emotions raging in Lisa's life, one thing is clear-Frankie and Amy are *Playing for First* in her heart.

**Available now, only from**

Make sure to check out these other exciting Blue Feather Books titles:

| | | |
|---|---|---|
| Tempus Fugit | Mavis Applewater | 978-0-9794120-0-4 |
| In the Works | Val Brown | 978-0-9822858-4-8 |
| Addison Black and the Eye of Bastet | M.J. Walker | 978-0-9794120-2-8 |
| The Thirty-Ninth Victim | Arleen Williams | 978-0-9794120-4-2 |
| Merker's Outpost | I. Christie | 978-0-9794120-1-1 |
| Whispering Pines | Mavis Applewater | 978-0-9794120-6-6 |
| Diminuendo | Emily Reed | 978-0-9822858-0-0 |
| The Fifth Stage | Margaret Helms | 0-9770318-7-X |
| Journeys | Anne Azel | 978-0-9794120-9-7 |
| From Hell to Breakfast | Joan Opyr | 978-0-9794120-7-3 |
| Detours | Jane Vollbrecht | 978-0-9822858-1-7 |
| Possessing Morgan | Erica Lawson | 978-0-9822858-2-4 |

**www.bluefeatherbooks.com**

LaVergne, TN USA
12 October 2010
200467LV00001B/40/P